I0677118

4 AUTHOR ANTHOLOGY

EVERNIGHT PUBLISHING ®

www.evernightpublishing.com

Copyright© 2024

Everight Publishing

ISBN: 978-0-3695-1046-4

Cover Artist: Jay Aheer

Editor: Lisa Petrocelli

TELL ME LIES: MANLOVE EDITION

A Dark Bully Romance Anthology

Table of Contents

4 AUTHOR ANTHOLOGY

RED-LIGHT RIVALS

Faedra Rose

Copyright © 2024

Chapter One
Jackson

My mood is so sour I can almost taste it. The red lights across the street flicker on, and The Red Bastille's sign glows. There's already a growing crowd lining up on the pavement, waiting to go in, both men and women alike. The Red Bastille is a gentleman's club with an upper-class feel. It might be targeted at men, but that doesn't stop the ladies tagging along, just as keen to drink, enjoy the music, watch the dancers perform, or experience their first threesome or orgy.

Fucking Sebastian. I wish there was a way to send that little shit out of business. He's such a fucking pretty boy. With a lithe build, colorful ink over every free inch of skin, and straight black hair cut at that annoying length where the prick is forever flipping it out of his eyes, giving him that dramatic, Emo flair. The women love him. He's as suave and smooth as silk. Just the right amount of predator and debonair ladies' man to come across as powerful, but not brutish.

Sebastian Crenshaw. My fucking rival. I should be content. The Dungeon—*my* gentleman's club—has its own breed of clientele. Here, we don't serve cocktails or have glittering disco balls. The Dungeon is all about BDSM. Like me, most of my paying customers are muscular, heavily tattooed in monochromatic designs, and are affiliated with drug cartels and outlaw MC clubs.

The Dungeon is all about leather, black lace, and every dark and fucked-up kink imaginable. Whether it's leading bitches around on leashes, spanking or flogging asses red, fucking publicly, or enjoying any one of the playrooms on offer. If someone wants it, The Dungeon will happily oblige almost any level of deviancy and debauchery—including breath and edge play. We always have a handful of fully qualified medical staff on premises, just to be safe, because kinks are fun, but ultimately, we want everyone getting home in one piece and still breathing.

The music thrums through my club, and I pour myself a shot of bourbon. I have three staff behind the bar tonight, but I like to make an appearance, and hanging out behind the bar gives me the opportunity to meet customers directly, as well as keep an eye on things. After all, this club is my life. It's my job to take care of it. I have security, of course, but The Dungeon is my baby.

Slugging back my drink, I lean on the bar, staring out across the street. Sebastian shouldn't bug me as much as he does. We have mostly different customer bases … but I guess his club has a broader intake than mine does, which means that little shit is practically rolling in cash. He gets the newly legal-aged teenyboppers, as well as the classier customers who enjoy the burlesque entertainment, not to mention the regular sex addicts who frequent any establishment they can.

The Dungeon caters to a very specific taste, and the only people who walk through my doors are those who know the dark and depraved pleasures the world of BDSM has to offer, or they're interested in finding out. I'm proud to own the premiere BDSM club in the city, but Sebastian just gets on my nerves. Some nights he even saunters over here like he owns the place, flaunting his wealth, using his disarming smirk, and jet-black gaze like weapons of mass destruction.

Everything about him makes me want to grind my teeth and break him in two. His club might rake in more than mine, but I bet that little Emo prick couldn't last one night in The Dungeon. *He'd probably break!* I muse. And then, like a bolt of lightning through my soul, a stomach-twisting realization hits me. *Fuuuck.* I've always known that I'm bisexual, at least since my late teens. But when it comes to men, I'm very, very particular. I'll fuck any hot, vivacious Goth chick with a bit of attitude. Men, however, are an entirely different story. For me, it must be about more than just sex. When I'm with a man it's about connection and compatibility in the way we complement each other as partners.

I'm attracted to my bloody enemy. God-fucking-damnit. My red-light rival knows just how to push my buttons in all the right ways. I pour myself another drink and slam it down, enjoying the fiery burn as it slides down my throat. How did I miss this for so long? We've both been in business for the better part of five years, and though we've had our mouthy run-ins, I've never thought of Sebastian as anything other than an arrogant little shit. But now? Fuck me. The tension, the fire between us, the rivalry … it's like all the dots are finally connected and I know without a shadow of a doubt that I'm into him.

Well, this sucks. You never mix business with

9

pleasure. It always ends in disaster. That's Business 101. And even if I did want to get to know Sebastian more personally before burying myself balls-deep in his hairless ass, who's to say he'd even be interested in me? I'm six foot four, I work out, have wavy, shoulder-length bleach-blond hair with dark roots, and live in leather. Spikes, handcuffs, and belts are my regular accessories. The owner of The Red Bastille, meanwhile, spends his life in suits, tight-fighting pants, and turtlenecks.

Maybe we're too different? I wonder. I look like a fucking biker, and he looks like he could be the next 007. *What if he likes*—I cut myself off mid-thought. I'm not going to get myself caught up in knots over this guy, no matter how beautiful he looks in my mind bent over a cage as I eat out his ass. He hasn't made a move in all this time, so why should I?

He obviously has his priorities sorted with The Red Bastille, and I should focus on mine—The Dungeon. *That's not to say I can't have my fantasies...* Abandoning my tumbler in the sink behind the bar, I take my leave and head for my private office on the second floor. I have a mind to beat one out before things really start picking up in the club. So, whether that pretty little shit would like it or not, for the next five minutes, he's going to be my fantasy bitch.

Chapter Two
Sebastian

The night is ramping up and The Red Bastille is a hive of music, pageantry, liquor, and sex. My club offers something a little more refined than most. With burlesque and stripper shows, live music, and private themed rooms, it attracts people from all walks of life. You're as likely to see an elderly couple come in for the burlesque, as you are a new sex-mad couple keen to explore their limits. It creates a uniquely appealing environment—one where everyone feels safe to enjoy themselves.

Twirling my cane, I saunter through the crowd, dipping my hat, and laughing along to the same old jokes. My scene might be a little more punk and metal, truth be told, but I'm a businessman, and I run The Red Bastille for the people and for profit. Though I'd never admit it, I'd much rather visit a club like the one across the road— The Dungeon.

The owner is my rival in a manner of speaking, but it's all a charade. All for fun. Jackson Maguire is a great big beast of a man. Heavily inked, with the body of a fucking gladiator, shoulder-length permanently scruffy beach-blond hair, and the bluest eyes I've ever seen... I enjoy raising his ire. He's damn sexy when he's worked up and all that animalistic growliness comes out to play.

I consider myself an alpha male, but of a different breed than the glorious god that is Jackson. Where he's muscle and brute power, I'm suave and manipulative. Some would define me as a Switch, which is perhaps even more accurate. I always get what I want, even if it means submission. Even to the point where the other party involved thinks it was their idea all along.

The power play is what I enjoy most. The back and forth, the tension, the flexing of wit. I just wish The Dungeon master could see how interested I actually am. *What I wouldn't give to be ridden by that beast.* To feel him pummel my prostate into oblivion would be the greatest of sins and wickedest of pleasures. I'm not ashamed to like what I do. Man or woman, ultimately it doesn't matter. Humanity was made for loving, and I'll enjoy whomever I want, whenever I want.

Taking a colorful cocktail from a waitress's silver platter as she walks by, I slam it down, replacing the empty glass on the bar. *Perhaps I should pay The Dungeon a visit?* I wonder, with a sly grin. While I like to make an appearance at my own club, my presence isn't required. I have a hierarchy of management that always has everything under control. From replacing the urinal cakes in the bathrooms, to stocking the bar, to paying the entertainers, to organizing physical security on premises, it's all orchestrated to perfection. I just need to enjoy myself. And that's exactly what I'm going to do.

Sauntering out of The Red Bastille and into the cool night, I breathe in deep and sigh. This is going to be ridiculously entertaining. *I can hardly wait!* When the street is clear, I cross, blowing kisses and winking to all the ladies still waiting to get into my club as I go. I step up onto the pavement directly outside The Dungeon. There's no line here, no crowd of eager and excited patrons looking forward to a night of drinks and entertainment.

No, very few people indeed even use the front door. It's mostly for show. All the regulars and hard-core party people enter from the alleyway behind The Dungeon. It's more private and has a dirtier and nastier appeal. But you know what? I'm me. I'm fucking fabulous and I have no shame. I'm going to stroll in these front doors and make a scene, because why the fuck not? I can't wait to see the look on Jackson's face. It's going to be priceless.

Cane in hand, I push the doors inward like I own the place. A deep, throbbing base washes over me, as a sensual and erotic wordless vocal melody sends a shiver through me. "Love it. Love the vibe," I say to myself. As I drink in the dark beauty of Jackson's establishment, I smirk. *This is definitely me.* Flicking my hair from my eyes, I casually take the stairs down to the bar and slide onto a stool.

"What can I get for you, Mr. Crenshaw?" asks one of the bar staff.

"How about something tall, tattooed, and with the bluest eyes you've ever seen?" I answer.

The young woman bites her lip and her eyes sparkle. "Mr. Maguire is in his office," she answers. "Would you like me to see if he'll come down?"

I wink. "No, thank you, doll. I think I'll surprise him," I say rising from the stool.

"Ah, we're supposed to let him know if he has visitors," she calls after me, a little look of panic on her features.

"Don't fret. This one's on me, promise," I say, looking over my shoulder before passing through the club. Limbs, lashes, and moans fill the air as I disappear down the dark hall toward the stairs that will take me to Jackson's office. He's going to freak! Taking the stairs two at a time, I straighten my suit, flick my hair aside, and burst in with my usual level of extravagance. "Damn," I breathe.

The Dungeon's master is sitting at his computer, sans pants, slowly wanking his thick, pierced cock to a particularly alluring picture of me. To say the sight is hot would be an ungracious understatement.

Jackson looks sidelong at me, a deepening smirk on those gorgeous lips of his. "No one else would be so bold as to bust into my private office," he says in his deliciously husky voice.

I close the door behind me and flick the lock.

Jackson raises an inquisitive brow. "You've got some nerve, Sebastian," he says, not missing a stroke.

"Says the big burly bastard jerking one off to a photo of his red-light rival?" I retort with a smirk as I saunter across the office.

Chapter Three
Jackson

I watch, intrigued, as Sebastian comes to sit on my desk. "So, to what do I owe the pleasure?"

Sebastian smirks. "It seems we might have been thinking along similar lines," he answers. He glances down at my cock in hand, before giving me a devious smile.

I relax back in my chair. "It occurred to me this evening that not only do I find you irritating as fuck, but also hot as fuck," I say. "All these years I've been wanting to knock your stupid pretty lights out, and now, well…" I gesture at the screen with my eyes. "Now, I just want to fuck your ass until you cry."

"You talk a big game, Jack," says Sebastian casually, hooking his cane onto the desk beside him. "But how about I put your cock where my mouth is?"

Using my boots, I push myself back in the chair, providing more space. "Well, there you go, sunshine. Have at it." I gesture, goading him.

The owner of The Red Bastille removes his jacket and drapes it over my monitor, covering the screen. "You're not going to need that when you've got the real thing," he says, sinking to his knees between my legs. "Damn," he says for the second time since entering my office. "A Prince Albert. Nice."

I remove my hand from my cock and recline further, putting both arms behind my head with the cockiness of a king on his throne.

Sebastian takes my cock reverently in his pale, colorful inked hands.

"Nice manicure," I retort, admiring the contrast of

his black painted nails against my skin.

My rival simply looks up at me with those jet-black eyes and my cock twitches in his grasp in response.

In the next instant his hot tongue swirls around my head, flicking my Prince Albert on his way around. I bite off the urge to moan as he trails his tongue up either side of my eight inches, lubricating my cock with his saliva, before taking me straight to the back of his throat—and beyond—like a seasoned fucking pro.

"Fuck," I moan, unable to help myself as he takes me all the way. Licking my lips, I lower my arms to trail my fingers through his glossy locks. "Oh, Sebastian," I growl. "Where did you learn to suck cock so good? Fag college?" I feel teeth graze my length in warning.

Sebastian smirks as he comes up for air, working my cock with his left hand, his gaze unwavering. "And where did you learn to give compliments?" he asks. "Asshole school?"

I tighten my grip on his hair and pull his head back, but he stubbornly refuses to break eye contact. "Get back to work, bitch," I command, before forcing his head down again. With both fists entangled in his black locks I have complete control. The power is titillating. Shoving him down, then reefing him back up, I force him to deep-throat me whether he wants to or not. My sac tightens and my ass puckers at the fucking vacuum this bastard is achieving even as I roughly manipulate him like he's nothing more than a useless, dirty fuck-sock.

I moan and Sebastian relaxes then tightens his throat in response, undulating his muscles to clutch at my thick, pierced cock. This bitch is a fucking expert cocksucker. And I'm almost jealous thinking of the lucky fuckers who've had the divine pleasure of experiencing this before me. Who am I kidding? I *am* jealous. I've had a few amazing blowjobs over the years from a handful of particularly gifted women who take to cock like air, but getting down with a gorgeous Emo cunt who is clearly a natural and talented Switch? *I've fucking hit a gold mine!*

I close my eyes, head back, as I pump the poor fucker, thrusting in the chair as I force his lips to the base of my cock. "Oh God, you fucker." I snarl. "I'm going to come."

In the blink of a damn eye Sebastian takes back control. Prying my fingers from his hair—his strength surprises me and turns me on—to take back his own rhythm. He slows it down, returning to long, languid, deep strokes, before sucking hard on my oversensitive cockhead.

"Fuck," I hiss.

He holds me momentarily hostage, his long, pale fingers wrapped firmly around my wrists, pinning them to the chair as he works at his own leisure. His confidence and defiance are everything.

I've been with just a couple of men, and they've always been submissive. They've had their fire and their attitude, it's true. A good sub knows how to play and act out for the purpose of achieving punishment and pleasure … but this is something else. It's like dancing with an equal. And it's abundantly clear that Sebastian Crenshaw knows this dance like the back of his hand.

"Sweet fucking Christ!" My entire body tenses, and I arch my back in my executive chair, causing it to creak with the shift of my weight. My orgasm builds like a wave at my core, gaining wicked speed and momentum until it threatens to crest, and I can't hold back any longer. "Sebastian!" His name slips like a prayer from my lips, and I grit my teeth as he stays deep, forcing me to spasm in his throat as my deluge of cum erupts hot and fast. *Shit!*

Without missing a beat, he undulates his throat

again, ramping up my release from a toe-curling orgasm to the utmost ecstasy.

"Fu—" I can't even finish the word. I make fists against the leather cushion, clenching them hard as the last of me spurts down his warm throat. When it's over, I slowly allow myself to relax. Still breathing heavily, I look down at Sebastian in blind appreciation and lust. And as he painstakingly cleans my cock with his tongue, his gaze reaches mine and I'm lost in those bottomless pools of darkness and their cocky allure.

One way or another, I'm going to find a way to make this happen much, *much* more often. And I don't give two shits who knows about us, either. But for this delicious moment, I'm going to pretend like it's our dirty little secret.

Chapter Four
Sebastian

Licking my lips languidly, I lean down once more to place a wicked, tantalizing kiss on Jackon's cockhead, before I rise to my feet. "Well, that was a little bit of fun, wasn't it?" I ask, casually leaning against his desk as if I didn't just blow his damn mind.

"You're a fucking cock-demon," he answers. His broad, inked chest heaves with desire as he catches his breath.

"I think that's the nicest thing you've said since I walked in this room."

Jackon grimaces ever so slightly. "I've hated you for fucking years, Crenshaw," he says by way of an apology. "And now, you're locking my office door and giving me some of the best head I've had in my life. Forgive me for being a little thrown."

"You hated me, seriously? You hardly know me," I reason with a small shake of my head. I reach into my pocket and retrieve a spliff I rolled earlier in the evening. "You indulge?" I ask.

"Always," he answers, pulling a beautiful, custom-engraved The Dungeon zippo from his ass pocket. Flicking back the cap, he lights that baby up, offering the flame to the joint between my fingers.

Leaning forward, I puff to get her going. Satisfied, I take a few long drags before exhaling a plume of delicious, sweet-smelling smoke, then pass it to Jackson as he puts his lighter away. "So," I say, staving off the silence. "What did I ever do to shit you off so bad?"

Jackson inhales and exhales, filling the office with

the telltale smell of good weed, before he cracks a grin that has me swooning. "I honestly couldn't fucking tell you," he answers. "It's just everything about you. You're cocky as hell, not to mention a bloody pretty boy. Your club has patrons for days, and you're always in the damn media. You with your fucking perfectly fitted suits, your cane, and your Emo-ass hair ... you just get under my skin."

I smirk, and reach for the spliff, hanging it loosely between my fingers as it slowly burns. "And you only just realized you were attracted to me tonight, for real?" I ask, one brow cocked in amusement.

Jackson pushes himself up from his chair and makes a show of putting himself away, slowly zipping himself up and re-buckling his belt. "Watch it," he says. He wanders over to the floor-to-ceiling windows of his office that look directly over The Dungeon. "This club is my life. It was easy to hate you. You were—*are*—competition. It's just business."

"Is it?" I reply. I saunter to his side to watch the depraved and kinky activities going on below in The Dungeon's lush, Gothic space. "Our clubs serve very different types of clientele, Jack. The Dungeon is a true haven for the debauched BDSM lover. The Red Bastille is just for fun. It's all pizzazz, entertainment, and a little sex on the side. It's a good night, that's it. My clients aren't yours. Some may grow to be, one day. But my club is for those new to the scene—those who are exploring. Your club is for those who already know they're different, know what they like, and aren't ashamed of it. I don't know why you ever felt threatened by The Red Bastille. The difference between our establishments is night and day."

Jackson grabs the last of the spliff off me with a wry smile. "Well, when you put it like that, I don't bloody know, either. Though I wouldn't call it threatened, pretty boy. I just didn't like your showy cabaret shit."

I roll my eyes and slip my hand into the tight back pocket of Jackon's leather pants and squeeze his hard ass. "So, friends then?" I ask. "Unless you want to keep up the enemies charade?"

Jackson drags the joint to death, snuffing it out beneath his boot on the matte black tiles, before blowing the smoke in my face. "I don't know what you're fucking talking about," he says, seizing my wrist, and removing my hand from his ass in the blink of an eye. "We aren't friends, Sebastian. We never will be."

"How about friends with benefits, then?" I offer, letting my inner brat out to play.

"I said, I don't do friends. You're either my enemy or my lover."

I sigh. Jackson is so hot when he puts on his grumps. "All right then, you win, big guy. Enemies it is."

Jackon releases my wrist and wraps his huge hand around my throat, forcing me to the tips of my toes. "Oh, you are a bratty little shit, aren't you?" he croons by my ear. "I'm only too happy to play," he warns.

"Then put your Dungeon Master moves on, bitch," I breathe, defiantly holding his eye. "Because I might bend, Jack, but I don't break."

Jackson's mouth crashes into mine as he pivots— still choking me—shoving me against the one-way glass that overlooks the club.

My mind melts at his perfect control and brutal power. I haven't been manhandled properly in a good, long while. I've missed it.

Releasing my throat, his voice takes on a deliciously husky and dangerous tone. "You're a bit of a pain slut, aren't you, Sebastian?" he whispers into the crook of my neck, nipping and biting at my tender skin in the most erotic way imaginable. One hand gropes my ass, while the other teases my cock through my tailored trousers. I spread my legs automatically without shame to give him better access. "What of it?" I rasp, craving more.

Jackson squeezes my package firmly and looks deep into my soul. "Tonight, you're my whore, Sebastian. I'm going to show you how we have fun here, away from all the feathers and frou-frou shit."

I grin, riling him. "All I hear are words, Jack. *Show* me," I challenge. Jack's palm sings across the side of my face, and for a moment I see stars, before a deep, hot throb develops in the cheek where he struck me. *Fuck, yeah.*

"It's *Master* to you, slave boy," he snarls. "And next time you disrespect me, I'm going to take it out on your ass."

Chapter Five
Jackson

Turning my back on my new plaything, I fetch a simple and elegant black leather collar and leash from my desk drawer. *This will do nicely.* "Get here, slave," I command.

With his deep, dark, and soulful eyes, Sebastian obeys.

I secure the collar around his pale neck and attach the leash. "Let's go have some fun," I say. I lead him from my office, down the stairs, through the dark labyrinth of halls, and back into the thrumming and decadent hive that is the heart of The Dungeon.

Our entrance draws a handful of curious, appreciative glances, but otherwise, the patrons of The Dungeon are too used to public displays to pay us much mind when they have their own deviancies at hand. Approaching the bar, I tug Sebastian along. He looks so beautiful. Without his cane and jacket, he looks much more casual. With his black silk shirt open at the cuffs, and his tailored trousers, it's like the Emo movement met Fabio. He just oozes an undefinable and unapologetic aura of confidence and sex appeal.

"Juliet, two shots of Green Fairy, please, doll," I say to young woman manning the bar.

"Oh, I see Mr. Crenshaw found you," she answers, already decanting our absinthe with style and elegance. "I wanted to give you a heads up, but Mr. Crenshaw is not one for following House rules it seems."

I smirk as I slide my slave's drink across the bar to him. "It seems I'm going to have to teach him some manners," I say, giving him a sidelong glance as I slug back my shot. The liquor burns down my throat, potent, satisfying, and familiar. "Thank you, Juliet. Enjoy the show." I wink.

Sebastian downs his shot without a word.

"Will do, sir," she answers without a second's hesitation.

I grin. Juliet is a cutie, and one of my regular subs. We get to mix business with pleasure often. Which is just how I like it when it comes to those beneath me. "Come," I say, leading Sebastian up from the sunken bar, and to one of my St. Andrew's Crosses. In the form of a giant X, it allows all four limbs to be bound in a standing position. "Take off your clothes. Back to the cross," I order, unclipping the leash from his collar.

My slave for the night obliges without question, his fingers deftly unbuttoning his black silk shirt, before letting it fall in a pile on the floor beside the cross. His trousers follow, as do his shiny black dress shoes. His form takes my breath away. His ink is magnificent and reminds me heavily of the Yakuza's famous full-body art. Thousands of dollars have been sunk directly into his skin, and his lithe, but muscular form only enhances its beauty.

"Like what you see, Master?" he asks, standing tall.

Like an angry bear, I attack, shoving him roughly against the cross. "You will only speak when spoken to," I warn, hand at his throat. "Is that clear, slave?"

Sebastian's lip quirks ever so slightly, but he reigns it in—for now. "Yes, Master."

"Good," I answer, though I'm utterly unconvinced that I can expect good behavior from this slave. One at a time, I secure his wrists, and then his ankles. The soft, but firm leather of the shackles serves to sufficiently restrain but protect the punished from chaffing or attempting escape. Standing back, I admire my prize. "I'd never damage such beautiful ink," I say, almost to myself. "But there's plenty of fun to be had without breaking the skin."

I grab a selection of my favorite floggers, paddles, and even a cane. *This should be fun.* As the music in the club throbs and swells, filling the air with seduction and illicit promise, I choose my first toy—the suede flogger. The sting will be brilliant and splayed, but not pinpointed enough to damage the skin. It's precisely what I want to start with. If my slave is a little pain slut, then we'll begin the dance with a nice warm-up. He'll want primed skin before the cane comes out to play. Cold skin with solid toys is, let's just say, like slamming your fingers in a car door on a frosty winter's morning. It'll cause immediate shock and have you yelling obscenities, dragging you from the headspace carefully cultivated by clever and calculated pain application.

"All right, slave. I'm going to ease you in nice and gentle. We play a little rougher here in The Dungeon than you lot over at The Red Bastille are used to."

Sebastian smirks but says nothing to counter my subtle slander.

Closing the space between us, I trail my fingers over his semi-erect cock, and earn a twitch and a quiet moan. With a devious grin, I lick up the side of my slave's cheek, before whispering in his ear. "What's your safeword, pretty boy?" I trail the suede flogger's soft tails over his cock as the seconds pass between us.

"I've never used my safeword," he answers proudly.

"Be that as it may," I say with a note of subtle admiration. *My boy toy isn't afraid to go hard!* "I should know it, just in case. Let's say it's House Rules."

Sebastian sighs. "It's *ambrosia*."

"The mythological food of the gods? Intriguing.

Very well. Now, we can play." Standing directly in front of my trussed-up morsel, I tease the tails of the flogger through my hand. Then before I can give away my next move, I strike. The flogger bites at his sac as I swing underhanded, rolling my shoulder the way a bowler would. I bite my lip in desire when Sebastian hisses between his teeth, his body tensing, and his fists clenching.

"Have I got your attention, Mr. Crenshaw?" I ask, my tone dripping with desire.

His cock jumps involuntarily, and his sac becomes firm, shrinking away from the pain. Sebastian smirks. "You've always had my attention."

With that nice little perk to my ego, I twirl the flogger around as I pace the platform where the St. Andrew's Cross is mounted. "You've got a honeypot for a mouth, don't you, my pet?" I counter. "We'll see what pretty words spill from those lips when I'm burying myself balls-deep in your ass?"

Sebastian's lips quirk in the cockiest way possible. "I guess we'll find out, Master."

Chapter Six
Sebastian

"Challenge accepted, slave," says Jackson.

In the next breath the flogger sings against my inner thigh, making me flinch and grit my teeth. "Master," I say. "May I have a bit?"

Jackson fetches one from its place on the wall nearby. "Very well. Wouldn't like to damage those pearly whites," he says. "Open up."

I allow him to place the silicon bit between my teeth, bite down, then relax, adjusting to the sensation.

"Will that suffice, or would you prefer something mounted to a harness, or a ball gag, perhaps?" Jackson offers, his glacial blue gaze boring into me.

"This is good," I manage around the bit. "Thank you, Master."

Satisfied, Jackson returns to his position.

I can't help but admire his form. Everything about him exudes raw masculinity and power. I can't wait for him to manhandle me later. He can toss me around as much as he likes, and I'll love every damn moment of it.

His inked muscles flex as he strikes again and again, the deceptively soft suede tails of the flogger kissing my skin with a sharpness and precision only a true Dom and Master can inflict.

Heat radiates through my skin, and my bite pressure on the bit refreshes with each blow. Before long, my legs are aflame from ankle to crotch. There's not an inch of them that doesn't feel lovingly and brutally flogged. Rather than any one spot being more painful than another, it smarts most when Jackson purposely, and with a glint of knee-weakening malice in his eyes, flogs an already hard-whipped area.

He knows how to extract an exquisite amount of pain without breaking the skin. Which is just as well, because if this cunt fucked my ink, he'd be paying for the fucking plastic surgery to fix the damage. My beauty and charm are a part of my business, and patrons pay a hefty fee for a private show with this body. I don't blame them, I'm hot as fuck.

"Motherfucker!" I swear, eyes ablaze, the bit falling from my lips. My cock is on fucking fire.

And Jackson stands there, teasing the floggers through his fingers, watching me with the utmost amusement. "Feisty," he muses aloud with a smirk on his face. "It suits you. But I'm afraid that bad behavior can't go unpunished, can it now, my slave?"

Slowing my breathing consciously, I nod. "No, Master."

"Well, how's this?" he says. "I'm in a fantastic mood, so I'll let you choose your own punishment from a selection of options." Jackson reaches back to tie his long, beachy blond hair into a messy man-bun, then leaves me to my own company as he fetches an assortment of toys, accessories, and implements. When he returns, my anus puckers and a shiver runs through me.

"So, option one. You stay this way, and I introduce the nipple clamps and breath play, as I jack you off for all and sundry to see. Option two, I flip you around, and we see how many anal beads fit up that ass of yours. And option three, now that you're all warmed up, I take you back to a private room so I can fuck the literal shit out of you and remind you who's boss."

I bite my lip in thought. I haven't played hard in a good while, and all three options sound like an epic time, but I've wanted Jackson to bury himself balls-deep in me since I walked in The Dungeon's doors… "Three," I answer confidently, holding my master's gaze.

Jackson's eyes sparkle in the dim, mood lighting of the club. "Excellent choice," he growls, his voice low.

Its gravelly timbre turns my insides to jelly in an instant. *I am so ready for this.*

My Master spends the next couple of minutes releasing me from the bonds that hold me to the St. Andrew's Cross, before reattaching the leash to my collar. "Come, slave," he says, tugging me along.

As we walk away a man dressed in skimpy leather appears with a utility belt of cleaning products, and he's sanitizing and wiping down everything we touched during our short session. And before we've disappeared down the dark labyrinth of halls to find a free room, the cleaner is already done and gone, like he was never there.

We find a private playroom and Jackson leads me in, then uses the key card in the wall slot to lock the door behind us. The room is luxuriously appointed. A king-sized, four-poster bed at the center boasts wrought-iron craftmanship, and lush red satin sheets. With its Gothic design and the incredible metallic roses that spiral their way up each post, it looks like it could belong to the Devil himself.

A whipping post features off to one side of the room, while a sawhorse used for spanking and bondage takes up a similar appointment on the opposite side. And hidden away in an alcove by the door is a contained shower recess for cleaning up after particularly messy play.

A shiver runs through me, and I lick my lips in anticipation. The thought of more furniture play is erotic, and just thinking about it has me hardening again. But we're here for the big bed, and the rough and tumble that will take place there.

"Get on the bed, slave," orders Jackson as he unclips the leash from my collar.

I obey without question, and like a good slave, despite the fiery kiss of the flogger still burning my flesh, I kneel in the middle of the bed. With my head bowed, back straight, and palms facing upward—resting on my thighs in submission and supplantation—I'm ready to receive or give as instructed.

The anticipation of our union hangs in the air, thick and tangible as Jack retrieves a pair of leather handcuffs, and a connected pair of nipple clamps.

I wince at the sight of the clamps. *Damn.* Those bastards hurt. But it's likely I'll scarcely fucking notice their bite once Jackson, the tattooed Viking, is burying all eight inches of his pierced cock inside of me!

Chapter Seven
Jackson

My God. Sebastian looks like a literal dark angel, like desire incarnate, and I feel my heart begin to race at the mere sight of him. With his perfect posture, his elaborate, colorful tattoos, and his unexpected obedience, I can't help but feel something. Though, I'm not quite sure what that *something* is. He has a magnetism, an allure, or some kind of gravity. And it threatens to suck me in so deep that I could almost drown if I dared succumb to its wild abandon.

With my cock growing harder with each passing second, I clear my throat, flick my hair over my shoulders, and approach the bed. "Raise your wrists," I command. My voice is huskier and contains more gravel than I expected, but it's all natural. This fine, lithe, fit beauty of man brings out the beast in me, and it's proving difficult to reign it in.

Sebastian raises his wrists to be bound, head still bowed. He doesn't move a muscle, and I can't help but admire his control. He might be a Switch, but he is a supremely trained submissive.

With his wrists bound, I yank on the chain between them, and he jerks forward, but maintains his balance, teetering on his knees, halfway between pulling back and falling forward. "You've spent a lot of time on the bottom, haven't you, pretty boy?" I ask.

"I have, Master."

"And do you have a current significant other?"

Sebastian hesitates before answering, licking his lips. "I have many playmates, Master. Some I have known for years, but none of them are ... my lover," he emphasizes.

Interesting. "I see."

"Master, may I speak?"

Intrigued, I acquiesce. "You may."

"I've watched you from afar, and dreamed of this moment, Jackson. Promise me you won't hold back. I want you to fuck me like the world's ending and there's only us."

A growl escapes me, and I bend down to whisper against his ear. "Oh, my beautiful dark angel. You have my word. There will be no holding back. Tonight, we drown together." A shiver ripples through my slave, and I release the chain, allowing him to kneel comfortably once more.

With a sudden and wicked smile, I pick up the nipple clamps from the bed. "Almost forgot these. They're such an exquisite agony, wouldn't you agree, slave?"

"Yes, Master. They are."

Left first, then right, I pinch the clamps wide, then allow their metal maws to bite down on Sebastian's precious pink nipples—aside from his palms, the soles of his feet, and his face, they're one of the very few naked, ink-free areas of flesh on his body.

Sebastian grimaces, pursing his lips, but remains silent.

"That's my pet," I praise. "You have a good pain threshold, but I do hope you won't be so quiet when the real fun begins. Now, face the headboard and present yourself to me. I'm going to get undressed and grab some lube so we can get the show started."

"Yes, Master." Without hesitation my slave adjusts his position, elegantly bending at hips to rest on his forearms, cuffed wrists together, his perfect ass in the air, knees spread to shoulder width.

"Fuck," I breathe as I undress casually, allowing myself time to appreciate the view. He's simply breathtaking. My boots come off first, then pants, and finally my simple black t-shirt, until I'm as bare as the day I was born. Similarly covered in ink, we make for a spectacular pair. We're both living, breathing works of art. Squirting a wad of clear lube into my palm from a pump on the wall, I clamber onto the bed behind him. With a wicked grin, I bring my lube-free palm down hard across his right ass cheek.

Sebastian hisses through his teeth, and his body temporarily tenses before relaxing again.

Satisfied, I slather my fingers in the lube, then spreading his cheeks, I smear a generous amount over his pretty little asshole. My cock twitches in anticipation. I work one finger inside him, and then two, ensuring he's well lubricated and ready to take my pierced beast.

My slave moans beautifully, his breath quickening as I fuck him with three fingers, pumping with increasing intensity to get him nice and riled up. Sebastian's back bows, his posture deepening to open himself to me and my deviant ministrations.

"Do you like that, slave?" I ask. My lower lip is slack with lust as I grip his left hip for support and finger-fuck him.

"Yes, Master," he answers obediently.

"Do you think you're ready for my cock?"

"Yes, Master. Please," he begs. "I want your cock. I need your cock."

The absolute dominance of my position overwhelms me. *I'm really going to fuck my enemy.* I'm going to claim my rival's ass and fuck him into submission. It's hard to believe after all these years. I went from hating him and wanting to smash his pretty face with its perfect black Emo eyeliner, to fapping over him in my office, torturing him in my club, and now…

Primed and ready, I press the head of my cock to Sebastian's puckered hole, and it pops in with just the perfect amount of resistance. "Damn, you're tight," I groan as I shuffle forward on my knees, easing my cock in further. And then with just the first inch in, I pause, my strong hands gripping his hips, savoring the sensation of his ass choking my cock.

Sebastian tries to push back, but I hold him fast.

"Not yet, pet," I growl. "Not yet." When I'm sure I'm not going to bust my nut, I lean slowly into him, burying my beast inside his ass one painstaking inch at a time.

My slave whimpers quietly in need. "Please, Master," he begs. "I hate this slow tease! I need you to jackhammer the shit out of me."

"Speaking without being granted permission," I say, the smirk on my lips evident in my subtle growl. "Not smart, slave. I think punishment is in order. And you know what they say. Be careful what you wish for." Without another word I thrust with all my might, burying myself to the hilt, before grinding against him with knee-weakening force. A deep groan escapes me.

An unholy grunt slips from Sebastian, and he shudders beneath me in the most delectable way, still desperately pushing back for more.

"You thirsty little cock-whore."

Chapter Eight
Sebastian

Jesus Christ. As Jackson slams into me, grinding himself against my ass, I'm violently bucked forward, almost collapsing to my chest on the bed under his sheer grunt and weight. It's hot as all hell. I can't remember the last time I was with a real, muscular babe like Jack. More often, I'm with women, or other well-dressed, suave men. The sort who wear suits and drink expensive spirits. The kind who own private jets and penthouses. And while they're my bread and butter—my loyal patrons and valued business donors—they're nothing like this. They're nothing like my brutal, inked Viking god, Jackson.

Even as he degrades me, I revel in it. The thought of being his thirsty little cock-whore only serves to make our union even more sinful and me painfully harder. Again and again, he thunders into me, his delicious Prince Albert piercing heightening the ecstasy to mind-boggling levels. Jackson's control and dominance is absolute, from the strength he punishes me with, to the way he grips me with his unforgiving hands. *And that voice!* God, that alone could almost make me come. His deep, husky gravel has me dribbling all over the sheets like a bloody teenage simp, just begging to be his slave.

Whether he's praising me or degrading me, it's equally as hot. As long as I'm his, and his attention is mine, I'm in bliss. Sharp, stinging pain sings across my scalp, jolting me from my fuck-crazed reverie.

With a fistful of hair, Jackson reefs back, causing my back to arch and bow. "Do you like that, slave?" he asks, pulling me all the way up until he can nip at my ear.

"Do you want more?"

Head titled back, my cock at full mast, I moan. "Yes, Master. Thank you. Fuck me, harder. Make it *hurt*." A heartbeat later and my nipples scream with blinding agony. Pain like fire pinches them between merciless metal jaws as Jackson tugs on the dangling chain connecting them.

I bite my lip, but it doesn't stop the genuine whimper that betrays my desire and penchant for pain. *I really am a masochist.* Pain thrills me in ways nothing else can.

"You sound so sweet when you whimper like that for me, my pet," he growls in my ear, before shoving me to my stomach on the bed. He roughly forces my legs together with his knees and plows deep, the tension of my clenched ass cheeks adding to his pleasure—and mine.

Garbled noises shred from my lips as he spears my innermost sanctum with renewed fervor. He's not the biggest cock I've had up me, but it's thick, pierced, and he uses it well. There's no point being hung like a fucking horse if you can't fuck to save your life. Sex is about so much more than the simple act of sawing in and out of a hole. It's about connection and power play, and for some, love.

And God, Jackson knows how to fuck. He ruts me like a demon freed from the pits of Hell. His thirst to break me open, forcing my body to succumb to his will and violence, grows by the minute. And Christ forgive me, but I'd let this man fuck the very ventricles of my heart if I could just watch the spectacle as a damn ghost! There could be nothing more beautifully erotic than being utterly destroyed by this exquisite beast. Except, maybe … for being destroyed *and* treasured by him.

"Where have you gone, pet?" whispers Jackson in my ear.

His delicious weight crushes the breath from my lungs, and I gasp. "I don't know," I breathe.

"Don't lie to me," he snarls, wrapping the crook of his arm around my throat, stifling my breath.

It becomes harder and harder to breathe. Autoerotic asphyxiation. *Fuck, yes!*

"Give me an answer, slave, or it's going to be light's out for you. And you don't want to know what I'd do to you if I had free reign over this ass."

"Tempting," I rasp, ever the brat.

"Sebastian," he says, running his hot tongue up the back of my ear as he continues to pump me, crushing me with his weight.

"I want you to break me," I cry out, wincing as the metal nipple clamps crush painfully between me and the mattress.

"Well, that can be arranged," Jack breathes. "But it's more than that, isn't it?"

I try to shake my head but can scarcely move in his brutal headlock. If he wanted to kill me right now, I'd have no hope of escape. I'm completely at his mercy. "I want you to want me, too." Darkness encroaches on my vision, and my mind swoons inside my skull, the edges of reality slipping away from me with every passing second.

Jackson eases off my throat, then, and with a deep breath the world starts to come back, the brightness overcoming the oblivion that would consume me alive.

"Are you with me, pet?" In the next instant I feel Jackson pull out and he flips me over.

Blinking against the lurid red glow of the room, my bearings slowly return, and I find myself staring up into his brilliant blue eyes. "I'm here," I whisper. I reach up tentatively to touch his dirty-blond beard with my still-cuffed hands.

"What are you on, Sebastian? Seriously."

I stare, still vague. *What does he mean?*

Rubbing his erect cock against mine, he catches my lips with his in a passionate, all-encompassing, and breathless kiss. His tongue plunders my mouth, seeking, probing, caressing, until I'm not sure whether I'm awake or passed out—lost to some beautiful dream.

"Wow," I say, dazed when he steals his lips away.

"I want you, Sebastian," says Jackson, continuing to frot me toward ecstasy. "I always have, from the moment I first saw you. When you opened The Red Bastille."

A moan slips from me and I close my eyes as my second orgasm of the night builds to excruciating heights. "But would you really want to be my lover?" I ask, my breath hissing past my teeth.

Chapter Nine
Jackson

I groan, hanging my head for a moment as my impending orgasm sends thrills of electricity through me, my muscles tensing and clenching, ready to let go.

"I'm going to come, Master," says Sebastian, his gaze suddenly panicked.

"No. I forbid it," I say. "Hold it until I say so."

My pet whimpers but nods, pursing his lips in that exquisite agony only one who engages in edging can understand, as he dances upon the precipice beside me. "Yes, Master."

"I told you we can be whatever you want," I say in partial frustration, answering his earlier question. "I gave you the option of enemies or lovers, and you fucked around with the idea of friends with benefits," I growl. "Then your bratty ass suggested enemies."

"That's not what I want," he says, running his hands over my inked chest, his gaze pleading. "I'm sorry. I'm sorry I was a brat. I want you to hurt me, but I need you to claim me. I want to be with you, Jackson."

His admission forces my breath to catch in my throat, and my heart to race. Owning Sebastian would be nothing short of a dream come true. He's beautiful, a talented businessman, a flexible lover, and an absolute deviant at heart—just like me. As much fun as the concept of remaining rivals is, owning his ass in an official capacity is worth *so* much more.

"I want to be your only lover," I say, catching his lower lip between my teeth. I grind against him, giving it a little love bite. "I want you in my Dungeon whenever I need you, not the other way around. And I want you outside of the club, not just behind closed doors. I want you to truly be mine—and not just my sub—my boyfriend."

Sebastian gasps, his fingers pale and splayed on my flesh in desperation. "I'm going to come," he sulks, biting his lip until I see blood bead.

"Do you accept my terms?" I press. My own orgasm is ready to explode out of me with enough violence to tear my cock off.

Sebastian's eyes are wide and full of desperation and honesty. "Yes, yes. I'll be yours, Master. I'll be your boyfriend. You'll be my only lover, I swear it. I swear to God."

His words are like a balm for my soul, the answer to a wish I didn't know I'd ever made. My red-light rival has become my lover, and it's all I want in this moment. *It's everything.* "Come with me," I command. I fuck my slick, throbbing, rock-hard cock against his until my ass clenches, my sac tightens, and my second orgasm of the night spews out of me in violent spurts, pumping my cum up Sebastian's colorful chest.

At the same moment, as if we were both too far gone to hold back a second longer, my boyfriend bucks beneath me, writhing and cursing under his breath as his liquid love mixes with mine in a delicious, glistening mess.

"Fuck," I growl. Supporting my weight, I rest my forehead to his. With my eyes closed, I savor this moment. I didn't get to finish in his gloriously tight, inked ass, but it doesn't matter. *Not one bit.* Because now this ass, and the man who owns it, are mine. *Sebastian Crenshaw is my boyfriend.* The words repeat in my mind as my breathing slows, and the blood returns to the rest of my body. "That was something else."

Sebastian tips his head back, and raises his face to

kiss me, and I let him. "It was," he breathes when our lips part.

Rolling off my perfect pet and onto the mattress beside him, I throw one arm above my head, using it as a makeshift pillow, and stare at the ceiling, lost in my bliss.

"So, what now?" asks Sebastian, his gaze searching, and lust glazed as he turns onto his side to watch me.

"Now, we get cleaned up and ready for act four."

"There's a fourth act?"

"Baby, we haven't even gotten properly started."

My boyfriend snakes his hand across my chest, then he props himself up on one elbow, a cheeky expression playing upon those gorgeous lips of his. "Well, before we hit the showers, how about you let me clean you up enough so you're presentable to walk the halls of your own club?"

A growl rumbles up from within me, and I feel a second fire burst to life, awakening with the heat and need of a slumbering dragon. "What did you have in mind?"

"Just let me take care of you, lover," he answers. He scooches closer, his head lowering and his tongue flicking out to languidly lap up the fast-cooling jizz on my belly.

I put both hands up behind my head and get comfortable, ready to enjoy the show.

Like a hungry little whore, Sebastian avidly cleans me, his gaze flitting up to meet mine every so often, a deviant, bratty gleam in his eyes.

It's hot as hell, and I can't wait to reward him for his diligence and good behavior. "You really are beautiful, Crenshaw," I say appreciatively. "I can't believe you've wanted me all this time and never said anything. We've wasted so much time."

My new boyfriend licks his lips and tuts with a delectable smirk. "And I can't believe you've hated me all this time," he retorts.

I shrug against the bed. "Love … hate … you know what they say. It's a fine line."

Sebastian laughs, and it's like music to my ears. "I think that's pleasure and pain you're thinking of."

I roll my eyes. "Same fucking thing."

"There," says my pet proudly, sitting back on his fine ass. "All clean."

I sigh. "I really am lucky you set up shop across the street from me."

Sebastian bites his lip. "Hang on," he says. "It appears I've missed a spot." And then he takes my half-soft cock into his mouth and begins to suck it clean, never batting an eye at the fact that he's chowing down on the taste of his own hot little ass.

So much for never going ass to mouth! I chuckle internally.

Chapter Ten
Sebastian

I have a fucking boyfriend. The thought spins around in my mind like a whirling dervish, obliterating any sense of clarity. The gorgeous Viking bastard and Dungeon Master Jackson Maguire is mine. And I am his. And now I'm in bed with him, sucking on his beautiful cock for the second time in one night!

His pierced beast begins to harden in my grasp, finding its strength again as I lavish it with the ardent love of my lips and tongue. Before long it's as hard as forged steel, and I can't help myself. With a mischievous wink at my moaning brute, I mount him—taking control. With his cock in my hungry mouth, and my needy ass hovering above his face, I foresee an early act four.

"What's this?" Jack asks.

And I thrill, careful not to bite down as a resounding *smack* sings across my inked ass.

"I didn't know you were serving hors d'oeuvres."

I moan as my Master spreads my cheeks and buries his face between, his hot tongue seeking the very depths of me as he penetrates and loves my quivering hole. *Is there anything he can't do?* I wonder, lost to the sensation of a mouthful of cock, and an assful of tongue.

It's not long before my master's fingers find their way inside of me, pumping my prostate with wicked precision as his free hand cups and massages my achingly firm sac.

I groan around his cock, the words "oh my God" sounding like nothing more than a pack-raped jumble of syllables.

My knees feel like they're going to buckle under

me as wave after delicious wave of pleasure assaults me. But I can't bow or break. Or I'll be impaled, spit-roasted between his cock down my throat and his hand up my ass.

"That's it, pet," he soothes, another two fingers working their way inside me.

I gasp around his cock, driven to double my efforts and deep-throat him, allowing him to butcher my throat until he reaches his own ecstasy. At this angle his thick eight inches hits my gag reflex repeatedly, but I force it down, bending it to my will with trained prowess. You don't learn to be a true submissive without knowing how to take a big cock and relax your throat for a pounding.

"Yes. Fucking Jesus," Jackson swears as he raises his hips to slam me harder.

But I can take the abuse. And I love it.

Soon his huge bloody tattooed fist is silent ducking its way up my ass, and it's been so long that it feels like I'm being split in two. I feel so full. There's just so much inside me, it's almost too much to bear. Tears leak from my eyes as I'm ravaged by a sickening combination of pain and pleasure.

Our conversation from earlier comes roaring back. There's a fine line between pleasure and pain. And it's so abundantly true. Every inch of me wants to escape the deluge of torment against my body, and yet in the very same breath is pushing back, begging like a slut for more.

"Fuck!" I scream around him, as his hot cream fills my throat—forcing me to swallow like a demon on speed just to combat gravity—and the deepest, most horrific orgasm I've ever experienced steamrolls me. Mind, body, and spirit. I'm fucking floored.

Somewhere in the distance I can hear Jackson's

voice—it sounds concerned and insistent, but I can't make out what he's saying. There's just darkness. Nothing but darkness, and a shrill, piercing, yet deafening silence that suffocates me, leaving me breathless and panicking within myself. It's Heaven and Hell all at once. I'm trapped, seemingly frozen between one heartbeat and the next. I've never felt anything like it in my life and I'm scared.

****

When I open my eyes next, the room is bright, the red glow gone, and every fucking inch of me feels so used that I don't know where I begin or where I end.

"Sebastian."

I blink again as my eyes adjust to the light. My throat feels dry. "Jackson?"

Then he's there, raising me up carefully, cradling me against his body, an open bottle of water pressed to my lips. "Drink," he says. "You gave me a fucking heart attack."

Without thought, I obey, sipping at the cool, refreshing liquid, before raising my hand to wipe my mouth. "What happened?" I ask, a strange and elusive lightheadedness still clouding my thoughts.

"More," he commands, without answering my question.

Again, I drink. Each small sip revitalizing me. I sigh and lick my lips when a third of the bottle is gone.

Jackson tosses the still mostly full bottle off the bed. No shits given. "How do you feel?" he asks, his brilliant baby blues searching mine.

I shrug in his arms. "I guess … dizzy. Not all here yet," I answer. "I feel light and heavy at the same time. It's bizarre."

"You had some kind of fucking seizure," says Jackson, worry etched on his features. "You came like a fucking firehose, bucking and gagging all at once. Then you went all fucking rag doll on me. You just collapsed, floppy as shit, like a broken doll. I called the fucking ambulance. They're on the way."

"Jesus Christ," I breathe, laying my palm against my forehead. "What the fuck? I'm in perfect health."

"Apparently not," says Jackson, brushing my black locks from my eyes.

Swallowing against the pain in my throat, I smile weakly. "I really wish you hadn't called the ambulance.

And then the Dungeon Master is back, his unmistakable brand of authority and dominance fills the room. "We take no chances here, love. This wasn't your run-of-the-mill subspace zone-out. Something's wrong, and I won't have any patron of The Dungeon not properly cared for, especially my damn boyfriend."

A chuckle bubbles out of me as I reach up to touch his face. "You called me your boyfriend," I tease.

"Watch it, brat," says Jackon, humor lightening his tone. "I'm still your damn master. Don't fuck with me."

I almost laugh at that, at the playfulness hidden behind my Jack's brutish exterior. But then the door to our private room bursts open and a team of trained paramedics storm in, swarming me like crazed ants fighting over a sugar-glazed donut.

Chapter Eleven
Jackson

The paramedics bundle my brand-new boyfriend onto a gurney and wheel him through the emergency exit and out into the alleyway behind The Dungeon where the ambulance is parked.

"I'll follow you," I say, squeezing his hand, before they wheel him away. *Better safe than sorry.* I quickly wash up, before collecting Seb's clothes and phone from my office where my cleaner so thoughtfully put them—having found them discarded by the Saint Andew's Cross earlier—I pop them into my black leather satchel and sling the bag over my body.

Picking up my phone, I hit the speed dial for my assistant manager. "Hey, Darren. Yeah, sorry to interrupt you. But I need you to come in now. We've had a code red here, and I need to follow a patron to the hospital. Can you make it in? Thanks, man. I owe you one. I'll text you later. Okay. Bye." Slipping my phone into my bag, I grab a bottle of water on my way out and slam it down, tucking my motorcycle helmet under my arm as I go.

I stroll through The Dungeon's lounge, and jog down the stairs to the bar. "Hey, Juliet," I call. "I'm heading out. I'm going to follow the ambulance to the hospital. I called Daz, he'll be in shortly. You think you got everything under control?"

Juliet nods. "We're good, boss. Nothing's going down between your bouncers and the security team."

That's true. I don't imagine there's anything those boys couldn't handle. I hired the best. "All right then, Juliet. I don't know if I'll be back in tonight, so if not, I'll see you tomorrow."

"No problems, Jack. I hope Mr. Crenshaw's okay."

"Me too," I say, before disappearing out the back of the club. Two minutes later I've got my helmet on, and I'm revving my Harley. Tearing out of my personal garage at the club, and out onto the main road, traffic is light. It always is in the city. Most rely on public transport or catch taxis or Ubers. No one wants to drive when they're coming into social central to get smashed and either fuck or dance the night away.

The multicolored and neon lights around me flash by as I weave my way between traffic. God, I love my bike. Nothing is as freeing as straddling a steel horse and blazing off wherever the fuck you desire. Outside of managing The Dungeon, it's what I live for. I'm a one-percenter without a club or chapter, what most in the culture refer to as a Nomad or a Lone Wolf. I'm not down for being bound to others when I have my own goals and ambitions, and notions about how I want to live my damn life. *I'm no one's bitch.*

For the most part, I'm left in peace. Patched members make up a fair few of my most loyal patrons, and those guys would defend me and my establishment if push came to shove. Especially as I deal from my club. No one outside the specific clientele I sell to would know that I make the best crystal meth in the city. It's pure as fuck, and my product ends up all over the nation. Transported in bulk by a select few—men I can trust not to rat me out and bring down the club.

Pulling into the hospital, I park my bike, pay for a damn ticket, and head inside. Approaching the administration desk, I remove my helmet and tuck it under my arm. "Hi. I'm looking for Sebastian Crenshaw. He was admitted not long ago. The ambulance picked him up from my club. I'm a friend."

The administrator smiles politely. "I'm sorry, sir, but only relations and family can visit at this time. He's still being monitored."

I clear my throat. "I'm his *partner*," I clarify. "Sebastian is my boyfriend."

"Oh," she says quickly, pursing her lips. "I'm sorry for the misunderstanding, sir. He's on level two, room four of the Jonathon Herbert Ward."

"Thanks," I say, turning on my heel. *God, that felt so strange to say aloud.* But it's true. Crenshaw is my bitch, baby. And I'm here to make sure he's all right. Taking the elevator, I find Sebastian's room in no time.

He's in bed, hooked up to fluids, with a pulse monitor on his finger.

"Hey," I say, as I knock on the open door.

"Hey," says Sebastian, a smile lighting up his face. "I didn't actually think you'd come."

I frown, dropping my satchel on a nearby chair, and place my helmet on top. "I said I was coming, didn't I?"

"Yeah, but we just…"

"Just hooked up? Just made things official?" I ask.

"Yeah, that."

"I always keep my word, Seb. If I say something, I follow through. And aside from being my boyfriend, you're someone I respect, and have known for years— even if from afar. I wasn't going to not check up on you. I mean, it's kind of my fault you're here in the first place."

"How do you figure that?" says Sebastian.

"Have you forgotten that earth-shattering, brain-blitzing orgasm already?"

Sebastian cracks a grin and shakes his head. "No, no, I absolutely have not," he admits. "Don't know that I ever will."

With my hands in my pockets, I wander closer to the bed. "But seriously, what've they said? Do they know what triggered the seizure? Are you epileptic?"

Sebastian shakes his head with a grimace. "It's the first one I've ever had to my knowledge, and they say I seem fine, but they want to keep me under observation overnight, just in case it happens again."

"You know, I've heard brutal orgasms can cause seizures. It's really fucking rare, but it does happen."

My boyfriend smirks. "Just my luck, huh? It must be God's way of saying, 'fuck you,' right? Experience the most mind-blowing orgasm of your life and he's like, 'Nope. There'll be none of that shit,' so he smites me like a motherfucking cunt."

"Well, if I believed in that sky fairy crap, it sounds just like the sort of shit he'd do," I agree with a lopsided smile. "I mean, he got shitty that one time and wiped out all of humanity. Flooded fucking everything, apparently. Bitch seems easily triggered. Probably just sore cause he's missing out on a good deep dicking."

Sebastian cracks it at that and it's fucking good to see him smile again.

Chapter Twelve
Sebastian

"You're rough as fuck, Jack. I've always loved that about you. You're the perfect counterbalance to me."

"I never thought of it that way before," Jack says honestly, sitting down on the bed beside me. "Up until tonight I've always viewed you as competition. As the total opposite of everything I am."

"But that's just it," I interject, reaching for his hand. "Opposites attract, Jack. We always want what we don't have. But together we *can* have the best of both worlds."

"Are you certain you want this?"

"Us?"

"Yeah," says Jack, his heavy brows furrowed.

"Yes, I want this. I've wanted this since I first laid eyes on you. Who wouldn't want to fuck the big, burly, tattooed biker running the city's premiere BDSM club?"

Jack's gaze drops to his boots. "Is that all you want? Sex?"

I retract my hand gently, sitting up straighter in my bed. "Well, what exactly is on offer, Jack? You said *lover*. You said *boyfriend*. You meant exclusive. But what does that mean?"

My Viking beauty's gaze flicks back to me. "I want it to mean everything."

"Feelings? Dates? Movie nights? The whole deal?"

"Exactly. I want to spend time with you, get to know you. Take you out on my bike and show you what freedom really feels like. I want to make you a part of my world, for real."

"And I'm not supposed to have any other lovers, *serious lovers*, but you?" I ask.

"Right."

"What about my playmates? For business."

Jack grimaces. "I know your club is different," he says. "You have billionaires to wine and dine. I can't expect you to change your way of life for me. Your business has to come first."

A small smile creeps to my lips. *Idiot.* "And how about you? What about your lovers? Would you give them up for me?"

Jack's baby blues burn like glacial ice into my very soul. "I would."

I'm floored. "I'm sorry. Seriously?"

"For you, Sebastian, I could be exclusive if that's what you wanted."

Wow. Ripples of shock send little chills through my bones that fizzle out at my toes. "You really want me that badly?"

"Did I stutter?" Jackson asks, his gaze hard.

"No, you didn't," I say, my mind racing a million miles an hour. "So, you'd give up your playmate lovers for me, but wouldn't expect me to do the same?"

"Our businesses are different," he answers simply. "I'd rather have you—be with you—than not have you at all."

My heart thunders in my chest and a deafening clarity sings through my entire being. He'd give up his way of life for me. For just the mere *chance* that we could grow to be something more... I'll be fucked if I'm not that damn keen, too! "I'll axe the playmates," I say without hesitation. "They're gone. I'm done. If you're giving up yours, I'm giving up mine. We'll have each other, and that's that."

Jack swallows hard, a beautiful, rare vulnerability

visible in his eyes. "How … but what about that side of your business? You're the fucking draw card, Sebastian. People don't just go to The Red Bastille because it's a great club, they go because it's *your* club. The paparazzi fucking love you, and the sheeple flock to be near you."

"Believe it or not, I didn't always fuck my clientele," I say. "It became a novelty and tool to assume greater gains and reach higher heights once I developed a name for myself. When I first started out, I was just me. The eyeliner-wearing, colorfully inked, suit-wearing Emo kid. And I can be that again if I want. It's my damn business. It will continue to thrive with or without the availability of my cock and ass. And if clients still want famous pie, I have more than a few friends in my Little Black Book who don't mind working a night for a big hunk of change."

Jackson stares at his black inked hands, wringing them in his lap, before meeting my gaze once more. "Let's do it, then," he says. "Together."

"Kiss me," I say, challenge in my tone and smile. "Let's seal the deal, sober, and beyond the walls we've built for ourselves."

Jack doesn't need to be asked twice. He scooches forward on the bed until he's close enough to embrace me. Raking his fingers through my hair, his other hand firmly seizes my chin, before he draws me into a passionate and stomach-fluttering kiss.

I sigh into his mouth.

He increases the tension on my scalp ever so slightly, reminding me who and what he is: Jackson fucking Maguire, Dungeon Master. And while his heart might be soft for me, he's all steel.

Breathless and flustered, my cock throbs beneath the pristine white hospital sheets with renewed need. A fucking seizure won't keep me from my hot Dom boyfriend. Not a chance in hell. The sound of a woman clearing her throat interrupts us, and I feel heat flush my cheeks, as Jackson breaks our kiss.

"I'm sorry to interrupt," says a nurse in soft blue scrubs. "I'm just here to check your blood pressure, Sebastian, and take your dinner order."

"Oh, God, no," says Jackson. "Don't worry about the order. I'll go and grab my boy something decent if that's okay?"

The nurse smiles, clearly charmed. "Of course. He's not on any dietary restrictions at this time."

"Excellent," says Jackson rising from the bed and straightening his cuts. "All right then, I'll leave you in capable hands and fetch you something for dinner. Any requests?"

I grin, my mouth already watering. "I'd love some sushi," I say, hopefully.

"Consider it done," says Jackson. With a gleam in his eye and a wicked smile, he walks out of my room, tall as a king with a country to conquer.

Chapter Thirteen
Jackson

When I return with a bagful of sushi, the nurse is long gone and Sebastian is lying back in his bed, reclining comfortably, watching TV.

His gaze snaps to me as soon as I enter the room, his smile bright. "Hey," he says, raising himself to a seated position.

"Hey," I answer, placing the bag on the wheelie table beside the bed. "Here, let me help you." Sebastian's expression is adorable as I fix his pillows for him.

"Thank you."

"My pleasure," I say.

"So, what've we got? I'm starving."

"I got a bit of everything. I didn't know what you'd like. For all I fucking know, you could be a damn vegan or vegetarian." Pushing the adjustable table over his bed, I start unpacking the bag's contents onto its clean surface. "We've got some raw salmon nigiri, and a variety of maki. California roll, prawn and avocado, teriyaki chicken, katsu chicken, spicy tuna, and even veggie roll. So, take your pick."

Sebastian's eyes are as big as saucers. "It looks *so* good," he says emphatically. "Thank you, babe."

Babe. My stomach flip-flops, and I can't help the easy grin that accompanies the ridiculous and unfamiliar sensation. "It was no trouble."

"Here, sit with me," says Sebastian, moving across and patting the mattress beside him. "We can watch trash TV together."

"Japanese maki and trash TV? Sounds like the perfect first date."

Sebastian's smile is as blinding as the damn sun, and his happiness is fucking contagious. "Definitely. And for what it's worth, I eat everything and anything. Don't let the suits and flawless makeup fool you. I'll just as happily eat a truck stop pastie as I will eat a five-star steak dinner. I'm easy."

"So I've noted," I say, giving him a gentle nudge in the ribs with my elbow and a wink.

My perfect boyfriend laughs, then plops a slice of the salmon nigiri into his mouth, closing his eyes. "Mm," he moans, a smile of utter bliss on his face.

With a contented sigh of my own, I pull our drinks from the bag. "Bubble tea?" I ask.

"You drink boba?"

"Ah, yeah. I fucking love all things Japanese," I answer.

Sebastian grins and stabs his giant straw into the cup's thin plastic film. "Me too!" He takes a deep slug, several tapioca pearls shooting up the straw. "Oh my God. Peach is my favorite. How did you know?"

I stab my own tea. "I didn't. It's just my favorite."

"Bloody hell, Jack. Who fucking knew you'd be my perfect man?"

I shrug and take a drink, reveling in the sweet, milky beverage that I've secretly enjoyed since my early teen years. "It's not me who's perfect. It's all you, my brat."

"Well, to each his own," says Sebastian, flicking his ebony hair from his face with a very atypical air of bratty defiance.

"Watch it," I say, a laugh escaping me as I shake my head. I squish a liberal amount of wasabi onto my spicy tuna roll and give Sebastian the side-eye. "You just wait until you're out of here and given a clean bill of health," I warn. "I'll take out any attitude on that sweet ass of yours."

For the next few hours, we eat and drink and laugh until we're red-faced and thoroughly satisfied. Sebastian rests his head on my shoulder when we're done, and it's not too long before he starts to drift off, safe in the comfort that I'm here.

At ten o'clock the same nurse returns, and she places a hand over her heart, mouthing "Bless," as she stops on the threshold. "I'm sorry," she says aloud. "But visiting hours are over. You'll have to say your goodbyes, but you're welcome to come again at eight a.m."

I nudge Sebastian. "Hey, I have to go, Seb. The fuzz is here."

Sebastian's eyes flutter open and focus on the nurse at the door. "You're an idiot, Jack," he says, righting himself.

"An idiot who spent all night keeping your ass company," I remind him.

"Thank you," he says. "For everything. Aside from the whole seizure thing, I had a blast. We'll have to do it again sometime."

"Definitely," I say, echoing his earlier sentiments as I get to my feet. "If you need a lift home tomorrow or anything, give me a call," I say. "Your phone, clothes, and my card are in the bag there," I say, gesturing to my satchel.

"I will," says Sebastian.

Leaning over, I place a kiss on his forehead, and ruff up his perfect hair. "Good night, sexy. Hear from you later, then."

Sebastian beams as I walk by the nurse and offers me a cheeky wave.

Taking the elevator back down to the ground floor, I head for my bike, only to find a damn ticket stuck to my windshield. "Motherfucker," I breathe, but I'm not the least bit annoyed. Fighting the law is my default position, but right now, I couldn't care less about a damn parking fine.

Spending the entire night with Sebastian was everything. The whole world suddenly feels different. Like possibilities, paths, and an entirely new level of happiness that wasn't available to me before, now shine bright and clear toward a future I couldn't possibly have dreamed of, like the beams of a lighthouse in the darkest and most treacherous of nights to guide lost ships at sea safely home...

Chapter Fourteen
Sebastian

Having been given the "all clear" by the hospital and discharged, I leave none the wiser as to my sudden and unexplained, orgasm-induced seizure. Unless I suffer another seizure, they can't formally diagnose me with anything. For now, they're deeming it a rare and unlikely event. And I'm free as a bird to go on living my life until such time treatment is deemed necessary.

Gripping Jackson's waist, we zip through the streets of Los Angeles, the city of lost angels. A more befitting name for our home, I couldn't imagine. On the back of my boyfriend's Harley, I feel as if I have wings. It's a rush I've never experienced, but I am fucking loving it and could see myself getting used to it. It's exactly what Jack said. Riding is freedom, and now I've had a taste? It feels as though I'll never have my fill.

Soon, we pull up to the apartment building I call home. The Harley rumbles beautifully, purring to sleep as Jackson turns off the ignition, and we dismount.

"That was fucking wild," I say as I remove my helmet.

"I told you it was sweet."

"I might have to get one of these bad boys for myself."

Jackon smirks. "I'm a Nomad, baby. I ride alone."

"That's cool," I respond. "I think I'd prefer to ride alone too."

"So, we'll be riding alone together, then?" says Jack, cocking a brow.

"Them's your words," I say, smacking him on the ass as I dance out of his reach. "Want to see my place?"

Jackson glances down at his watch.

"Got somewhere better to be than this ass?" I ask, giving him the look.

Jackson swings his keys around his finger before pocketing them. "You're so fucked," he says, stalking toward me.

I grin. "That's what I'm hoping."

As we enter the complex, Jackson glances at the buttons in the elevator, then raises his gaze to mine. "You're in the fucking penthouse, aren't you, brat?"

"Damn straight. Best views in the city. Plus, I love jacking off at the window with everyone beneath my cock."

Jackson slams the top floor button, and the doors close behind him. In the next instant he shoves me against the wall, his weight trapping me as his one hand grabs a fistful of my hair, and the other slips down the front of my tailored trousers.

I moan into his mouth as our lips crush against one another.

His mouth opens to me, and he stakes his claim, aggressively kissing me as he begins to stroke my cock. Then his teeth are at my throat. He nips, grazing my flesh with his teeth, sucking on the skin hard, forcing my blood to the surface and leaving me with a love bite—marking his territory like a baser beast.

"Oh my God," I gasp, my hands straying to his long, dirty-blond locks. Like the cheeky little shit I am, I slip my hand down his leathers and start playing with him, reveling in the feel of his semi-erect cock as we grope each other like rabid teens in a hotel elevator on Spring Break.

Minutes of frantic, desperate passion reach a fever pitch as the elevator pings, stopping at my own private floor. Stumbling into the hall, I reach into my pocket for my key card and chaotically swipe it as Jackson continues to ravage me.

Pushing the door open, he kicks it closed behind us, his eyes blazing. "I'm claiming that ass again," he says, peeling off his leather jacket, and then his simple black t-shirt, dumping them on my expensive furniture. "But this time, I'm filling it with my hot cum."

He continues to strip, his now-erect cock emerging from his leathers with an intimidating jerk. "Get naked, brat. Now. Or I'll skip the lube when I go to town on your ass."

"Joke's on you, cunt," I retort, before biting my lower lip. "I love a good dry fuck!"

"Swearing at your master? You're *so* screwed."

I grin, awaiting the cat and mouse game that is the dance of a true master and slave. And then the chase is on.

Naked as the day he was born, inked from the neck down, Jackson charges at me, his blond locks flowing behind him as his epic, muscular form powers forward. He looks every inch the fucking Viking juggernaut.

I turn on my heel and make to jump over the couch, but I'm not quite quick enough, and in the next instant I'm yanked backward by my black silk shirt. I hear the fabric rip as Jackson slams me onto my back on the couch.

"You really want me to rough you up, don't you?" he growls, tearing my shirt wide open, and sending black pearl buttons flying in all directions.

"Where would the fun be in behaving, Master?"

Jackson throws my shiny black business shoes across the room, and reefs my trousers off, giving me a chance to escape, and raise the stakes.

I dive-roll, making for the cool, clean white tiles,

and start to scramble.

But that big fucker is as powerful as a bloody bear, and he launches himself, landing on top of me, and pinning me to the floor.

I put up a struggle for the excitement of it, but he soon has me overcome.

He pins my hands behind my back, holding them tight at the base of my spine as he spreads my legs roughly with his knees. A second later he's spitting into his hand and slathering my hungry hole. Another second, and the head of his cock is pressed firmly to my entrance.

A moan slips from my lips as he leans into me, using his weight to his advantage.

"You might be my boyfriend, but for the next twenty-four hours you're my red-light rival. You're stealing my clientele and strutting around in those fucking suits like the pretty little bitch you are. And you're going to suffer for it, Crenshaw. I'm going to show you just what I'd do to my enemies. I'll break you and then make you beg for more."

With my face pressed to the tiles, a thrill-like fear races through me. He is so fucking hot when he lets his inner Alpha out to play. Then his cock surges forward and I cry out, my breath forced out of me in an inelegant grunt. I instinctively try to climb out of my own skin in an attempt to elude the burning eight inches that sear up my fucking poor ass.

Buried to his full length, he grabs a handful of hair and roughly shoves my head against the floor, until my cheek is smooshed and I'm wincing in a heady mix of pain and pleasure. Jackson smiles. I can hear it in his voice, even if I can't see it on his face. "That's a good little bitch," he croons, making me weak at the knees. "You want this, don't you? You preen and primp, playing the Switch when it suits," he says between plundering thrusts. "But really, you just want to be taken. You want to feel owned by someone strong enough to claim you."

When I fail to answer, he reefs my head back, sending searing threads of lightning across my scalp.

"Tell me you want me to fuck you until you can't shit straight," he snarls. "Tell me you want me to fill this hungry little bitch asshole until you're leaking all over your pretty penthouse."

I gasp as he fucks my hole without mercy, his Prince Albert piercing hitting the most sensitive and vulnerable places inside of me.

"Answer me, you fucking slut," he demands, leaning back onto his knees. Sharp, brilliant pain radiates from my toned ass cheeks as he slaps one, and then the other. Again and again, until I'm swearing like a fucking sailor.

"Fuck you, motherfucker!" I hiss, indignant in face of the pain as the thrill of the lifestyle role-play has me uncomfortably hard against the cold tiles.

Jackson forces me onto my knees, maneuvering me as easily as a wolf stalking sheep.

I raise myself to my hands, pushing back against his aggressive cock, despite my protests. I can't help what I love. And I love a badass dominating, bullying, and possessing me. I won't lie. Not with words, or with my body. Not to my Jack—my boyfriend—my master. I've wanted this, all of this, for too fucking long to play coy now. This is our game, and I'll play hard.

My master pulls me back, bringing me upright with him, then his hands are around my throat, and I'm grasping at them desperately as they begin to crush my airway, suffocating me. But I'm not trying to pull him away. I'm not fighting for my life. I'm latching onto an anchor, a lighthouse in the dark, a point on the horizon to which I can cling until the vicious onslaught is over. By anchoring myself, I can lose myself to subspace and feel oblivion tugging at my consciousness.

Head back, choking as Jackson thrusts his powerful hips, burying himself in my dry ass over and over, I feel the darkness encroaching. There's nothing but cock and a sense of disembodiment. It's surreal and grounded, and everything and nothing simultaneously. It's like being caught on the cusp of a dream or nightmare. The kind where you find yourself seemingly lucid, but unable to awaken and save yourself from the demons who would fuck you in ways that make terms like "unholy" sounds like child's play.

The light suddenly returns, and I gasp like a sailor broaching the surface of a hellish sea. My body thrums, every nerve afire as Jackson groans behind me, one arm now wrapped around my chest, the other hand having found its way into my mouth. He thunders inside me, pulling at my jaw like I'm cattle. My legs begin to quiver uncontrollably, and I feel the wave of ecstasy building inexorably within me. It bursts forth, erupting from my cock like a congealed cream sprinkler.

"Holy fuck," Jackson growls. He rails me hard, one final, magnificently brutal thrust sending us sprawling forward together, and crashing to the floor.

Still reeling, not entirely retuned from my venture into subspace, I lay trapped beneath him, a mangled, fucked, and exhausted pile of once humanity. Slickness smears under my cheek—cold as the floor—and I shudder internally. I feel every bit the dirty piece of trash of my fantasies. Used, abused, and left lying in a pool of my own cum like a whore. *Fuck, yeah!*

"Did that do it for you, baby?" comes a husky whisper in my ear.

A smile betrays me, and I sigh, nodding. Not capable of giving voice to anything remotely coherent in my current state.

"You're welcome," says Jackson. "You did so well, baby. You're a good slave."

The praise sings through my soul, warming my heart and fulfilling every secret and debauched desire I've ever dreamed of in a scene. And as Jackson pulls out, leaving me leaking all over myself and the floor, I let go, falling down the dark and endless rabbit hole of fuck-crazed exhaustion.

Lurid red lights flash behind my eyes as I give in, plummeting through oblivion like a star falling from the heavens. *We're going to have one hell of a party tonight.* For the first time ever, The Dungeon and The Red Bastille are going to join forces, and Los Angeles will hear us raving and fucking until the sun rises over the city of lost and damned angels. And we'll be there, together among it all—proud as fuck—announcing our deliciously deviant enemies-to-lovers union to the world! No fucks given.

The End

BROKEN

L.J. Longo

Copyright © 2024

Chapter One

"Hey, bartender, give me a quick blow."

The bar mirror reflects me and liquor. Between my bright-blue hair and the bottles, it's like a warning sign of forbidden pleasure. I'd just come from a jog, but even in my running shorts and sweaty graphic tee, I'm the damn finest man in East Quay, Galway City's finest gay bar and male revue. Even when it isn't empty as a church.

Paul stares in astonishment. Like a knocked-over scarecrow. "W…what? Chard, no."

"I was kidding." Shit, did he think I meant it? "Unless you wanna do it."

Paul will always do in a pinch.

"Did you forget I have a boyfriend again?"

Used to do in a pinch. Before the boyfriend. I'd met the guy once and rate him a low six. Paul could do better, because Paul could do me. *Let's not get too carried away, gym bunny. He doesn't like you.*

I ignore the nasty voice in my head and tease. "Give your boy toy a call. Maybe he's down for a threesome."

"Knock it off, Jeremy."

Once the "Mr. Paul Thayer voice" comes out, I swivel away and survey my empty playground. Older gay couple happily eating an early dinner in the booth. A coven of lesbians crowding a high-top. In a few hours, this will be wall-to-wall bodies, and it's not bragging to say I'll have my pick.

"You're antsy today. You taking your meds?"

"I am." The jittering energy in my muscles means I'm due for an episode. Maybe I can outrun it. "Guess I better hit the gym."

"Were you skipping leg day again?"

"Dude!" I spin on the stool, earnest and offended. "Some lines you just don't cross."

He's about to defend himself, when our boss emerges from the back with a crate of clean tumblers. Judith Churm lost any fucks she'd given about gender to the first round of grunge and when she enters the room, you sit up and pay attention.

"Hey, Chard. You on for the teaser tonight?"

"Sure am."

"Great. Paul, grab the tequilas?"

Once he left, Jude picks up the rag he'd left in the disinfectant and redid all his work. Her gaze sweeps her empty empire.

"How's the cross-fit class going? Anyone drop yet?"

"My students don't quit," I scoff. I love bitching about the overcrowded cross-fit class and Jude—because she's a good friend, great boss, and exceptional bartender—listens attentively as I tell the tale.

Until the door chimes as a customer enters.

The entry wall blocks him from my view, but Jude cackles, "Oh, here's someone for you, Chard. This cheap bastard comes in every Tuesday to see the teaser, but never to the show."

A little guy came into the bar, returning her wave. Not "little" like Paul's boyfriend. Not soft. His jaw and nose could cut wire. Scrappy. Except he's nestled in a cozy green flannel and a coat several sizes too big. Trying to be mistaken for a butch dyke, but wearing a thick beard. He's out of place, not just in a gay bar, but with himself.

"How's your week been, Larry?" Jude asks.

"Pretty damn dead. With this congress, there's not—" The man notices me leaning on the bar and he forgets it's impolite to stare.

Jude calls him back with a warm, "The usual? Sour and a cheesesteak?"

"Yup." He stands at the bar, as far from me as possible.

I study him in the mirror. The dude's face is wrecked. Scarred by dozens of little gashes and divots, including one big white spot breaking up his left eyebrow. His upper lip is permanently split, like a piercing gone wrong. Must have been in a car crash.

In the mirror, his eyes meet mine. Pale blue, cold, and angry.

I don't look away at once, maintaining eye contact with his reflection. I'm not used to people frowning at me. It makes me uneasy.

Paul emerges, arms full of tequila bottles.

Feeling uneasy makes me mischievous. "I guess you can blow me since you're providing the liquor."

Those angry baby blues swivel away from the

mirror as the guy turns toward me in shock. "What?"

"But that's a lot of tequila, even for me, Paul." I act like I'd only just saw the little man sitting there. "Sorry, I was teasing my buddy."

"Who still has a boyfriend." Paul wanders back into the storeroom for another armful.

"You ever meet Chard in person, Larry?" Jude set his drink on the bar.

"No." He doesn't touch it until she skewers a cherry on a tiny straw and drops that into the glass. "Seen him dance."

I smile over, turn to accept his praise, and extend my hand. "Chard Stagger."

He takes my hand. "Laurence Trockel."

That name is unfortunate.

Something's wrong with his fingers. The tips of the gloves are empty. *What the hell is this guy?*

I smile brighter to drive away any revulsion I betrayed. "Trockel? Interesting name."

"It's awkward, but it's mine."

The only name more awkward I can think of is Jeremy Sowenburger, but I don't trot my real name out for strangers. "What brings you to East Quay every Tuesday?"

"What do you think?"

Oh, hostile ... sexy!

He clears his throat and backs off. "I meet some friends here. We see the teaser."

"You can sit if you like." I gesture to the stool beside me.

"No." He doesn't even deliberate.

Even straight men never shut me down so hard.

He stirs his sour, sucks the cherry off the straw, almost seductive. He'd do for a quickie. A three or a four.

"So, Chard," he bites my name, accusing it of

being fake. "How long have you been stripping?"

"About twenty-nine years. I never liked clothes."

His full smile is unexpectedly charming. Raises him to at least a five.

I lean nearer. "How long have you been watching strippers?"

"Ever since Jude hired a cook. I come for the cheesesteaks."

Christ, was he actually straight? "The half-naked beefcakes don't interest you?"

"Never said that."

He is not.

With another five minutes to amuse him, he'd be putty in my hands. But Jude brings him dinner, and he takes the plate and his drink to the high-top in the corner.

I watch as he sets up a computer and doesn't cast me a second glance. If this is a tactic to pique my interest, it fucking worked.

****

After my run, my shower, and my afternoon meds, I return to the bar too early for my call. I hang out with Paul, ignoring the wistful hints from the Latino rocking a fedora, indifferently declining the drink from the bear in a red tank, and wait to more kindly reject the very young twink being pressured by his girlfriends to approach me.

Trockel lurks in his corner, his cut-up face illuminated by the blue glow of his tablet. He rubs his beard with gloved hands but never lifts his eyes to the room. I can't shake the taste of our encounter, and I hate that.

"You know, I realize that as the studliest stud who

ever studded, you might never have faced this particular dilemma, so here's a tip." Paul put two empty shot glasses in front of me. "You buy these shots, carry them over, give him one, then you don't make fun of him."

"I'm in a gay bar and I'm a goddamn male stripper. I do *not* buy drinks."

"In two hours you can pull it out of your thong." Paul fiddles with a bottle. "You'll want a snakebite. It's the only other thing I've ever seen him drink."

"What happened to his hand?" I wiggle my fingers at Paul.

"Christ, you're an asshole."

"Wait, wait…" I reach for his arm. "I'll give you a twenty later."

"Thanks for the generous tip." He turns away to perform his alcohol alchemy.

"You can take it with your teeth, and you're welcome."

Paul set down two neon-green shots. "Do us a favor, and don't break the little guy, all right? That hard-on you're trying to get rid of counts as a concealed weapon in at least three states."

****

I fall into my Queen Bee strut to mask my nerves. I haven't been rejected by any kind of man since I grew into my height and built up my muscles. I wasn't ready to take a "no" from this guy.

"So, Trockel, do I call the shots since I bought them?" The green potions rap loudly on the high-top.

The little guy jolts, and only just stops himself from punching me. *Stressed much?*

His face remains hard and unapologetic and he glares at

the shot. "What does that even mean?"

"I'm still work-shopping that line." I sit across from him. "Want me to try another?"

He raises his unbroken eyebrow, unimpressed with me.

I lean nearer. "What do we talk about for the next ten minutes before you come upstairs to my apartment and give me that blowjob we were talking about earlier?"

He doesn't have the courtesy to look flustered. "Terrible line. And I'm meeting with someone any minute now."

What does this guy want? The confusion makes me twice as determined to get my hands on his ass. Even though he was barely a six.

"So, are you unavailable?"

He sips his whiskey. "Would that stop you?"

No. Not always.

"Of course. But if you're just intimidated because I'm hot—"

He gives me a very not intimidated smile and picks up the shot. "Tell you what, since you bought the shot, why don't you tell me what you want to do for me? Drink first."

Snakebites are lime, high-proof, and truly vile. I slam the empty on the table, making him flinch again, then loom over the little man.

"So, first, I want to remind you why you come to see *my* teaser every week and give you a private show. Then I'd like to find out what's under all this flannel." I stroke the fabric where it lay over his chest. Under the cozy fabric, there was nothing soft. All bone and tense tight muscle. The desolate hardness of his body turned me on more than I expected. "Maybe, if you like all that, engage in a harmless bout of wildly passionate, totally protected sex."

He regards me with steely eyes, as if beautiful men drip on him every damn day. Then shrugs. "All right. No need for any of that other crap. I'll suck your cock."

I'd never received anything but a resounding, "Yes, please," and the occasional puppy-eyed, "OMG, really!" I feel cheated.

"But later," he says indicating his tablet. "I'm busy now."

"Hey!" Jamie, the revue's cute gender-indeterminate DJ, leaned on the high-top with the disgusting grace of a former ballerina.

I cringe, embarrassed to be seen chatting up Laurence Trockel, certain Jamie would assume I was taking advantage. But damn it, the man had not been easy.

Then they say, "Sorry for being late, Laur. Public transit."

Trockel all smiles and warmth now, stands and embraces Jamie. "Hey, no worries. I had a real-live East Quay Cutie to entertain me."

The change, instant as putting on a mask, astonished me. I hate the remarkable ease. I want some of that for myself.

"Chard, you getting interested in advocacy?" Jamie unpacked their backpack, glancing at me uncertainly.

I could stay. Force myself into the conversation, and possibly into whatever advocacy was. *Not good behavior.* Yeah, that's the mania making demands. So, I clear the table of the shot glasses.

"Thanks for the drink." I wink. "Gotta get dressed so I can take my clothes off."

His brow arches again, but he doesn't correct me.

Jamie relaxes, my presence at his table explained

at last. Once their world turns in the correct orbit again, they launch into a conversation about a homeless shelter and some kind of logistics with a shuttle bus.

So, I wander upstairs, alone. Not what I expected.

I knew who I'd be dancing for. Show Laurence Trockel what he was rejecting.

No, not Trockel. Jamie with their knack for renaming people had it right. He was Laur—unique, secret, and mysterious. A sane man could get inordinately attached to someone named Laur.

And I was not exactly sane.

Chapter Two

"Listen up, ya slackers and sluts," Jamie plays the room like a soundboard and every head turns as the lights dim. "Do y'all want a taste of the East Quay Cuties?"

Of course they do. Why else would they pay a cover charge on a Tuesday?

While the crowd shouts, a thin trail of light appears making a path from our "man cave" to the stage. The path clears and Jamie cross-fades from the house-mix to my song.

"Y'all wanna know who's on tap tonight?"

They roar. My name is among the screams.

"I'ma give y'all a little hint."

The opening of P!nks' 2012 masterpiece, "Slut Like You" titter over the dark room and the regulars lose their minds.

Deep voices whoop and howl. High voices shriek. I hadn't even stepped into the light and someone starts to chant. "Stagg-er! Stagg-er!"

Jamie won't encourage a chant until I'm safely on the stage. "Chaaard Stagger! Coming out!"

That's the cue. A little before my time in the music, but Jamie knows I don't give a shit. I'm no ballerina.

I step out of the man cave and into the light walking with a confident swagger into the mob. Their roar drowns out all trace of the music. By the time I start dancing, they're a frenzy of lust. Most of them keep an awed distance, as if I'm something beautiful and contagious to be witnessed at a distance, as if the heat of my body burns.

Still, I encourage audience participation. Lean into the groping of a very drunk group of nurses, beckon those pink-faced boys, offer lewd hip-swivels to the bride-to-be who is absolutely coming for my dick until her maid-of-honor protects me.

I spend too long in the masses. The other Cuties dart to the stage, afraid the crowd would tear them to pieces.

Isn't that part of the appeal?

Jamie gives me the cue to get my ass on stage. "Chard Stagger? Show us…"

The regulars join in. "What you got!"

What I "got" is mania. I'm barely in control of myself, let alone the crowd. I always lose my clothes faster than the other Cuties and I've forgotten which choreography I planned. But I know my business.

There's an art to unbuttoning a jacket to make people scream. Anyone can yank off tearaway pants, but it takes a special combination of hip, knee, and back to pull off sliding them down, threatening to bare your ass, and making people adore you for not following through. I know how to make them squeal and I give it a hundred and ten percent.

When P!nk starts barking commands, I'm on my knees, as naked as the law allows, covered only by the skimpy red strap. At the edge of the stage, shoulders to the ground, hips in the air, cash fluttering down around me.

This bridge is bigger than the cash, though. This moment is for caressing my chest and thighs, for tracing nipples and the divots of my abs while the mirrors reflect everything for the audience in the back. The ones sitting at the high-tops, no longer looking at their tablets.

In this brief and sensual union of dancer and whore, I'm the melting center of the sex-starved crowd. All eyes for me. All minds consumed by my body and their dreams. My movements mold the mob's shared fantasy, my aimed winks and smiles feed the frenzy.

When the song ends, the roar is brain-melting.

Jamie breaks the spell by bringing up the lights and jingling a coin jar into the microphone. "Show him some love, folks. He works for tips. You can also tip Chard on your card at the bar. But look! His friends are here to help!"

The change is instant, like waking up from a dream. The eyes look away from me and to pockets, wallets, and money clips as they seek the means to pay for their pleasure. Three other Cuties join the crowd. If it was anyone but me, they'd come up to the stage and there would have been an excerpt from the actual show, but ... well ... it's me. There's a lot of cash to collect.

The song vamps as I swivel and dip along the edge of the stage and they pay for the privilege of being near me. Across the elevated catwalk, strutting my way to Jamie's wall of machinery. Normally, I clear my tips into their jar then complete my circuit and make a sexy exit.

Tonight, I say into the microphone, "I owe the bartender a twenty."

Jude looks confused and Paul turns fifty shades of red. He gestures frantically, *no*. But Jamie rallies the crowd to chant "*Pay up!*"

This crowd will not be denied.

I take a twenty directly from a patron and carefully arrange it in my thong, then cha-cha my way along the catwalk to the edge of the bar where Paul reluctantly waits. If the bar was cleared for dancing, I could step over—*Do it anyway, do it for the bit*—but it's not cleared tonight, so I stay at the edge doing a demure little Betty Boop swivel while Paul hides his face and inches closer to take the money.

I drop low and grab his hands, making the crowd laugh and cheer. When it's clear I'm not going to let him escape, Paul relents and takes the bill with his teeth.

The crowd's approval drowns not only the music but also Jamie's voice as they try to announce the revue's times. I saunter back to her microphone. With a gesture from me, the crowd hushes.

I make eye contact with Laur still sitting at his high-top sipping his whiskey. I coo into the mic, "I'll see you all at the show. Starts at nine."

Then I wink and kiss and dart out the fire exit to escape the crowd.

****

The fire escape goes to the alley. The alley wraps around the side of the building and into the man cave. When I step into the familiar darkness, the heat of the club tingles on my skin. The other three Cuties are still working the crowd.

I dab away the sweat with a baby wipe and rub off the tape keeping the thong publicly decent. My plan is to rush upstairs, take a shower, and make Laur sweat.

"Hey, Stagger, you ready for that blow?"

There he is, un-sweatable, leaning in the doorway. The whiskey tumbler refracts the light around a new cherry and straw, but the man himself is only a shadow against the wild dancing lights. *How did he get past the bouncer?* It freaks me out a little, especially with my luck with stalkers.

"You shouldn't be back here, Laur."

"The owner likes me more than you." He sips his drink and smacks his lips. "So … we doing this here or elsewhere?"

Right here. Right now. Fuck his face against that wall with the dance floor two feet away. Yank down those pants and rail him in front on the dressing room mirror, so he and anyone else in the club who happens to look in can watch the fuck machine that is Chard Stagger in action.

My mouth dries. If I'd been off my meds … if I hadn't been taking my cognitive behavior therapy so seriously … fuck, if I didn't know three other Cuties could wander in here any second…

"Upstairs. Now."

Laur, unimpressed by my authority, doesn't take a step from the doorway. In the backlight, he plucks out the cherry and sucks it off the straw again.

Christ, those lips were going to feel so fucking good.

"You sure you want me? You walk back out there and at least a dozen panties will drop. You're only getting a blowjob from me."

I tower over him and I promise, "I'll change your mind."

He smirks, colder than the ice tinkling in his glass. "Unlikely."

I reach out to caress his face. "I'll be very gentle."

He dodges my touch. "Oh, be still, my beating heart."

Then he drains the entire whiskey sour like it's a shot and then drops to his knees.

Hot damn. It is *happening here.*

It can't. If even one of those boys saw, they'd run right to Jude to complain about how her mentally unstable sex-crazed cash cow is misusing the space.

Shit. I don't have the self-discipline to stop him. Shit.

I can see the bar and Paul smiling to the patrons favoring him, still blushing. The twenty is tucked into his black shirt like a badge of honor.

Laur stands again, leaving the empty glass at the

edge of the door. Disappointment and relief ripple through me. Raging lust pushes out every other emotion and I beat down the desire to hurl him on the couch.

He looks at me, his left eye droops at the edge. "Well, I don't know where the fuck we're going. Lead the way."

Chapter Three

My apartment's vibe is sort of industrial. But it's also my stuff, so it's like a rainbow vibrantly exploded onto the black-and-metallic furniture. Very suited to a studio above a queer nightclub where the evening revels pulse through the floor.

Laur makes no movement to take off his coat as he takes in this view. Not unimpressed. Not suspicious. A strategic evaluation.

I step nearer to help him with his clothes, ready to kiss and undress, to ignore whatever disaster had happened to the rest of his body. This bout of wildly passionate, totally protected sex is the best he'll ever get.

Laur wanders out of my reach as if he doesn't notice me, strides up to my swiveling computer chair. "All right. Take your clothes off."

I scoff at his command and stick my hands into my shorts, pushing them a little lower and posing. "Is that all?"

His gaze travels over my body, pausing on my crotch and then back to my face. "Yup."

Laur pulls my computer chair to a clear space in the room, sits, and stares at me. The intensity makes me uneasy. I want him to want more of me, to consent enthusiastically to kisses at the very least. But if the only thing he wants is a private striptease, I'll wear down his resistance.

He stops me at the first sway of my hips. "Just normal. I want to see it all."

It all. Not *you*. The request ripples through me. Dehumanizing. *Who the fuck is this guy?*

I tear out of my clothes like it's a quick change. I only pause at the red thong.

Laur regards me with piercing, cold eyes and I

feel as if I'm removing my clothes at the threat of violence. Like his gaze is a loaded gun. I yank off the underwear and let it join the litter of my clothes on the clear hardwood. There. He can see *it* all.

The bass thumps dimly on the floor, and images drizzle through my brain. This man would be king of the hate fuck. Kneeing over me, slamming his ass onto my prick. Bent over my kitchen counter commanding me to go harder. These thoughts hit me like a bullet aimed and fired from his crystal-blue eyes straight to my cock.

Laur beckons me nearer using two fingers of his left hand. The right rests on his knee, the glove tips crumpled. I strut over to him, not suspecting any trap.

He cups my balls in his gloved hand, rolling them over the leather. His right hand, the really mangled one, strokes across my ass possessively. His grip would be unmistakable. Hot as a brand.

He does nothing but look. As if my cock is a piece of museum art. But he's a critic. Hard-eyed and unforgiving, he studies my cock to find the flaws in my family jewels.

I struggle to breathe, shaking apart from this … unexpected lust. By the time he slips his hand away from my balls, my cock is painfully rigid under his unkind judgment.

Say something!

I badly want to tease him back under my control, but not only can I not think of anything, I'm not sure I'd have the courage to speak. Somehow, this angry little man has taken complete power over me. *When did that happen?*

Finally, he takes pity on my anguished dick and strokes the base delicately. I suppress my relieved sigh, but he notices. He holds eye contact while he leans closer, his mouth inches from my bursting cock-head. His breath tatters what's left of my calm, when he whispers, "When you come, I'll swallow."

Fuck, that's hot.

Laur grazes just the tip with his tongue. Sucking with an artificial delicacy. Tightening his lips with a cruel softness.

I groan. The huskiness, the raw want in my voice startles me. I drop a hand on his head in the hopes of coaxing my cock deeper. My fingers slip as he stiffens and shifts away. But his grip—the fingers on my balls—tighten, bordering on pain. He glares.

Is he afraid of me? Worried I'll grab him by his scruffy beard and fuck his face? Or that I'll wrestle him to the floor?

Do it. Tear up this little shit's ass.

Should he be afraid of me?

I tuck my hands behind my head and smile down at him reassuringly.

Laur, who had never been reassured in his life, sucks a little harder. Runs his tongue in wet circles around my head.

"You're a goddamned tease."

He swallows my whole cock to the base and sucks hard as he withdraws, sending rockets of pleasure through my spine. Until my cock slips out of his mouth with a wet pop. "Naw. Teasing is your job."

Laur raps his tongue along my shaft in quick beats of bliss, but he also pinches at my balls. My cock is a rope in an overwhelming game of tug-of-war between pleasure and pain. When I can't handle the mixed signals, almost immediately I step back.

He smiles as mischievously as any twink, even with the beard. "I torture."

Drop this bitch and fuck him. Show him not to play mean games on men twice his size.

Before I can sort out if this is a good or a terrible idea, the champion of mean games yanks me closer and swallows my shaft completely. I forget how to think as he deep-throats with a ferocity I've never experienced. My cock is at his mercy.

I didn't expect that I'd be the one fighting back orgasm. I was supposed to exhaust his defenses, to convince him he wanted that beautiful cock inside him. But at this rate...

His hands leave me only long enough for him to remove his right glove. The only piece of clothing he's taken off so far. When he presses a bare knuckle between my clenched ass cheeks, I realize...

Oh, fuck!

Laur is a top.

****

I haven't been fucked since ... well, before I discovered P!nk's "Slut Like You." With his unnatural fingers exploring the crease of my ass, teasing around my pucker, I'm not sure I want that to change, but I can't speak. He might stop sucking my cock to answer.

And you want to make him swallow everything.

The need to come is relentless. My balls boil in his left hand and the right claws and pokes at my entrance without quite committing.

This time when I put my hands in his hair, he lets me touch him. But he does slither off my cock to remark, "You're very spoiled, Stagger."

Don't let him stop. Fuck his face!

The terror radiates through me and does nothing to quell the fire in my cock. He could just stand up and walk out. He still had on his boots and coat. I deserve to be abandoned for strutting around like I owned his ass. I open my mouth, uncertain what's going to come out.

"Please, keep going, Laur. Please."

Begging. Great choice.

Laur smirks and licks his lips, only accidentally brushing my desperate cock.

Apparently, it's the correct choice, because the man dives back into the best blowjob I've ever gotten. His left hand joins the right, squeezing the dense muscles of my ass and it's only now that he's stopped manhandling my balls that I register how tightly he'd been clawing them. The blood rushes back and they throb and tingle. Now those same fingers grip at my cheeks, spreading me open. I don't care. As long as he keeps yanking my hips into his face, fucking himself with my swollen cock.

"Thank you."

Laur rewards my politeness by shoving two of his blunted fingers past the resistance of my tight ass and twisting them deep.

"Fuck!" The pain pushes me over the edge. Not surrendering to orgasm, more like having it beaten out of me. Like he'd broken the dams of my restraint and now there's nothing left but the flood of cum and longing for him.

And he keeps going, sucking hard, gobbling my cock as it spasms, fucking me with his shortened fingers so that I wobble forward. He won't let me go until my cock softens and my strength is completely sapped away by the sheer force of the orgasm.

"Fuck…"

Laur only shrugs me off his shoulder, like my entire weight is an insect that landed on his arm. He rubs his mouth with the back of his gloved left hand, wipes the right off on the back of my leg.

His cold eyes lock on mine and I know I'll do

whatever he wants. If he says suck, happily. If he tells me to turn around and raise my ass in the air, it'll be done.

But he says nothing. He pushes the swivel chair back and finishes tugging his right glove over his wrist.

He's going to leave. Just like that.

I grab my chair to hold him. "Laur, how about I—"

"Not part of your deal." Laur stands and walks toward the door as if I'm not even there.

Oh, fuck ... fuck my stupid arrogance.

He's not the type to melt into compliance with a few well-placed apologies. I could beg and coax and it wouldn't make a damn difference. The diamond toughness of this angry little man won't relent...

Unless you make him.

No, I'm not getting more than that soul-shattering blowjob. Just like he'd said.

Laur adjusts his coat. "Want to see me again?"

"Yes," I say, too quickly. "Tonight? After the show? I could comp your ticket."

"So can Jude." He smirks, amused by the idea. "I don't like being teased."

That makes no sense. Not with the bulge in his jeans. Not with the way he watched.

"I'll come back next week."

Everything in my soul sinks through my knees and into the floor. "A week?"

If he notices, he doesn't care. "Do you dance again next week?"

I nod. Next week is Teddy's teaser, but I'm one of his backup dancers.

"Then I tell you what..." He stands near me, looking up into my face and then gives me a little push. I drop into the chair where he wants me. He touched my chin and I look up. "After you tease that whole room again, after you make those sluts howl like bitches in heat, I expect you in that bed. Facedown. Ass up. Wearing a blindfold and handcuffs and nothing else."

****

"Laur?" Jamie wanders through the costume closet. "I met him at some Pride advocacy thing. Maybe a protest. I don't remember."

I can't get the guy out of my head. How could Jamie just forget? "What kind of work do you do together?"

"He works at a government clinic helping people navigate the system. Like health insurance, housing, and shit."

"Oh." *Great. I'm obsessed with customer support.*

Jamie rejects a purple sequined suit jacket and keeps digging. "Why so interested?"

I'm not prepared to explain. "Just curious. Do you know what happened to—"

"No! But I'm dying to know. You gotta find out!"

"Huh?" Their enthusiasm is confusing.

"He won't talk about it. Jude knows, but she won't say. But, hey, Chard Stagger, no man can resist your charms."

I scoff at the idea. If there was one man who could... "I only had one conversation with the guy."

And one hell of a blowjob.

"Take one for the team, Chard. Find out his secrets." Jamie laughs, then picks up another costume to test. "But seriously, if you do fuck him, Chard, don't lead him on. He's really sweet and he doesn't deserve false hope."

Really sweet? Yeah, right.

****

By the next Tuesday, my mania reaches its peak and I can barely sit at the bar.

"Do you need the night off, Chard?"

I haven't felt this out of control since I started taking medication. A wild mess of impulse and reaction, fidgets and desires, and the whole swirl of madness centers on a man who might not even show up.

"Chard?" Jude is talking to me.

"No, thanks. I'm fine. It's better if I have something to do. Thanks for noticing. You know, you're a great boss. Just the best. Do you need anything out of the storeroom?" Then I gasp because I've said all that in one breath.

Jude smiles. "Who are you waiting for?"

"Nobody." If she knows, I won't be able to resist prying.

"Well, Mr. Nobody is going to make you miss your call."

"Shit! I came out here to tell you the fireman's hat is missing. Someone took it to a party—not me, I swear—and it didn't get—"

"So? Go as something else." She cackles with a mischievous delight. "Go as a soldier."

I don't get the joke. "Okay."

I'm ready to scurry when she grabs my arm. "Chard!"

I return to the stool and smile up at her.

She fills a tumbler with sparkling water. "No booze. Be sure you wrap it up. And have a fun night even if Mr. Nobody doesn't show up."

Great advice on all counts. "Yes. Thanks, Jude."

Who cares if my particular nobody is here or not? There's an entire room of somebodies waiting to see me naked.

Chapter Four

Soldier is appropriate. My body is at war with my mind. My brain sets fire to my legs, and my skin strangles my throat. I must move or scream.

But it's not my teaser night. So, I wait in the man cave, irritating Dex, who's sits in a sexy police costume and studies a textbook on finance, because he *has* a future.

It's a tough crowd—for Teddy. He doesn't know how to work a room. I hover waiting for Jamie's cue, hiding in the shadows when I'm dying to shine. Then I step too far.

And there he is. At the bar. Leaning on his elbow, chatting with Jude, whiskey sour in his gloved hand, angled toward the stage, his eyes on Teddy. Jealousy mixes poorly with my superior sex appeal. *Damn it. Let's show some restraint.*

I burst out of the dressing room.

Dex slams his book shut, then he realizes. "Ted's got another two minutes."

I pass the bouncer. Then Jamie—because they are an angel of improv—brings the lights up on the cave. The crowd notices and cheers loudly reacting purely to my moves and confidence. I ignore the path of Jamie's lights and saunter toward the bar.

Such a bad idea.

Dex hurries out to take the path through the crowd to the stage. Jamie moves fast to cue the bar lights. Jude desperately makes room, waving at customers to grab their plates, and running a dry rag over the shining surface.

Three people scrambling to keep up with my bullshit.

The bar's crowded, wet, and sticky. Food isn't supposed to be served when there's going to be a dance. But as I swing up in my soldier costume and my rainbow-colored combat boots, I don't give a fuck. Neither do the customers. They might have to hold their drinks, but there's Chard Stagger in the flesh dancing around their abandoned French fries. Everyone goes apeshit.

Everyone, of course, except Laur. He looks furious.

But he's looking at me.

My camouflage shorts are stuffed with cash by the time I reach his end of the bar. His face is stoic, unamused when I crouch in front of him, putting my cock level with his pockmarked face and swiveling further down.

Someone slaps my ass and I give him enough attention to warrant the twenty he stuffs in my shorts. Then I turn back to Laur and tease him with the cock end again.

Jude, pissed as she must be with me, can't help but laugh at her friend's predicament.

"Come on, Laur, don't make him beg," Jude says in her MC voice.

Laur smiles—at Jude, not at me—and reaches into his pocket and pulls out a single.

I drop to my knees, absolutely begging, grinding in the air too close on the cramped bar. He slips the bill in my shorts, not through the waist, but through the leg, sliding his hand up my thigh and pushing up until the bill pokes out the top of my shorts again.

Jude says over the thrilled squeals of the crowd. "That's inappropriate, Larry. I might have to throw you out."

"Meh, I outrank you."

"It's my damn bar!"

Of course! He's a soldier. Jesus fuck, I'm a moron.

****

Back in the man cave after the teaser, Dex gives me a glare that could make an intern cry then grabs his backpack and beats it downstairs into the revue. Teddy lingers like a puppy that's been kicked in the nuts and Jude stands by the kitchen door, arms crossed, like she's not done kicking.

I offer Teddy the jar full of cash Jamie gave me. "Sorry about crashing your number, man. Take my share of the tips."

He doesn't take the cash. "I will, thanks. But Jude told us about … special attention for a veteran, that was … he must have had a hell of a time. I'm glad you were here tonight to do it."

It's exactly the kind of shit that would soothe things over with the other Cuties.

Thank you, Jude.

"He usually sits at the high-top," I say by way of explanation and push the cash at him again. "Take it. Because of the surprise. Split it with Dex too, so he'll talk to me again someday."

Ted chuckles and finally takes the cash, then shrinks and flees downstairs. Not stripper energy.

Jude clears her throat and gestures with her head to the alley door.

Fuck, oh, fuck.

I follow her into the cool night air. My gut roils with shame, even through the beat of adrenaline. I have to focus, to look contrite, to not run away. *He might already be on his way upstairs.*

"Chard, I can't believe I had to leave the bar for

this shit. A minute forty early, crashing the new guy's number, *and* you jump on a full bar."

"I got carried away. It won't—"

"It better not," she interrupts. "There are rules for a reason, Chard. Common courtesy to your fellow performers."

"I made it up to…" I can tell I missed her point and shut up.

"How about food and health regulations? Safety regulations? If you tripped on a piece of ice or we had a health inspector in…"

She doesn't like my eye roll either.

"Hey! This is my operation. I don't wanna get shut down because you can't control yourself. Just because you're my top earner does not mean you can walk all over the other Cuties or that you can break the rules."

This is going to haunt the fuck out of you once you come down.

"Chard, you're great ninety percent of the time."

Try to remember she said that too.

"But you've got to get a handle on that other ten percent or take the night off when I give you the chance. I don't want to fire you."

My earnest nod doesn't placate her, but she needs to get back to the bar. And I need to get upstairs. Facedown. Ass up. Wearing a blindfold and handcuffs and nothing else. To be in my bed where he expects me.

****

Time and I have never been on speaking terms, but now it seems to be moving slowly on purpose. It's a particular kind of torture, asking me to hold a pose. Especially when I'm alone in the room.

I shift into a different pose, legs spread wider. Handcuffs a little higher.

Maybe he won't come. Maybe the soldier costume...

Why hadn't I realized that immediately?

Pissed him off. Maybe Jude told him how I'd endangered her business and he went home to punish me.

Maybe not even two minutes have passed and the chemicals in your brain are misfiring?

No. He's doing it on purpose.

Something shuffles in the room. I turn toward the sound, but thanks to the blindfold I see nothing. There's no other sound. I must have imagined it. I would hear the door open when he came in. Even with the nightclub in full swing, that door creaks like hell.

Then the scuff of a boot dragging. If he is here, it's uncanny how quietly he moves.

"Laur?"

I actively resist pulling off the blindfold. This is a test and I'm determined to wait him out. He already has too much power over my mind and imagination.

A hand brushes my hair and he asks, "So, tell me what's in the pillbox?"

"Jesus Christ, man!"

How had he not only crossed the room, but nosed around in my bathroom without me being certain he was there?

Laur chuckles and puts a hand on the back of my neck. I keep the pose, forehead pressed to the pillows. It's his left hand, an infinitely comforting grip. "Is it catching or a heart condition?"

"Oh ... no. Uh, not like that." Probably not wise to talk about this in detail yet, but how did I avoid—

"Glad to hear." His right hand trips over my spine. "So, when I fuck you, it won't kill you?"

My cock twitches violently from where it's squeezed between my knees.

"Oh, I forgot." The humor, the comfort vanishes from his voice. "You only want blowjobs from me, isn't that right?"

He's never gonna let that go.

He slaps my ass and commands. "Turn on your back."

I twist my arms so I can flip over and breathe in the darkness of the blindfold.

He trips his fingers around my nipples. His hand is cold and slightly damp. "Full disclosure. I was already in the apartment."

"W-what?"

"Saw my buddy talking to you in the alley. Seemed like a pretty important conversation, so I kept heading up the stairs and invited myself in."

Hadn't I locked the door? Did he know how to pick a lock?

"I figured the fake plant was there for a reason."

To hide my spare key. Right.

How had I not noticed him? I lived in a studio. I had taken a shower! Where had he been hiding? What had he been doing?

Something crunches and the sound terrifies me. Like bones or stone grinding together.

The hell is going on?

Then Laur's mouth surrounds my cock, just the head. This time it's not maddening. This time it really is torture. I'm so hard, so hot, so ready for him and the thing he'd crunched … ice.

"Fuckin' Hell!"

He sucks more of my cock into his throat and rolls the ice shards around my shaft while I writhe. They melt fast and my cock throbs harder. He attacks my dick with the same ferocity he had the last time and it's not long before I squirm. I don't want to come too soon ... again.

"Laur ... don't spoil me too much. I'd like to fuck you this time."

His mouth pulls away from my cock slowly. I can feel the disdain. "Presumptuous little shit."

I smile innocently. "It's my charm and good looks. I get away with everything."

He smacks my thigh. The sharp slap rings in my ears and on my skin. "I'll make a deal with you. I'm gonna fuck you."

He pushes at my hips and I roll back to where I started, facedown, ass up.

What's the rest of the deal?

"If you can hold off until I've had my fill of this ass." He grips my cheeks with both hands and fails to jiggle the solid muscles. "Then I'll let you fuck me."

"That's not very fair." I curl my legs closer to my chest to offer him better access.

"Fair? I don't believe in fair." Something cold and wet presses against my pucker and just as I'm catching up to his games, he's stuffed a whole ice cube into my ass. I flail from the shock until he grabs my hair and pins my face to the pillow.

"Stay down."

I whimper at his domination. Not that I'd never been domed before, it's a mainstay in the revue, but he's *so* good at it.

"Who would have thought a built guy like you would be so damned tender?"

I dare to lift my head to speak. "I don't suppose it matters, but it's been maybe ten years since anyone has played around with my ass."

That's probably a lie. I did a lot of stupid things before I stopped drinking and I don't remember them all.

Probably been more like two years. But when he starts squeezing at my cheeks now wet with the cold water…

"I feel so privileged." He nudges my legs wider, then kneels between my thighs. "Practically a virgin, then. Should I go slow and gentle?"

"Please?" I'm relieved he cares.

He shoves another ice cube into my ass, neither slow nor gentle. This time I grit my teeth and refuse to squirm.

Laur is amused. "Fast learner?"

I try to agree, but the sound is much more wavering than I intend. I clench my hole tight to stop from dripping.

Laur drizzles a piece of ice over my back, letting the heat of my skin melt it and making my skin flinch and dance from the chill. The puddle catches in the indent of my spine until I arch my back like a cat and it rolls down my sides.

The man hisses, appreciating the sight. One finger of his right hand teases the edge of my pucker, poised to penetrate. "Guess how many more of these I have?"

"I don't know and I don't care."

In his left hand, he cradles one of the ice cubes and rubs it over my nipples and then down my stomach. "This might even up the deal. Get you some of that fairness."

I know what's coming, but my body still roars in protest when his hand and the ice cube crush around my cock. The softness of his fingers. The unyielding chill of the ice. My poor dick is in completely alien territory and doesn't know if it hates or really *likes* what's happening. I sob and grind my head into the pillows unable to understand or deal with the roiling lust.

When I'm nothing more than throbbing heat, damp chilled skin, and the panting beat of my heart, he announces, "That was the last one."

"Oh, good." I relax a little.

He takes advantage to shove another in my ass.

"Fucking Christ, Laur!" A well-timed cheer from the nightclub below swallows my shout.

"Should I fuck you now?" Laur runs his fingers, wet and cold, across my lips and I suck the chilled water off the tips. "Or is that unfair?"

"Give it to me. I can take it."

He whistles appreciatively. "Good answer, kid. You were born to be broken."

Then he disappears.

There's nothing but the pulse and beat of the nightclub, the wet sheets between my knees, the chill in my ass, and the throbbing of my tortured cock. I stay perfectly still, straining to hear.

He left. You won't believe it for another ten minutes. So you'll stay here like a total loser, handcuffed and blindfolded, with ice melting in your ass and your cock hard as hell because you're a broken shell of a man who nobody will ever love.

Plastic crinkles behind me. *Oh, a condom. How thoughtful.*

That's the only warning I get before he sinks his cock to the hilt. His sharp tool squeezes the cold water out and pushes what had not melted deeper. I howl from the chill and the pain.

Not thoughtful!

"Fuck, that's a tight ass," he growls in my ear, crouched behind me, like a demented goblin riding my back, controlling my every movement with the jerk of his cock. "I did not know that about you, Stagger."

I gasp for breath, fighting through the pain and into pleasure. "I don't give it up to every man who slips a dollar in my shorts, you know."

He makes a disbelieving "meh" sound. Then hammers me with such ferocity that for a moment I think maybe I can outlast him. Maybe he'll get carried away and come first. He won't honor any deal he's made, but I can make him. Grab him by the shoulders and pin him to the floor. Use actual lube, like a fucking gentleman.

"Every time I've watched you shake that ass in a man's face, I imagined him fucking you. Even before you deigned to speak to me." He wraps his arm around my throat, choking me.

When I panic, he switches tactic immediately, releasing my throat and gripping my shoulder hard to keep me down. I fucking love that. He holds his weight over me and I can feel the missing digits, the surprising sharpness of knuckle bones too close to the skin.

"The way you spread your legs on stage and offer it up like that. Had no idea this piece of meat was just for me."

Yes. Just for him.

He slaps my ass and fucks harder and the cheap handcuffs clatter together.

"You know the worst part of a striptease?"

I moan in answer, past the point where I could say anything more complicated than "please" or "slower" or "fuck me."

"These boys get you so hot and bothered, and I bet not one of them has the goddamn common courtesy to give you a reach-around." He takes my cock in his left hand.

The mere presence of his fingers makes me croon with delight and sends a surge of lust to my cock. He strokes as hard as he fucks, and I have no defense against him. No hope of holding out.

"But you know what, Chard?" he coos in my ear. "Next time I see you strut across that stage and hump some drunk bitch, I'll remember."

He slaps my ass with his right hand. "Just for me."

I pant my agreement. So close. Hovering on the brink of total sexual annihilation.

"Say it."

"Just for you," I promise in a desperate pant, and with that for a cue, my cock twitches and releases. It douses the bedsheet and happens so fast and so powerfully, I'm briefly lightheaded. I marvel that no one below had any concept of the ecstasy happening over their heads.

"Yeah, go on and come, you little bitch. You don't get to fuck me." Laur growls and pumps my cock in the same brutal rhythm he pounds my ass, not relenting an inch just because I've surrendered to my pleasure.

Just when I was worried he'd rub my ass and shaft raw, he pulls out. I hear the shuffle of his boots, the ragged exhale, the snap of a condom. I stay down, overwhelmed by the force of my orgasm, dripping and weak in the knees. He grunts and his cum splatters on my back.

I'm not certain I like this. Like the faceless bottom in a porno. Not a person.

"Good job, slut, I had fun, I guess." He slaps my ass one last time.

I definitely don't like the sound that escapes me—a little too prissy, too close to a sob.

"Everything you expected?"

"Nothing I expected." I twist the release on the handcuffs and free my hands.

He's zipped up and by the time I ease my broken ass into a sitting position, he's across the room and buttoning his coat. I stare at him, his close-cut hair choppy from sweat, his face a burning red above the thick beard. He's the first man to fuck me since … to fuck me that brutally ever, and I hadn't seen any more of him than I had the week before. And even sitting in a puddle of cum and ice water, I'm desperate for more.

"Would you think less of me if—"

"Probably," Laur said. "But, yeah. I'll come back and fuck you again."

Not what I was going to ask.

Wasn't it?

"Next Tuesday?"

"Naw. I don't think so." He walks over again and crouches down to look me in the face. It's a feral movement, like a big cat or a demon. He grins. "Oh, I'll be here Tuesday. I always come in for my whiskey sour and cheesesteak on Tuesdays. But this … I'll hold off on a while."

He runs his left thumb over my lip.

Please kiss me.

I need a kiss, wanted just enough affection to not feel…

"I like a desperate whore."

Chapter Five

Late fall turns into a chilly, dark winter. Laur has no other coat besides the green one, but it gets puffier sometime in December. There's no Christmas gift exchange between us, but I buy some leashes and more restraints for him to play with, and he comes to the bar early one day without his laptop and has a conversation with me before he disappears for two weeks before the New Year. That's the most intimate we'd gotten after four months of once-a-week and fairly brutal fucking where I never see him naked.

"Jeremy, you're experiencing shame about something you're not sharing with me," Dr. Rooks, my psychiatrist, likes to pause and see if I'll rush in and fill in the gaps. She'd classify Laur as risky behavior simply because her idea of kinky sex was kissing without asking for permission.

"Have you asked anyone in your support network to help you navigate it?"

My support network is Jude, Paul, and my mother. And I realize with a muffled hum, I had not.

"And why not?"

Because you don't tell you mother about the kinds of things Laur does to a man. And you don't tell your boss that her best friend has made you his bitch, because if *he* wasn't telling her, *I* wasn't going to.

I'd kept it from Paul—I hadn't really. He'd just misunderstood. I'd wanted his advice on how to move things forward, but somehow he got the idea Laur was stalking me.

He'd reached under the bar for the pamphlets Jude kept there to give to people in an abusive situation. "Jesus Christ, man, every fucking freak in Galway City finds you and you don't do a damn thing to protect yourself."

"No, no. It's not like that." He'd been totally unfair. If anything, I was the one trying to stalk Laur, but no one could tell me anything about the guy. "I know the difference between Laur and those guys. I mean, he's intense, but—"

"Laur? You mean … the finger guy?" Paul imitated the way I had wiggled my fingers.

Remembering I'd started that gesture made me squeamish. "Yeah, him."

Paul blinked with confusion. "Really? He's the guy who comes in for cheesesteaks on Tuesday?"

"Yeah. His name is Laur."

"You're sleeping with him? Like regularly?" Paul couldn't wrap his head around the idea.

And I knew no one would understand. "The whole world is fucking crazy and I'm the one on medication."

"I'm just saying, a guy who looks like that … I mean, when you're … you know." He gestured to by body. "There's got to be a reason he's not crawling all over you, dude."

"Yeah, self-respect. All I bring to a relationship is … you know." I imitated him in gesturing to my body. "Absolutely fuck-all."

Paul's expression had softened but he couldn't refute. Your ex-boyfriend can't usually extol your romantic virtues.

Dr. Rooks asks, "Jeremy, are you with me?"

"Sorry, just trying to … what was the question?"

Her frown deepens. "Any thoughts of self-harm?"

"No." I've been too obsessed to ideate on suicide.

"Is it illegal? Or immoral?"

"Not illegal."

"But you feel like you're doing something

wrong?"

There it is. I found the way to reassure her. "Doctor, I'm Jewish. Even when I'm doing everything right, it feels wrong."

The old woman smiles faintly, reminding me of my grandmother. This is the side she likes to see. The one who cracks jokes she isn't allowed to laugh at.

"It's just boy trouble. I'm sure I'll share more another session."

****

After leaving Dr. Rooks, I run on the beach and ruminate over Laur and our not-exactly-a-relationship. It's as much a part of my routine as getting eight hours of sleep and a gallon of water every day. But as my sneakers beat the salty snow and hard sand, hope is easy to find. There's no meaning in my meaninglessness between the endless water and the sky, and that's a fine thing.

When I hit the end of the boardwalk and turnaround, another group of runners passes me in the other direction. They move like a pack of sled dogs, all with precision in their movements and dark masculine shorts and tops. Not like my bright-blue joggers and the rainbow-colored water bottle bumping against my chest.

I don't cast them a glance until one of the pack calls, "Larry, where you going?"

The one peeling off is the shortest man in the group. The thick beard and baseball cap don't quite hide all the scars on his face. Or his sarcasm.

"Y'all can find your way back without me. It's the straight line."

Then Laur is running beside me. My heart hammers with the surprise intimacy. I can't remember the last time I ran beside someone. If I ever had.

He doesn't say anything. Am I supposed to say something?

Are we supposed to run in silence? How did I act with this man in the daylight?

After about half a mile, he spits an accusation, "You run here often?"

The tone catches me off guard. "Huh?"

"How did you find me?"

Shit. He's angry already? I haven't said anything.

"I know Jude didn't tell you I run here, so how did you—"

"My dude, I run here every Thursday and I have for at least seven years. Usually, I'm about … I don't know, thirty minutes later?"

He narrows his eyes. "How long?"

"I just said. Seven years."

"What month did you start? How long do you usually run? Why thirty minutes early today?"

The rapid-fire questions short my brain. "Uh, I think probably May? Sometime in spring. Depends on the weather and I—"

Who the fuck is this guy to make me fall over myself to answer. "Laur, is this an interrogation?"

Laur looks surprised, and then shame softens his face slightly. "Yeah. I guess it was. Sorry."

He says nothing else, and we jog in silence. I internally panic.

Eventually he says, "That's my VA group."

VA group. Is that like an AA group? Like with group counseling? I get the image of Laur beating someone with the sharing stick, and smile.

"What's that smirk?" Laur notices.

"Nothing! Just … for four years, we've been running by each other or just missing—"

"We've been just missing. I would have noticed

you peacocking around."

As if I'm the freak missing fingers and shit.

It was a compliment. Because you're pretty and dye your hair bright blue, when it isn't fucking March, you run half-naked.

I glance over and down at him. I'm so rarely standing in his presence that I'd forgotten how much shorter he is. He blended neatly with that group, like camouflage to hide his scars.

His eyes are so blue, but also mismatched. His right eye, the one that droops, has a more uniform shade, and doesn't react to the sunlight.

"Shit, you only have one eye!"

Well done, Jeremy. There's the maturity and restraint you're known for.

Laur puts his hands on his cheeks in sarcastic shock. "Oh my God! Really?"

He wasn't wearing his gloves. I'd never actually seen the damage. His middle finger was missing the first and second knuckle but his pinkie was only missing the very tip, like the fingernail had been sawed off. There was an almost cartoonish squareness to each stump.

"You know, between the blindfold and the kneeling, you don't give me the chance to look that often."

His head whips around like he thinks his buddies are nearby to overhear. When I look again his cheeks are a little redder than before. *Aw, he's cute when he blushes.*

Before I say something calamitously dumb, I give him a warning. "You know, as long as I'm making a fool of myself—"

"Quit while you're ahead."

"My mama didn't raise no quitter." I grin at him. "How did it happen?"

I wait for him to answer. It seems like the right

time. With the calming sound of the ocean, the rhythmic thud of our sneakers on the boardwalk, the naturally breathy breaks in conversation. He doesn't have to look at me.

But he remains silent.

Some families with very young children are flying kites, huddled together up ahead near the parking lot.

Laur clears his throat. I wait for him to say something, anything, but I get nothing.

So, instead, I appreciate the sand and the sun and the fact that I'm doing something with a guy that isn't entirely sexual. This is very nearly friendly. Maybe I could end the jog by asking for his personal cell phone.

"Which lot are you parked in? North or South?" he asks eventually.

"Oh, I take the trolley. I don't drive."

He looks confused. "Like at all?"

My license had been put on probation for unsafe driving when I was in my early twenties. Even after I got it back, so many of my invasive thoughts involved the winding cliffs of Galway City and simply not turning, that I'd opted to sell the car and settle for taxis, biking, and the shitty public transit system. "I mean, I have a license, but I don't drive."

"Keeps costs down, I guess." He hums. Then smirks. "Want a lift home?"

I cannot imagine he'd drive me all the way up to East Quay and not fuck my brains out. "Yes, please."

****

Giddy as a golden retriever, I follow him into the lot.

What kind of car does he drive? Jeep? Motorcycle? Got to be a pickup. Assholes drive pickups so it's perfect for Laur. When he beeps his keys, a silver Corolla blinks back.

I laugh. "What a demure little car."

"Better than no car."

The front passenger side carries a box overflowing with various loose papers and manila folders. Two briefcases and a laptop are precariously stacked on top of the papers.

"Get in the back."

It's a cramped backseat for a gorilla like me to squeeze in. He opens the door on the other side, letting the sea breeze blow through the toasty backseat. I suspect nothing until the slick black rope loops around my neck.

I know this leash. He's used it on me more than once. My back and arms are stronger than his broken fingers. Still, I go where he drags me and curl up across the backseat.

"Comfy?" He rewards my obedience by slamming the leash in the door to keep me down.

****

His car rattles as we climb the main road. I flex my legs to keep them from cramping, and try to follow our path by looking at the tops of buildings and the open blue sky. We stop at a red light.

East Quay is a left at that light. Is his house straight up the hill or to the right into the residential parks? "Hey, Laur, take me to your house. I want to play with your toys."

"My toys are only for big boys."

I know he wants me to beg, but before I can, his phone rings and the car announces mechanically, "M.O.H.A. house."

"Fuck." Laur mutters. "I got to take this. Don't

say anything."

I nod and swallow hard, which makes my Adam's apple rub against the leash. The light changes and Laur turns to the right as he answers the call, speaking in a bright cheerful tone and in another language I don't recognize.

I expected a military supervisor, but instead it's a throng of children and whatever he's said disappoints them. A dozen little voices chatter all at once in various languages.

One girl takes over quickly. "Mr. Trockie, you say you like to talk to us?"

He answers gently. "Of course I like talking to you, Telenaz. But today, I have no time."

"But why?" All the children take up her chorus.

His good eye flicks to the rearview mirror and I give him a little wave.

He switches back to the language I don't know.

"In American, Mr. Trockie!" a very young boy chastises.

"Okay, okay." Laur chuckles. "How about this? One at a time, youngest to oldest, you give me a single sentence to describe your week."

The car angles uphill as the children take turns rambling mostly about food and school in English, in French, and that other language I haven't identified. Laur encourages them, replying in their language of choice.

We keep driving uphill. Does Laur live on The Ridge? Big fancy beach houses overlooking the ocean. Houses with private stairs down to private beaches where I've done private stripteases.

Eventually, after a multilingual chorus of pleading and goodbyes, Laur hangs up.

The softness in him vanishes immediately. "The hell are you smirking about?"

"Who are your little friends? The children of cultural attachés? Future spies you're grooming for world domination?"

Laur snorts. "Orphaned refugees."

"Oh."

"We try to acclimate them to life in the West. Sometimes we reunite the kids with the soldiers that liberated them."

"Did you—"

"No." Laur doesn't let me finish. "That wasn't my department."

The car dips and picks up speed. A highway and a twisting road. He lives near the cliffs. *I don't love that for me.*

Laur gracefully changes the subject. "So, what do you want to talk about for the next thirty or so minutes, that will convince me to take you to my house?"

"Well, I'm horny as hell so why—"

"Try again." He shifts his grip on the wheel to stroke his cock.

"It's damn cruel to tie a guy up like this and not fuck his brains out."

"Getting closer."

The sudden blood rushing to my cock does nothing to ease the cramps in the rest of my body. "Because my tight ass is only for you and you got hard the second you saw me on the boardwalk."

"You're very spoiled."

"Yeah? So punish me."

"By giving you what you want?"

"That logic is totally sound to me, but I'm a crazy slut."

"You're also a lucky slut." He slows, turns, and a shadow falls over the car. "I don't live thirty or so minutes away."

****

When he opens the door, I see an oily concrete floor for an instant before his cock is in my mouth. I swallow greedily, and try to adjust in the backseat.

"Stop squirming and suck," Laur commands.

I obey, and after a few minutes at my mercy, he's the one squirming.

"When do you go to work again?" He pulls his cock out of my mouth.

I smile up at him sweetly. "Gym. Tomorrow at four. Then East Quay Cuties. I get busy on the weekends."

"I bet you do." Laur offers his cock again. When I don't take enough, he forces the rest in. "So, this ass is mine for the rest of the day?"

I moan, too excited by the prospect to stop sucking his cock and tease.

Laur doesn't bother to hold back. With my eager mouth and his frantic thrusting, it isn't much longer before he takes a step back.

I wait while he strokes his cock with both hands. He explodes on my face and into my open mouth, then rubs the dribbles into my skin. I only shudder and moan accepting his gift.

The rest of the day.

Laur grins wickedly and lifts my chin to admire his work. "You're gonna go through Hell before I let you come."

He's not wrong.

As soon as he marches me into the back corner of his basement, past the tidy laundry and behind a heavy curtain, I recognize the homemade dungeon.

"You know, I swiped left on this profile once."

"Good thing. I would have reported your profile as fake. Where do you want to start?"

"How about with a kiss?"

He pushes me instead toward demonic monkey bars.

Half his toys are designed for pleasure and the other half for pain. For the rest of the afternoon, he takes me on a personal tour of his dungeon. Binding me hand to ankle on the soft mats of the floor and teasing me with an incredibly wet stroker. Restraining me on the metal cage and whipping me until my ankles and biceps are somehow both made of fire and water, then dropping to his knees and sucking my cock. Without letting me come, of course. He still wants to fuck me over the padded bench first, then on the demon monkey bars, and finally against the wall held up by a collar and very mean-looking but very light chains.

When my ass drips lube and his cum and I'm too weak to stand on my own, he finally gropes my cock. I moan in exquisite agony and know, I'll finally get some relief … as long as he doesn't take his hand away

"If you don't let me … I think I might cry."

He takes his hand away, but only slightly. "I might wanna see that."

"You're such a bastard," I whimper and hump my cock against his open palm.

"Yeah." He firmly grips my cock and I give an unfamiliar high-pitched whine. "But you love it."

I can't disagree, mostly because I'm coming. The blinding pleasure I've come to crave. The purest rush of sex and explosion. My whole body shakes and drenches his hand and leaves me choking against the wall, because I don't have enough strength in my legs to stand.

He unbuttons the collar and I slump against the soft padding of the wall and drop like a stone. My wrists stay in the plastic chains over my head. I could sleep until morning. Except that Laur joins me on his knees and dangles his cock in front of my mouth.

I raise my eyes to him. He gives me an innocent little shrug and offers his cock hopefully.

"Who's spoiled now?" I say, then start sucking and begin my torture again.

Chapter Six

As soon as I open my eyes, I know the mood stabilizers have not been repressing mania. The garbage in my brain is not aided by the man standing over me unknotting the ropes on my wrist.

"You could have gotten out of this, you moron." He only needs to use one hand and the other holds a hot coffee. I have the fear he'll pour it over me.

"Did you want me to?" I'd fallen asleep certain he'd come back any minute with a new device to punish me.

Laur wears a suit today, like a bad cosplay of a billionaire dom fantasy. He sips his coffee. "I'll drive you back to East Quay on my way in. Can you be ready to leave in forty minutes?"

No. I can't leave this bed.

Ah, shit. I missed my meds. My first dose in, what, two years? Because I was tied up at my—

Not my boyfriend.

By daylight, my not-boyfriend's house is far cozier than I'd have guessed based on my experience in the basement. He decorates mostly with neutrals and really likes living plants— loads of ivies, spider plants, and other vines. A quick peak out the bay window shows a meticulously mowed lawn completely fenced by American flags, the top of the roofs across the street, and in the distance the ocean. Great view. There's a bike path curling along the cliff. I get lost in the mad fantasy about settling into a house like this with a man. Maybe this house and this very man.

Don't get your hopes up, Champ. People don't tie up their future husbands in the guest room.

"I wouldn't make a habit of running thirty

minutes earlier in hopes of catching me again." Laur hands me an orange juice.

Does he remember I don't own a coffeemaker? Seems like a small observation from a fella who speaks at least three languages.

"My buddies have been texting me all night. Bunch of worrying bitches."

I'm still debating the importance of the orange juice in my hand. "It's not likely. My shrink isn't very flexible."

"Shrink?" He snorts and pours his coffee into a thermos. "The fuck do you need therapy for? Being too pretty?"

Does he think I'm some anxious middle-class kid wearing mental illness as a badge of honor?

Take a minute, Jeremy. He doesn't know.

My stomach is gnawing itself open, I haven't slept, and I'm coming off mood stabilizers for the first time in two years. I do not take a minute.

"Four suicide attempts, recurring episodes of mania, depression, and other antisocial and risk-taking behavior related to bipolar disorder. I wasn't diagnosed until I had to be talked down off a bridge."

Laur puts the coffeepot down and turns his whole body to see me. "East Bay Bridge?"

Weird answer.

But accurate. I nod.

"Yeah." He returns to his thermos. "That one's a problem for us, too. How d'you like the safety mesh?"

I remember the shining metal net, a strange hammock built to preserve my life. Seeing it between me and the water had been enough. I called Paul, even though he'd broken up with me three months prior. I'd started walking back as soon as he answered and he'd convinced me to check myself into a clinic before I was even off the bridge.

Yeah, remember how fast you went from wanting to die to wanting help.

"I saw it," I answer Laur.

Back off, Jeremy. You can still have a nice morning. You like this guy.

I do not back off. "You one of those Republicans who fought against it because it ruins the skyline?"

"Why the fuck do you think I'm a Republican?" That pisses him right off.

I'm exhausted by his anger. "I don't know. There's a lot of flags."

"I'm a damn patriot." He screws on the thermos cap. "But you're damn right I fought against them. A little fucking net isn't going to do shit to stop someone who is determined."

Because *I* didn't want to die enough?

"Someone—like a trained solider two months off his tour of duty—has the physical chops to climb down the mesh and execute his jump from there. We wanted a fucking fence."

He doesn't mean me. I know veterans are an at-risk group, just like LGBTQ+ youth, but I never considered the difference. Being trained to kill, conditioned to push through your limits, mixed with the pressure of being "all you can be"…

My people mix sleeping pills and booze and slash their wrists. What do his people do?

To the silence I offer, "I'm told any barrier is usually enough."

"Must be why guns work better than bridges, huh?" Laur smirks like it's a joke.

The idea makes me lightheaded. Like hovering above a dark pool of water and not being sure I can make myself swim. "Do you have guns here, Laur?"

"No." He glares as if I'm accusing him. "New Jersey has … very strict laws and I can't..." He clears his throat. "I can't pass the mental health exam."

Hot damn! Common ground. "Oh, cool! What's wrong with you?"

As soon as the words leave, I know they're all wrong, but still they land and burn.

"What's wrong with me? What the fuck is wrong with you? Asking a guy a thing like that?"

"I just told you," I answer defensively. "Bipolar disorder."

"Fuckin' moron." He swipes his thermos off the counter and picks up his keys.

"Forgive me, I thought spending the night in a guy's literal dungeon—"

"It doesn't."

Keys and coffee in hand, he stands refusing to look at my face. Lips pressed so tight they disappear. Maybe bringing me to his house was his version of vulnerability. How did it backfire so spectacularly?

"Your sneakers are on the doormat and your phone is on the counter. Meet me in the car. Five minutes. Do *not* bring this up again."

****

Neither of us has the courage or kindness to say something soft as he drives.

Galway City is desolate at this early hour. There must be days when he doesn't see the sun.

"Listen, Chard, um…"

So sorry. Chard's not here right now. Care to leave a message?

"I'd hoped this morning would go better."

"It's my fault." Entirely. Because I'm a moron.

"Not really. I'm—I don't know, a bastard at the best of times."

Oh, shit. This is an apology. What do people say when I apologize? "I … it's okay. Thanks. I shouldn't pry."

He snorts, agreeing. Then continues, "I don't know anything about bipolar."

We turn a corner and I recognize my safe space by the fluttering rainbow flags. About three blocks from East Quay.

"I'm conflicted here."

Shit. That means breaking up.

We weren't dating!

"On the one hand, I like, uh … engaging in a bout of wildly passionate, totally protected sex, once a week."

I nod, holding the knot of fear in check, because don't I want more? But not a lot more? Just what we'd almost had this morning.

"But on the other..." I'm on his blind side and he can't look over. "I'm … I am aware … I don't know—a friend of mine—a doctor friend of mine, talks about self-destructive tendencies. Like a fire in a person's head. And the best you can do is find someone to help keep it a nice warm bonfire."

I like that metaphor. *But what the fuck is he trying to say?*

"But there are other people who kind of throw … uh." He had a word he wanted, and chose something different. "Gas on the fire."

I frown. "I can manage my symptoms just fine."

"Chard." He huffs out a breath, self-defeated and smiling. "I'm not talking about you."

Right. *His* self-destructive tendencies. *His* doctor friend. *His* experiences with self-harm and suicidal ideation.

"I'm the gas on your bonfire."

I wanted to be that *other* person. I'd never wanted anything more and I'd never had a goal so impossible to attain.

Laur says, "Maybe we ought to have this conversation when you're in a better state."

Right because I was off my routine, off my meds, and out of my mind.

"I shouldn't have said anything," He stops in front of the club, which looks sickly in dawn's early light. He doesn't turn off the car or turn to see me. "I'm gonna do what I want anyway."

"Good." I reach out to take his chin and turn his face toward me.

He fights, but he looks.

I smile. "Next time you kidnap me, let's make sure it's after five p.m. Or, you know, break into my apartment and bring me the pillbox."

He sneers from whatever fresh meanness is in his head. I meant to kiss him, but his expression grew blank and unreadable.

And that scares the shit out of me.

He said, "I've gotta go to work."

"Right." I get out feeling oddly unsettled but weirdly happy at the same time.

We had a kind of relationship and it scares him as much as it scares me. I'll take my meds, take a nap, eat something, and figure this shit out for both of us.

Chapter Seven

Meds, sleep, and lunch did not bring me back to normal. I pushed myself through the entire weekend, powering through my classes and performances.

And now on Monday, I've spiraled into a deep low. It takes a miraculous effort to take my pills while I'm standing to microwave a frozen pizza. And the whole time I stare at the sink as if the wet metal could provide an answer to the numbness of existence.

Paul comes before his shift and puts my pills and a glass of water on my nightstand. He notices, "You missed a day."

"Yup." I force myself to sit up and take the pills.

"Did you talk to Dr.—"

"Nope."

He looks at me like he expects me to dive headfirst out the window right then.

I try to help. "But I have before. The best thing is to resume the right schedule."

"Call out of work tomorrow."

Teaser Tuesday. "No."

"Jeremy."

"I like working," I protest.

"Okay, if you're up to it. Let's go for a run together then."

I see his tactic, his challenge, and I try to rise to it. Running would make me feel better, especially with Paul who is not an athlete. I'll just put on my sneakers. Just get out of bed and put on my socks and… The endless to-do list utterly defeats me.

"The gym will fire you if you ghost them again." Paul puts my phone in my hand.

He sits there coaching me through each step. The

gym manager knows about my condition, is very warm and accommodating, but I fully expect to be fired anyway.

"I'll let Jude know. Dex or Tony will cover for you."

"Thanks." I drop back into bed.

He leaves my pillbox on the nightstand.

What happens if you take them all at once?

I open my bedside drawer and slap the box out of my line of sight.

Oh, come on. Just a thought experiment.

****

Tonight, the sound of the club is particularly galling. I should be down there. That's my crowd.

I'm impossibly lonely. But I also hate every single person I have ever met.

So? Leave it all. Bet they'll blame that ugly asshole. Maybe that will teach him not to be so mean.

"Oh, fucking hell." I hate my own thoughts and know it's hopeless to try to escape them.

Maybe I could put on a DVD to drown them out.

Don't lie to yourself. You're not leaving this bed. No matter how sad and disgusting you get, you're stuck here.

At the deep low of the cycle. I had to keep telling myself that. Cycle. I'd come round again soon. Feel better for a while.

Then swing right the fuck back here again.

Endless and fucking awful. Angry, lonely, and pathetic. I'm the worst kind of douche and no one wants me. I'm lucky I'd fooled the ones I had. It'd be a blessing to every single one of them if I walked into oncoming traffic—

Or had the determination to drop onto the mesh and execute my jump from there.

"Fuck!" I roll off the bed and sprawl on the bare floor.

You do you, boo. Sometimes a change of scenery helps.

I thought about the only man who'd ever told me no. About gas on bonfires. And his conversation with the refugee orphans, and his sex dungeon, and the morning after, which might have been the start of something good, if I wasn't a moron.

I spiral into helplessness, hopelessness, and that sick loneliness that comes when you are desired for the night, but not for longer, worthy of fucking, but never love.

Then my door rattles. It's a jarring sound and I turn my head to look under the bed, through the bookshelf, and to the door. It doesn't help. All my lights are out. No one is home. Certainly not Chard. Probably drunks from the club looking for a place to bone.

There's a scraping sound. Someone moving my fake plant. Jude and Paul had keys, but they're both working. Maybe it's one of the Cuties sent up to check on me. Probably Teddy.

I call, trying to sound cheerful, which makes for a desperately dry and unpleasant sound. "I'm fine, thanks. I took my medicine and I don't want to go anywhere quiet."

"It's, uh … me."

Laur.

I lift my head and catch a whiff of myself. Jude would have told him I wasn't home, or was unavailable. And he'd probably scoffed and said something about owning this ass and having it when he wanted.

Yeah. I can't navigate this asshole. How could I

have a future with him? He needs someone to tend his inner fire and keep life bearable. He needs someone like Teddy.

Fuck. I drop my head back to the floor and don't answer.

"It's Larry Trockel."

Ignoring him won't work. "I'm not in good shape right now. Can we meet next week?"

Too soon. You can't crawl out of this pit—

"Yeah, Jude mentioned you'd been off since ... uh, last time I saw you. Can I come in?"

No. I really need a shower. "I don't think you'll like me this way." *I know he won't.*

"Down?"

It's a simple word, but it speaks volumes to his understanding. Had he researched bipolar and learned it like a new language?

"Well, I know, Sunshine Boy. Let's meet the rest of you."

Don't let him fool you. No one can stand you like this, Jeremy. No matter how beautiful you are the rest of the time. This is the real you and everyone hates it.

Yeah. He'd been gone a half hour, tops. But it is actually very sweet.

Let him in at least.

I say nothing.

After another minute passes in silence, he says, "I got your keys and I'm coming in."

I get off the floor and flop onto the bed—*pointless exercise in failure.* My hair is greasy and it hurts my scalp to run my hands through it.

"Don't get up on my account." Laur doesn't turn on the lights. "I found your spare key under the fake plant."

I thought of his house, so full of life and light and

plants. "I have enough trouble keeping myself alive, I can't bother with a living plant."

"Ooh, dark." He takes off his coat and throws it over a chair. He has a brown bag from the bar and the whiskey sour. "Eat anything today?"

Pathetic. "No."

"Mind if I do?"

I consider sinking to the floor where a worm like me belongs. Instead I stand up and walk over to him.

"Sorry. I won't be good company. Can I get you any—"

"Nope. Don't apologize." Laur chugs his whiskey by the sink then fills the tumbler with water. "Just sit with me for a bit."

I sit at the kitchen table. I know what he's doing as soon as he opens the bag. The cheesesteak smells so good. He puts half in front of me and I pick it up.

"If you can stand it, drink some water, too." Laur pushes the tumbler nearer to me.

So stupid.

Of course I can stand it. Water is probably what I need more than food. Hadn't I been thirsty while I sprawled there on the floor and just too damn... "Thanks."

I drain the little glass in one go and it feels so good in my parched throat that I look at the sink. A million years ago, while waiting for pizza to heat—was that yesterday?—I had stared at the wet metal. Maybe hydration had been the answer to the numbness of existence.

What are the steps to get another glass? Stand. Walk to the sink. Pour the water.

"Want more?" Laur takes the empty glass.

"Yes," I answer belatedly, then drop my head on the table.

"Can I be a hundred percent honest with you?"

I mumble affirmatively.

"You mind looking at me while I'm a hundred percent honest with you?"

I lift my head to see he's filled my huge water bottle. I drag it over and suck on the straw.

"Jude said you were out of town. I came up here to break in."

"You did?" It wasn't the first time.

"Yeah. My big idea was to get your key, plant some of my nasty toys under your bed, and go through your mail and figure out what the hell your real name is."

That amuses me. "Jeremy Sowenberger."

"Sowenberger?" He made a face of exaggerated horror. "Oh, no! We're cousins."

He went on gamely when I only gave him a weak smile. "Jamie renamed you?"

I nod. "It sounds like broken glass and burnt things, but was actually salad."

There *was* a joke in that and I totally botched it.

"Jamie likes their nicknames." He goes on, "Never thought I'd get one shorter than Larry, but hey."

"It suits you." Just like broken and burned things suit me. I swallow most of my cheesesteak in a few bites.

Before the silence quite solidifies, Laur said, "I introduced Jamie to Jude, you know?"

"Wow." He must have known them both a long time. That put things into perspective with Jamie and I suddenly realized why Jamie "forgot' how they met."

"You helped them find housing, didn't you?"

Laur nods and drinks water from this tumbler and makes a face when he realizes it's not booze. "Then we sued the homeless shelter for gender discrimination."

"And Jude? Was she in your army group thing?"

"My unit? Dude, we didn't even serve in the same

branch." He chuckles. "We met after our final tours. In rehab."

I stare at him blankly.

Laur carries the conversation. "She likes to say we learned to walk at the same time. But she only had a broken leg."

"Right. Driving a supply truck that crashed. Her knee bothers her sometimes and she lets me massage it." It's taking advantage, but I can't stop myself. "What happened to you?"

Something deeper than rage flashes across his face, but he sucks in his lip to keep control. "Two shattered tibia, multiple severe muscle lacerations, left fractured femur."

"I bet you make jokes the whole time about how it would be less painful if they just cut them off."

Laur sits straighter. "How—"

"I was going to school to be a physical therapist. I did great in the practicals, but I flunked out."

"Pity, you'd be really good at it. Encouraging. Fun to be around. Just like the gym."

He means it as a compliment, but it rings hollow. I don't feel encouraging, fun to be around, or—

"I need to take a shower." I shoot up to act on the impulse.

"Sure." Laur flounders. "Uh, should I stay?"

He's desperate to leave. But I don't want to be alone.

So you'll take advantage of this poor bastard? He doesn't even like you. He wouldn't be here if he didn't like me. *You're right. He likes fucking you.*

"Jeremy? Do you want me to leave?"

I want to feel normal, I want him to be mean. I don't have the mental capacity to deal with this nice version.

"You don't have to stay and you don't have to leave."

"Can't say I love that ambiguity."

"Well, that's what I got for you right now." I went into the bathroom.

"How about after your shower, we watch one of your films?"

I smirk at the idea, pulling off my stuck-on clothes. "I only have kids' films."

A man who'd been blown-up and had his legs nearly demolished, probably did not appreciate Disney and Dreamworks.

"Great. I'm a huge fan of Studio G."

No fan of Studio Ghibli would call it that. "What's your favorite?"

His voice is farther away as he investigates the stack. "Um ... *Pony-o*."

I laugh out loud, wondering if he got it wrong on purpose, melted either way by his lie. I step into the shower. I stay in there until the water is nearly cold then wrap up in my towel and not my dirty shorts.

He has *Ponyo* cued up and a bowl of popcorn in his lap.

Maybe he likes you after all.

****

I jolt awake when his leg spasms.

I remember when the popcorn was done, I took advantage of his compassion to inflict intimacy on him and cuddled up with my head in his lap.

Now he massages his thigh and knee and grits his teeth against the pain. "Sorry."

The whole room is dark. The nightclub pounds only faintly below, a sure sign it was past two in the morning. I might have stayed sleeping on his lap all night. And he might have let me.

He flexes his legs gingerly, stretching the hamstrings and ankles. But he smiles at me. "Wanna lie down for a bit?"

"Are you going to leave?"

"I mean … I ought to. Work in the morning. But I'll come by tomorrow, maybe."

"I'd like that."

He stands when I do and crumples as his knee buckles. Then takes the popcorn bowl to the sink.

"I can do that."

"I'll leave it in the sink. You go to sleep."

I obediently go to bed. The towel slipped off long ago and I don't bother to put anything else. There's something so strange in being stark naked with your lover in the room doing dishes.

I zone out, thinking about this level of connection … is it real? Or just polite? I only realize I've posed when he finishes the dish, sees me, and his mouth falls open.

Well, you're a hot mess, but at least you're hot.

The sight of me radiates through him and I know he's not going anywhere. And maybe that's exactly what I need. A little bout of wildly passionate, totally protected sex.

"You sure you have to go?"

"I…" Then something twists in him. "Yes. I have to go. But I'll be back tomorrow."

"Okay."

Laur smiles on his way out. "Good night, Jeremy."

****

I wake again from a light doze when I hear the

trash cans banging in the alley. It feels like mere seconds have passed, and the sky is still dark. But it's too late for a drunken fight in the alley. When someone shouts, I yawn and drag myself to the window to decide if the police need to get involved.

All I see is Jude, holding her head with frustration, getting behind the wheel of a little sedan to drive one of her drunks home.

Nothing unusual.

****

"How you doing, big guy?" Jude greets me nervously at the beginning of my shift as bartender.

I got to my classes, went for a run, ate, drank, and medicated at the proper times with only the mildest sense of the yawning darkness crippling my every movement.

"Better today." And I'm going to make Laur his whiskey sour today. Won't he be surprised? "Gonna be better tomorrow."

Jude nods solemnly and sits on the other side of the bar as if she were a patron. There's a tension in her shoulders that I don't love.

She's gonna fire you.

I smile, obviously false. "What'll it be, Boss?"

"My friend isn't going to bother you anymore." She can't lift her eyes.

"Huh?" *Who?*

"Paul mentioned…" She shakes her head and I realize her cheek is bruised. Someone had hit her. "I saw him leaving last night and we had words. He should *not* have taken advantage of you in that state."

"Advantage?" Did she mean Laur? Laur wasn't going to bother me? Laur had taken advantage? What did she think? Had Laur hit her? "No, no. It's not like that.

He comes up every Tuesday."

"Yeah. He told me. It's not healthy, Chard. I told him last night you were out of town and he went up there to break in."

"Well, yeah, he does that."

That doesn't placate her.

"If I'd seen his car earlier, I would have gone up there myself and … listen." Jude puts her hands on the bar and can't raise her eyes. "Most of us who went over there made things better. Dig wells and pave roads and shit, but his unit—"

"I don't want to hear this from you."

"Well, you won't hear it from him," Jude says. "His people did some real fucked-up shit over there. Especially the good commanders like Larry. It's hard for the best of us to adjust to civilian—"

She stops herself and shakes her head. "That doesn't excuse or justify anything. He has no right playing mind games with you."

"Mind games?" We'd watched a movie and I fell asleep on him.

"I know you tanked after you ran into him Thursday. I run after the VA meeting too, and when you didn't come home that night and wouldn't answer your phone, I put together where you were. Then he comes here on Tuesday and goes up there to break into your apartment."

"I invited—"

"I told him you weren't there," Jude protests and the bruise gleams in the bar lights. "What the fuck was he doing even going to the door?"

I can't deny it or defend him. "I … so, he's not coming tonight?"

"He's not coming back at all, Chard." She sighs. "You're a match made in Hell, dude. You see that, right?

He spends every second with you thinking about how ugly and broken he is and that makes him meaner than spit. You spend every second you're with him trying to earn the approval or affection that he does *not* have the capacity to give, and it's going to make you hurt yourself. You've been off-kilter for months."

"So, you forbade him from coming to your bar?"

"No, Chard," Jude's voice softens. "I took him for coffee. Talked about what I've seen in him and what Paul's seen in you. He decided he wasn't coming back."

"Oh..."

Well. That's a different kettle of fish.

Jude says after a moment, "Sean's here. Take the night off."

"I don't..." I look back at her solemn eyes and think about the last time she'd offered me the chance to not work—the first time I'd been really off-kilter for the man.

"Yeah, that's probably for the best." I nod. "Probably all of it ... for the best. Thanks, Jude."

That's it? Aren't you going to fight for this shit? Just...

I didn't deserve a goodbye.

But I fucking want a goodbye.

Chapter Eight

As winter thaws into a chilly wet spring, I take longer and longer bikes rides. It's become my habit to go to the intersection by the beach and explore the bike paths along the residential neighborhoods. Looking for a lawn full of flags.

Sometimes when I pass one of those cliffs I think about aiming the bike and pedaling as fast as I can and not turning. The cheerful little voice in my head screams: *Yes! You can do it. The end of suffering is near. There's the finish line. Show Laur you have the determination to die!*

And there's another voice in my head, a collected scoff that sounds remarkably like Laur. *Why the fuck would you do that? Don't be so dumb. Go home, eat some ice cream, and start over again with someone new. You'll do better next time.*

Since the meaner voice seems like better advice I would go home.

Still, in less than a month, I find it.

That's right--939 Cypress.

At first, I'm hesitant. There's no name on the mailbox. No mail in the mailbox. But that border of flags, lining his perfectly manicured lawn like a fence. The roofs of the neighbors on the next street down. The view of the ocean in the distance.

I have found his house.

Now, what would a sane person do?

Not look for his house in the first place. Not be in love with a man who has the emotional range of a clam, fucks you like a prescribed dopamine rush, and refuses to have a real conversation except on special occasions.

Certainly, a sane person wouldn't be parking his

bike and walking up to the front door.

Well, like I said, I'm not exactly sane.

He draws the curtains after dark, like there's some secret inside suburbia. I'm certain he'll see me on my way to the door. *And probably yell at me.*

He has no welcome mat. No fake plant. No place where he might put his spare key. There's a smaller window off the porch. Not curtained like the bay window, and there's Laur.

As soon as I see him, I know I should not be seeing him. He's so unguarded, so cozy and relaxed. Fluffy red bathrobe, hair wet from a recent shower, a sturdy metal cane, and glasses thick as Coke bottles. The book in his hands is a pastel-covered, *Achieve Your Best Self Through Kale and Zen* guide.

Oh, and he's missing his fucking eye. There's a concave darkness not terribly hidden by a drooping eyelid. He looks like some twisted Halloween version of a 1950's father.

Run away.

My hand is already on the doorknob. But rather than rattling, the knob turns.

Oh, hell! How did a man this paranoid not lock his door?

"Laur, hey, it's me?"

"Chard?" He sounds genuinely surprised, then swears. "Fuck!"

He rises and stumbles, trying to get to another room. But I've already entered the living room. The book is nowhere to be seen, and he's halfway to the hallway, his left hand balled into a fist to hide his absent eye.

"I didn't know you wore a contact." It's weird to catch him off-guard and I cover by acting confident, leaning in the arch between the kitchen and the living room, smirking as he flounders toward his bedroom.

Which he stops doing immediately. He lowers his hand, embarrassed to be caught hiding. "What the fuck are you doing here? Get out of my house!"

"Before you say something mean, I'm sorry I surprised you." I hold up my hands the way you do when greeting a frightened dog. "I just didn't have your phone number or any way to reach you."

"Yeah? Because I never gave you a way to reach me. It was a mistake bringing you here."

When I don't answer—because how do you answer that?—his good eye swivels away from me and toward his bedroom.

"If you're not comfortable, I don't mind if you—"

"I'm plenty comfortable in my own house," Laur says. "What I'm not comfortable with is you just showing up. Out of fucking nowhere."

"Out of nowhere? Really?" I resist. "We've been a thing for over six months, Laur. I wanted to see you."

"You piece of shit."

His aggression startles me because I meant, *I wanted to have a conversation, to have you tell me to my face why you determined not to be part of my life.*

Then I realize what he heard was, "I wanted to surprise you and see your broken legs, your eyeless head, you ugly freak."

When I'm at my low, I'm apathetic, dead inside, helpless. When he's at his lowest—

He hovers nearer to it than I do. He's triggered by the slightest cringe from a stranger at the bank, a gawking child in the supermarket, the way a beautiful stranger in a bar hits on him. The depths of his self-loathing come when he feels less than human. And right now, without his glass eye, without his gloves, without the accessories that cover his brokenness, he feels his shame. And he feels it as rage.

I say lamely, "I didn't think this through."

"You sure fucking didn't." Laur points at the door. "Now get the fuck out."

If I do, I'll never come back. "Laur, if you're gonna abandon me, I have a right to—"

"You have no rights," he scoffs. "Not here. Not with me."

I stare helplessly, my mouth opening, but no words coming out.

He rages nearer. "You think you can just walk up to me and offer sex like you're God's damned gift to humanity. Well, guess what, buddy? I don't think you are. I've seen plenty of men as built and goddamn pretty as you get blown to fuckin' bits or torn up with barbed wire. Fuck. I've been the one placing the bombs and pulling the wire. You see a body different when you know how to take it apart. Your beauty isn't worth shit to me."

His single eye glowers wide, his fists clenched, like he wants to use them.

When I don't immediately crumble, it makes him furious. "So, what else you got, Chard? Your balanced mental state? Your attentive and loyal personality?"

He doesn't look away but shakes his head as if saying *no* to the words that have already passed his lips. But he is also somehow relieved, as if something has been decided. He's said the worst things he could, and there's no taking them back.

I swallow hard, having trouble facing this man. He's not the same person who watched a children's film with a depressed man. Was he taking his meds?

At a complete loss, I try, "So, you're really angry, and I think we should talk about it?"

He sneers. "I do talk about it. The whole thing.

With my VA group. With my psychiatrist. I see no reason to discuss the things that make me a man with a cum-rag like you."

Okay, maybe he's not done with the worst things he can say. I don't dare answer. What other abuse can he hurl at me, and how long can I stand it?

He's trying to frighten me off, to chase me out.

But if I can just stand here until he exhausts his meanness…

"Will you just go away!" Unprompted by anything—anything from me—Laur attacks.

When his hands connect with my chest to roughly shove me away, some wires get crossed. My body misreads the signals and I'm faintly aware I should not be getting hard.

Laur is my lover, after all, and he's always been rough with me.

It surprises both of us when I grab his wrists on the second shove.

Laur— I'm reminded— is a little guy. He lurches in my grip and cannot get free. The man hurls curses at me. Nothing special. A garden variety of "son of a bitch" and "piece of shit" and variants on the theme. He barely noticed it, but he's at my mercy.

I test this theory by pushing his arms behind his back and pulling him toward me. He moves stiffly, too brittle to resist and surprised to find himself moving against his will.

I hold both his wrists in one hand and look down at his face. What will he do? He jostles and wrenches. It's a strain on my grip, but he's not going anywhere. When his flailing makes his robe flap open, I yank it with my free hand to help it along.

"What the actual fuck, Chard?" He gapes at me…

"You know our safeword." I reach between his

legs.

****

Laur stares at me speechless, his one eye wide with astonishment, the other lid half-raising with symmetrical instinct. Then he flings one arm free and jabs at my head. As a soldier, he knows to go for my throat or my eye. But his punch is loose-fisted and uncommitted. After I take the blow, I grab his arm again and bully him onto the couch.

As I pin him under me, forcing his legs wide around my waist, he hides the side of his face in the pillow and glares. "Knock it off, you piece of—"

I grab his face in my free hand and force him to look straight at me. Raw fear passes over his face as I lean in to kiss him. It reminds me of that day in his car, when I meant to kiss him and his cold, blank expression scared me off. He'd been terrified to be kissed. Now the fear melts into anger. He knees me in the stomach and thrashes away. Not enough to hurt me, not enough to shake loose.

We wrestle a moment before I pin him again, my hips and hard cock anchoring him as I tug at the robe and tangle it around his arms to restrain his motions.

Laur vibrates with anger and inarticulate swearing. Is he too mad to free himself from the stupid fluffy robe, or is he just playing along now?

I fight to get his boxers off his legs and force my hips between his thighs, then hold him immobilized and helpless. With the underwear stuck around one ankle and his legs spread wide around me, with his robe wrapped around his arms, he is finally naked.

He shuts his eye and bears the indignity of being looked at.

Beneath the extreme tan lines, his pale skin is dotted with pink and brown divots and gouges in a patchwork of missing pieces and scar tissue. His muscles are taut as wire and rock-hard because of how I've pinned him. His right nipple is pink and raised like a tiny button, but his left is a white slash of scar tissue. Some word has been carved into his side, uneven, slicing cuts. It is not a language I understand.

My gaze wanders the cratered landscape of his naked flesh until it lands on his cock. That rigid pole is instantly familiar, and a territory that makes my mouth water with desire and my hand instinctively reach. I stroke him, and he grunts, out of breath from his struggle, but infinitely tough and masculine, even raw and exposed as he was.

I remember the first time he'd commanded my body. Remember how I'd whimpered his name. I lean over his ear to remind him, "Laur, I want to fuck you."

He smiles, a wry and unsurprised expression, "You're still a presumptuous little shit."

I rub my hand lower, cradling the base of his shaft in my palm and stretching my fingers toward his ass. "Think I can get away with it based on charm and good looks?"

Laur swallows hard and nods slightly. I press my lips to his Adam's apple and he flinches away from the gentleness.

"Do you remember the deal you made with me?" I tug at his right leg spreading him wider.

He clenches and twists, but not enough to stop my finger from finding his hole. "I don't make deals, with pus—fuck!"

I shove the finger inside and keep him firmly anchored as he writhes and struggles.

When was the last time he'd been fucked? A

malicious, vengeful pleasure flowed over me, spreading like venom through my blood. Before he'd met me? Never? I twist and poke inside his tight ass, and he hisses and grunts.

The pain makes him smile, though.

There's something disgustingly wonderful about being wanted to the point of violence. And as hideous as he thinks he is, there is no denying that he is wanted.

I whisper, calm and nonthreatening, even as I thrust in and out of his squirming ass with my index finger. "Remember how you said once you were done with my ass, I could fuck you?"

Laur cackles because, of course, he remembers. "Is this revenge, then? You pathetic…"

I add my middle finger to the party in his hole, and he finishes with a loud. "Bitch!"

"Ghosting me?" I nibble at his ear, cooing. "Breaking up with me through your best friend?"

"We weren't dating." He flinches away from my affectionate whisper.

I shove both fingers in deep and hard, and his breath comes in a broken, high-pitched gulp.

"Seems like you're done with my ass, Laur." My voice is as soft and loving as the kiss I press on his cheek. "Now, I'm gonna tear you apart, little guy."

He scoffs. "You're not man enough to fuck me."

I smile, keeping him pinned with one hand, while I open my pants. "If that's what you need to tell yourself, sweetie."

His ass is hard, muscular, and as closed as a damn door even with the working I've given him. My cock—having been tortured for half a year—is more than up to the challenge of breaking in. As inch after inch of my shaft squeezes through his barely yielding hole, Laur's breathing changes. Not gasping for breath or grunting in pain—these sounds are beneath him—it's a focused deep breathing, punctuated occasionally with high-pitched yelping spikes as I force my cock deeper.

Christ, it feels good to be fucking a man again.

When I look at his face again, he's relieved, almost calm, as if some terrible battle has finally been lost, and he doesn't have to worry about it anymore.

I can't resist bowing over him to kiss his lips. I've gotten as far as cupping his cheek before he erupts into violence again. Striking my hand, pushing at my chest to get my mouth away, all while tightening his knees to keep my cock in place.

I don't fight back, but I don't let him move me. Keeping him pinned is like very violent resistance training. "Why won't you let me kiss you?"

"Because I don't want to be kissed. I want to be fucked," he answers, very coldly. "Will you just fuck me, you sissy fuck?"

I'm not going to say no to that. I clench his thigh and impale him on my full cock in one motion. Laur's jaw drops open with an intoxicating mix of surprise, pain, and pleasure, but not a sound passes his lips.

Buried to the hilt, I swivel my hips. That dancer's curl that makes an audience lose its mind. There's nothing sissy about that move to the man whose ass is on the receiving end. Hard and invasive, but Laur only grits his teeth and takes it.

When I pull my cock away, he takes another deep meditative breath. I thrust back in before he can release it naturally, forcing the air out of his lungs. I don't give him a chance to catch his breath. If he wants to be fucked raw and rough—and he fucking does—I won't disappoint him. Not when it feels so good, so brutally masculine, to tear apart his mean, little ass.

His cock stands straight between us, rock-hard

and never wavers as he takes my assault. Aside from his cock, Laur gives me nothing to express that he enjoys my deep hard thrusting. He keeps his eyes closed and his head back. I want his gaze, I want his song of desire. And his silence only makes me go harder.

He doesn't ask me to stop.

Quickly, relaxed by the barrage of my cock and slicked by my pre-cum, his hole softens, and my thrusts go smoother. That's when his pain totally melts into pleasure. He moans quietly and strokes his cock unobtrusively, without shame but without making a show of it. Practical.

If I hadn't been watching him like it was the last time I'd see him naked, if I had just brought him up to my apartment and gotten to have him like every other man I'd ever fucked, I would have been too interested in my own overwhelming pleasure to notice when he was coming.

It happens when he opens his eye to look at me. The sight of me towering over him on his couch, his legs thrown around my tapered waist, my shirt half-rolled up my defined abs—like I'd been distracted mid-striptease. The sight of me fucking him. That's what makes his whole body tighten and twitch with tension, that's what makes his cock spill onto his stomach in a thick white puddle.

My beauty didn't matter? Not fucking likely.

His whole body goes limp and he doesn't fight when I pull him into my arms. Easier to fuck him … and to kiss him.

Laur doesn't kiss back, just lets my lips explore his lips and chin while my cock spears deep inside him. I grunt, so close to coming…

When I intrude with my tongue—he tastes like whiskey—he opens his mouth with an aggressive disinterest. And when I make the kiss more insistent, balls-deep in his ass and fucking harder than ever, he finally kisses back. Just a tentative tilt of his head, the slight movement of his tongue, the shyest suck of his lips. He's left his hands pinned above his head, long after we'd fucked the restraints loose, but now his hands slide around my back to stroke over my t-shirt.

I erupt just as the shortened fingers of his right hand caress the back of my neck. The firing of pleasure, the release of all that sexual tension … it's like my body is being pulled in two and it's only his uncertain embrace that keeps me from shattering.

"Fuck…" I hear the newly wet slap of my cock entering his ass. "Forgot about protection."

"I don't care." He holds me closer and rocks slowly, milking my cock inside his ass.

The anger is gone from him now, and his voice, deep and calm, near my ear makes the lust in my belly roil again, even if my cock is thrumming with pleasure and totally spent.

I pull out and his arms slip away from me. He falls on the couch like I'd fucked the life out of him. His cum glistens on his belly and chest, mine drizzles from between his widespread legs. My cock, still wet, twitches. I want him again tonight.

Laur sighs, the happiest sound he's ever made, and turns into the pillow. He's about to fall asleep. Absolutely filthy from sex and more innocent than I'd ever seen.

I want him again, right now.

"Hey! No!" Laur violently thrashes out of his stupor when I grab him under the legs and around his back and pluck him off the couch. "Fucking hell! Put me down!"

I smile mischievously and carry him across the

living room, like a dainty child.

"Chard—Jeremy, I mean it, don't…"

"Which one is your bedroom?"

He scowls at me. And I remember being tied up in his guest room. So I open the other door. His bedroom is dark, with blackout curtains and not even an alarm clock to cast a glow, so I leave the door open and bring him to the bed. I drape him on the bed with another kiss, amused by how much this irritates my broken little princess.

Laur kicks off the last of his clothes, the stubborn shorts hanging on his legs. Then Laur crosses his arms and his legs at the ankle as if re-locking the safe of his body. "Don't do that ever again. I don't like it."

His words horrify me into stillness. "Fuck you?"

"What?" The darkness on his face turns to confusion. "No, no, that was great. I've been waiting for you to get the nerve to do that since the night we met."

News to me. That night when I'd thought about grabbing him and tearing off his clothes … he'd wanted that too.

But he doesn't want something else. Never wanted it again. Didn't like it.

When he sees I'm not following he clarifies, as if it was obvious. "Don't carry me."

"Oh," That *was* obvious. "Okay. Sorry. Why not?"

In the half-light of the hallway, I see exhaustion and post-sex relaxation defeat his caginess. "Because the last time a fella had to carry me I'd just lost a couple body parts and had my legs pulverized."

"I … sorry."

He waves his hand like it was nothing.

Now that he's calm again, it's awkward and unsettled. Maybe I should go. But I want to stay. Was it all right for me to touch him again?

Laur clears his throat, looking very small in his bed. He says with much less bravado than he had a moment ago, "Well, aren't you gonna ... you know ki ... do it again?"

He can't even say kiss. I smile at his macho repression. I place my knee on the bed and lean over him. "Do what thing?"

He stares me dead in the face. "You fucking know. Don't play games with me."

I love playing games with him. And mine aren't as mean as his ... I think. I come no closer, forcing him to either ask or kiss me himself.

Eventually he relents, unable to look me in the face when he commands very softly, "Kiss me."

I start on his neck, licking at the little scars I can see even in the dim room and travel from one to the other across his neck and face. He breathes in his slow meditative way, eyes closed, trembling from the slight touch of my lips on his skin. When I suck at the cut on his lip, he opens his mouth and invites me to kiss him this time.

We both melt into that kiss, his arms folding around my shoulders, my hand lifting to cup his face. I'm surprised when we part that he's looking at me with grief.

"Why did you come back?"

I don't answer but lean in to kiss him again.

He digs his hands into my hair and pulls me away from his body. "Seriously, Jeremy. Why?"

I run my fingers over his face. "Maybe I love you."

"Maybe?" His brow arches sarcastically.

"I have trouble committing to statements." I shrug and nod. "But you're right. I love you. Full stop."

He sighs as if that answer is the worst thing he'd ever heard. Then adds in a truly exhausted tone, "Well, I guess you can keep going then. Since you're insatiable and I'm inexhaustible. I'll fuck you again."

I smirk and reach for his cock, but as soon as I move forward, he flinches away.

"Actually, um ... do you mind..." He looks toward the door, then taps the lamp on his nightstand, bathing the room in warm light. "Getting the lights in the other room first? And, um ... maybe bringing me the cane by the chair out there?"

"Oh, shit!" I jump up. "Sure. No problem."

I come back with his whiskey and his cane, walking slowly in the darkness toward the soft light of his bedroom. I'm not surprised to see a beige patch over his missing eye. Like those bandages they made us kids wear when we had pink eye.

I slot the cane in the umbrella cage by the nightstand and hand him the whiskey. "For the record, I think you should go full Nick Fury and embrace a black leather eye patch."

He smirks, sips the whiskey, and strokes his cock. The full hot-asshole energy is back and in force. "I think you should either be stripping or sucking my cock."

"You gonna give me the beat or should I sing to myself?" I scoff, but immediately fall into the pelvic thrust of a little striptease.

"Just normal, Chard. I like it when you take them off normally."

"I don't understand that at all." I bend over to pull my shirt up and over my head in that hunched way that does nothing for a man's figure.

"You don't really?" he asks into the whiskey tumbler.

I drop out of my pants and kick off my sneakers without so much as a shimmy. "No, I don't. People literally pay money to see—"

Then I get it. Everyone in the city and their gay cousin could see me dance my clothes off. He's one of the few who's ever seen me just take them off.

"Good, you got it." He uncrosses his legs, giving me room to come between and take over servicing his cock. He finishes his whiskey and sets it down on the nightstand, then his eye slides shut and he murmurs, "Christ, that's good."

I've hardly done anything, but I know what he means. Having another person is infinitely better than being alone, definitely when it comes to a hand on your cock, but also…

I kiss him below his ear. "I got this crazy idea."

"Happens to mentally disordered people like us." He rubs his hand over my neck and back but does not stop me from kissing.

Or from talking. "When Jude said we were a match made in Hell, I realized we made a good couple."

He leans back to look at me. "Really? That's how you take that advice?"

"I've never been any match before!" I refuse to budge. If I withdrew this low-burning pleasure, Laur wouldn't allow me to speak. "Look, I know this is probably a disaster and will hurt us both in the long run and I just ... I'd like to ... try it anyway."

His brow arches sarcastically. "You wanna be my boyfriend?"

"Yes," I agree, overly eager.

"I wasn't asking you, just confirming that you want, like, not just sex but dates and seeing movies together and shit? Like in public?"

"Why is this so hard for you to believe?"

"Well..." Laur fumbles for an answer. "You could … anybody in that club would just…"

He pushes me away again, but moves with me, so

that I end up on my back and he leans over me. No longer accepting kisses but giving them tentatively as if the taste of my skin might poison him. "You really never dated anyone before?"

I shrug. "Just Paul, and I don't know if he would call it dating. It certainly wasn't healthy. And no one else … you cared. You remembered I didn't drink coffee."

He tsks. "Anyone who doesn't have a coffeemaker either drinks tea or orange juice. Anyone could figure that out. I broke into your house."

"Well, I stalked you and then jumped you in the privacy of your home."

"And I'm still mad at you for that, by the way." Laur opens the drawer of his nightstand and pulls out a tiny jar of Vaseline.

"Ooh, you gonna drag me into your dungeon and punish me?" I spread my legs to accommodate his greased fingertips. I moan lewdly when he pushes inside, considerably easier than when I'd finger-fucked him earlier.

"I think you like my punishment," Laur whispers into my neck.

His ear is near my mouth, and I moan lustily for him as he stretches and opens me.

He presses his lips against my neck. "I bet all the guys you slept with took one look at you and decided they weren't worthy."

"Sure." I roll my eyes. "Or they got a look at my medicine cabinet and ran."

"You've got it under control."

It's my turn to lean back to look at him with disbelief.

"When you don't have your routine fucked up by, you know, assholes with dungeons."

He runs his hands over my chest, and I rock my

hips into his fingers. What a strange and intimate way to have a conversation. Even as he pushes in a third, I know I want more than his fingers can give me.

"I'll be a rotten boyfriend," he admits, getting rough and twisting. "Emotionally constipated, mean as hell. I might have a drinking problem, too. Not to mention ass-ugly."

I place my hand on his neck and pull him down to my level to kiss him. The taste of whiskey burns against my lips. He shifts between my legs, pulling out his fingers and angling his cock.

"I might be shit at monogamy." I pull away from the kiss and confess. "I have very poor impulse control."

He pins my shoulders and pushes his cock inside. I gasp from the sharp pain as his cock plunges farther than his fingers have been able to reach. Laur groans from the pleasure, arching back away from me. I feel the tremble that rocks through his body and wonder if it was his shredded muscles spasming or the sex.

Laur looks at me, helpless, with love, I think. "We'll get good at forgiving each other."

"Yeah." I nod and swivel my hips to offer more of myself to his cock.

He grunts and starts to thrust. He could be truly brutal when he moved, but he's clearly trying to keep it gentle. Problem is, he's gripping my thigh as if he's worried I'll slip out of his clawed grip.

"Touch yourself," he commands.

He means my cock. He wants to watch me cum. But I obey only the suggestion, moving one hand over my chest and abs as I rock back into his hard thrusts. Squeezing my own nipples, rubbing my neck and side, dancing around his cock.

"You sexy bitch," he growls and fucks harder.

"Touch me, Laur," I beg.

He strokes along with the pace he's set. I gasp and feel the orgasm rising faster than I thought possible, like everything in me wanted to flood out and drown this man.

"Fuck me harder!"

He obliges. The pain and the ecstasy rise between us to frightened heat. We're both panting for breath and groping at each other, bodies slick with sweat sliding in his sheets.

Then he says, quietly, almost conversationally, "Okay."

"Huh?" I'd lost track of the conversation around the time he'd started mauling my cock.

"You're my boyfriend," he says. "We're gonna be just … gonna be exclusive and I'm gonna come inside."

"Yes…" I tighten my legs around him. "Please."

"I'll try not to be an asshole to the man I'm fucking, and you'll try not to be a slut. And it's going to be impossible because we're both broken as hell."

He pauses in his panting speech to fuck me with rapid and shallow thrusts, shaking the whole bed with the force. I growl and welcome his cock, so close to coming, all I can think of is this passion threatening to immolate me.

Then I burst between our bodies in a stream as erratic as my panting breath and his pounding hips.

"God, I love it when you come while I'm fucking you," Laur croons. "Yeah, boyfriend. And we'll go to dinner tomorrow night or some shit. "

"I work at night," I remind him, rubbing my cum over my abdomen and flexing.

"Yeah, you do." He remembers my job with a sharp stab of his cock, and leans his head back and moans. I bet he's imagining my dance.

He laughs, and I brace myself for his meanness.

"Brunch, then?"

"Sure. You can wear your sweater vest, and I'll put on a fancy hat."

He bows over me and kisses me again, a sloppy, desperate kiss. I wrap my arms around his head to lock him in that kiss, and he keeps pummeling my ass, until his body wrenches and he erupts inside me.

He tries to slip away and put distance between our bodies, but I throw my thigh over him and keep him close.

****

Mornings, it turns out, are the hardest time for him. Stiff from not moving all night. When I see how wobbly he is first thing, I thought he would certainly call off our first date.

But instead, he puts the keys to his car in my hand. "You can drive, right?"

He's quiet and hushed at the diner, locked in a conversation with himself that's fairly intense and not for me.

It's only after the coffee has been delivered that he finally says. "Okay. I'm gonna tell you about it."

"Huh?"

He looks across the table at me. Glass eye just as focused and intense as the real one. He lifts his hand and wiggles his missing fingers inside the gloves.

I swallow hard. "You don't have—"

"I know." Laur cuts me off. Then proceeded to sit in silence and stir his coffee.

I let him find his own way to the beginning.

"So ... I don't even remember which town. All the names kind of blended together, everything was "Ab" or "Ak" something or else "Qal'eh-ye." I called them all by their map coordinates. That tells you part of our problem over there, doesn't it?"

I nod earnestly as if I had ever thought once in my life about "over there." Hell, I didn't even know which Middle East place he was talking about.

"This terrorist cell ambushed us while we were setting up an ambush for them. We were mostly explosive experts and … the kind of group that doesn't have an official designation."

"Because of secrecy?"

He shakes his head. "Because of war crimes."

I'm not certain I want to hear this, but I also know I'll lose him forever if I don't hear this.

He watches me steadily, waiting for me to speak. When I say nothing, he points at his missing eye. "This only happened when they figured out who I was. Apparently, some of my old friends recognized me by the color of my eyes."

Laur lifted his right hand. "Happened one knuckle at a time over a couple of weeks. After they'd shot or beheaded most of the rest of us. They kept me alive, even though I pissed them off the most because I could translate."

He twists to point to his side. To the word carved there. But then untwists and sets his hands down. He doesn't want to tell me about that … not yet.

"And you know, it's never for knowledge. No one who gets caught knows shit. I certainly didn't. Neither did anyone I ever—"

His gaze falters glancing at the diner's door, then back at me.

"So, if it's not about intel, it's gotta be about vengeance and intimidation. You'd find the bodies—mutilated bodies, partly healed—and that's bad. But survivors are worse. I used to let people escape. If you're good you can follow them home to their friends and leaders. You've made them so afraid of meeting you again, they get reckless."

His gaze unfocused. I lean over to touch his knee.

Laur resumes as if remembering his place in a script. "Once they started working on my legs, I knew me and my boys were going to be a demonstration. Nothing as kind as beheading. Well, I didn't want to be a before-and-after on Fox News, so … well."

He grins and it's the most terrifying thing I've ever seen. "Let's say improvised explosives go both ways."

Jesus Christ, he did it to himself.

"I wasn't supposed to survive the explosion. It was the distraction my guys needed to escape. My guys weren't supposed to carry me out. I'd ordered them to run and escape."

"That's the kind of order people always ignore."

He's unimpressed. "People I talk to about this usually think that time is the thing that haunts me, you know. The pain. Watching the mutilation. That's why they left—"

Laur waves his hand dismissively. "It's not the prison. It's the town. Whose name I don't remember."

I tilt my head.

"The rest of the army found us within a day. And in the next hour they wiped that whole town off the map. I can't find it today. Those people didn't know what the fuck was going on. Some of them saw us escaping and gave us food and water. Bandages. Some little girl had a flag— one of ours, I mean. Young enough, she just learned to wear the headscarf, still had hair showing, you know? Not old enough for a burka and she wanted to show her flag to me, to this broken and bloody man who she certainly didn't think was going to outlive her. Then, the whole town goes up like the Fourth of July. And why? Vengeance and intimidation."

The words swirl in my head. What he'd said, what I might say. Silence is best.

"Anyway, that's what happened. Any more questions?"

"No," If I asked for more, I'd get it. But there's a door you can't close once you open it, a darkness that gets into you. He's given me enough of a peak to know why he keeps that door closed except with the people who carry that same darkness. "Thank you for sharing."

"Whatever."

I'd had some idea that knowing would bring us closer, but he was correct. I'm not sure what to do with that information and sit in silence for a moment.

But for now, that was the closest he could get to saying he loved me. Trusting me with something he didn't give away easily.

He's also correct about the place, doing it in public. The waitress comes back to take our order, and suddenly we return to the surface of life and not the dark depth that both of us already know too well. Back to smiling and setting her at ease. Then it's easy for me to ask him more details about his official job and for him to get the list of classes I teach at the gym.

And before the bill comes he reaches across the table and takes my phone.

"You ought to get some kind of security on this thing," he mutters. Then saves his number in my contacts as *that asshole who loves you.*

The End

SEDUCER

Lea Bronsen

Copyright © 2024

Chapter One

The town of Aranda de Duero in the north of Spain was built at a time when horses and carriages were the common means of transport, so most streets in the medieval inner-city center can't take large vehicles such as SUVs and trucks. Yet that's where I am, driving a limousine of all things (!) in the afternoon of a hot summer day, so you can imagine the hassle. The crowd and the traffic jam on these ancient, paved streets between low, pastel-colored walls. The noise. The irritation. My level of stress.

Blame it on my employer, a twenty-year-old brat so spoiled she couldn't be bothered to walk the few hundred meters from her hotel to tonight's film première. *Mira-Me* is her name, aptly meaning "Look at me" in Spanish, and celebrity is her game. She's a Generation Z starchild: TikTok influencer slash reality show contestant slash attempted pop star slash model. A product of the previous generation's lack of parenting skills, she's self-adoring, abusive, and fake through and through, her facial fillers competing with over-the-top makeup, blown-up boobies that any sane guy would deem unattractive unless he's desperate to get laid, and clothing straight out of a *Playboy* magazine.

Playboy? Okay, so, if I sound a bit outdated, it's because I grew up before the era of the Internet and smartphones and Snapchat streaks. But that's okay, I'm not here to impress anyone, and I don't need to feel younger than my thirty-eight years. The only thing I worry about at the current stage of my life is obeying and pleasing my boss. She's a Madrid native, I an American, so the potential for cultural misunderstandings is huge in addition to the obvious clash of generations.

Just to make things clear, I'm male enough but there's nothing sexual between us. Not just because I'm more attracted to men, or because of our age difference, but because she has her life and I have mine, and we meet halfway when she needs a bodyguard or a chauffeur. Or a fixer when she's dying for some junk food, or when she needs help to kiss the porcelain on an early Sunday morning because she's had too many *margaritas*. Although she's old enough to take care of herself, her parents find my presence reassuring.

Me? I'm only happy to have a job to pay my bills. I've had a complicated life.

I glance into the rearview mirror. She's in the backseat nose-deep in her phone, most probably checking her social media likes and comments, fluffing her platinum-blonde hair and making glossy fish-lip selfies for her hundred-thousand-something worldwide fans. She sports a sparkling, golden tank dress that compliments her tanned skin and matching gold hoop earrings with heart charms. We're late for the show, so I'm in a hurry, it's important she gets there on time so she's the talk of the event. Or else she might as well stay in her hotel room and plan her live-broadcasted and overly dramatic suicide.

There's an obstruction on the street, with several cars stopped ahead. What the hell is going on? There's an incredible crowd filling the narrow space, too, a lot of people looking excited, most likely a demonstration. Just what I need. How long is this going to take? I glance at the digital clock on my dashboard: 7:15 PM. Mira-Me needs to be at the cinema by 7:45 at the latest. That's thirty minutes. Not sure we're going to make it. Groaning, I thumb through the map app. Parallel streets lead to the same destination, but I'm stuck in a growing line of vehicles and can't turn around.

I lean on the horn. Get moving!

Slowly, we inch forward. The clock says 7:20. We really don't have time for this. If she doesn't make it on time, the lil' lady in the back is going to make a scene. At home, away from the public eye, she doesn't worry much about anything—other than the obligatory makeup and dressing *séances* recorded and published live—but she's damn picky about her *entrée* into the "real" world of fame, where eccentric gala-dressed celebrities are flattered by showers of camera flashes and the whooping of waiting fans. She wants to be best looking, the most commented of them all. She's such a diva. A brat, but a diva.

I snicker and look out the window. There're people everywhere looking at me weird, like I'm the one acting strange. So, I slam the steering wheel. What do you want? My hands fly into the air like I'm an Italian *mafioso*, like I'm offended, like they don't know who they're messing with. I work for an important person, peeps, so lay off. Well, "important" in the social media slash cultural élite world, but otherwise...

I use the horn again. Where are the police when you need them? I used to be a cop, but due to a certain unacceptable behavior in the line of duty a few years ago, my badge was taken, and I've done jobs as bodyguard and chauffeur since. It irks me that I can't just slam a blue light up on the hardtop and press my way through the disturbance.

I'm about to open my door and peek over the car in front of me when it jumps a few meters forward and stops again. Cursing, I tail it and hit the brakes. Everyone's attention goes to a weird creature in black-and-white checkered clothes who just appeared on the driver's side and leans into the open window. Is that who is creating such a chaos? He or she slips out the window again and displays a disturbing, white-painted face with exaggerated black makeup and a big, weird nose. A clown? From the person's height and build, it's a man.

He swivels to the crowd behind him with a ten-euro bill in hand and blows through a whistle. It sounds like a questioning tune, as if he's asking whether they think it's enough money for a tip. On the back of his pants, the name ROBIN is sewn in capital letters.

People boo. Not enough money.

He makes a face and turns back to the driver with a disapproving whistle. This seems to be his favored means of communication. He doesn't speak a word.

Who cares? His show takes too long. Making pranks is cool when you have time, but now it's directly uncool. I hope we're not subject to a whole tribe of circus people taking over the street and harassing bypassers.

I honk again to attract his attention. As he turns to face me, the car he was pranking seizes the opportunity to drive away. The street fills with laughter and I'm alone with the clown. He gives my limo his full attention, standing in the middle of the paveway with his hands on his hips, legs spread, considering my vehicle up and down. A wide grin appears on his white-painted face, and he makes a seducing wolf whistle as if to say the limo is extremely beautiful, or extremely expensive, or both.

The crowd cheers. They love him. He plays the fool, a quirky and mischievous creature. He must be good at reading situations and adapting to them, because it seems he knows what he's doing and what the audience wants from him. At his side, a cameraman films the scene, changing focus from him to the crowd and me.

I want to drive on, but he blocks my path whistling that loud, flattering tune. I can't exactly run him down. He circles the hood and pulls at my door handle, his whistle turning to a low, inquisitive tune, like he's busy thinking and investigating. Of course, my door is locked, and you can bet your ass I'm not going to open the window. Loud laughs fill the space around me.

I groan. Can't these people see things from my perspective? Don't they know how it feels to be in a hurry and afraid of losing their jobs? They probably do, but this is the time of their life when they're at the circus, they want to forget, they want to be misled, and they don't care what other people are enduring.

He tries the back door, and it opens. Dammit, Mira-Me unlocked it, the stupid brat. Sometimes, she can be such a pain. He mimics to the crowd that he's super lucky and slips inside before I can protest. I turn in my seat and tell him, "Get out, we have to drive." I don't know if he understands English, but I'm pretty sure the tone of my voice will get through to him.

Ignoring me, he rummages behind there, opening cupboards and checking stuff and whistling a happy melody while the cameraman films him through the open door.

Mira-Me squeals, hands in the air. What's he doing to her? That's it. I'm not just her chauffeur, I'm her bodyguard.

I open my door, get out in a hurry, and push the cameraman away. "Get out, you freak!" I call to the clown in the large backseat, a U-shaped leather couch with a table in the middle.

Seated beside him, Mira-Me rolls her eyes. "He's not a freak, Zane. He's a clown."

"You screamed!"

"No, I giggled. And *you* are ruining everything."

He bows his head to her with a mock-apologetic smile and lifts his hands in the air as if to say it's not his fault he's a clown, he was born like that or something.

"So, you understand English, dude." I pull at his clothes. "Get out."

He gives me a scrutinizing look, then whistles his happy melody and spreads his long legs on the couch.

I pull at his weird, pointy shoes. "Come on."

Behind me, the crowd cheers, and I can sense the cameraman hovering over my shoulder. I don't know what stops me from elbowing him in the gut and getting him out of my space.

I tell the girl, "Mira-Me, I'm gonna be pissed, and you don't wanna see that." I've never used such a severe tone, but she's only a kid, so for once the parent in me takes over.

She purses her lips, but I'm pretty sure she can see I'm not joking.

"We really don't have time." I try to sound persuasive. "You gotta help me get him out."

Her face lights up. "Oh, I know what we can do," she exclaims, voice high-pitched. She slips past him and out onto the street, where the crowd meets her stunt with a loud cheer.

To my relief, he follows her out, but fakes hitting the roof over the door before holding his forehead with a hurt mime.

She laughs and shows him her phone. "Photo!"

He whistles excitedly, jumping up and down like a kid. The stupid influencer is so damn smooth with him. She knows how to use the situation in her favor.

When they're done taking a selfie, he turns to me and grabs my sunglasses. There's an odd moment of hesitation where he stares into my eyes, his pupils a sparkling green amid the white makeup, a reaction so confusing I forget to protest. Then he seems to pull himself together and turns to give my sunglasses to someone in the crowd.

Several hands reach out, people shouting, "Robin! *Aquí*!" Here!

But instead of handing them, he takes another man's sunglasses and pretends exchanging them, then changes his mind with a big smile admitting he's naughty, and returns mine to me.

Everyone laughs. In other circumstances, I might consider the situation funny, too, but now the clown is just plain irritating. And he's making me the laughingstock, which only fuels my anger.

"Enough." I grab his arms from behind and turn him against the car door. I'm trained to use cop force, so it's no biggie plastering him to the metal and crossing his arms behind his back. Though I gotta say he's got some damn strong muscles working beneath the fabric of his clown costume. He obviously has physical training of some sort, like lifting weights. Intriguing. But I'm not in the mood to dwell.

He resists a little, but not as much as he probably could. Instead, he whistles a panicky, ear-piercing sound and bobs his head back and forth, mimicking fear. No doubt using the situation to his advantage to turn his fans against me.

"Leave us the fuck alone, you freak of nature," I sneer to his ear. "I've had enough of your stupid clown act."

Mira-Me shouts from my side, "Oh, my gawd, Zane, you're such a bully!"

I shoot her a sharp glance, ready to bark something at her, too, but she stands there with her hands on her hips and pouts like a spoiled three-year-old.

That's when the clown changes his game, suddenly rubbing his ass backward against my crotch and whistling that wolf tune again, like he's trying to seduce me. The crowd digs his improvisation and cheers loud. Mira-Me claps her hands, thrilled to bits.

Now I know he'll stop at nothing to make fun of me. Swallowing a grunt of annoyance, I pull him away from the car and spin him around on his feet. His long, pointy shoes cross each other so he loses his balance and does a clumsy dive into the crowd with a squeal-whistle of terror. Some people jump aside, hands flailing, others reach out to catch him.

Good riddance. With the whole street booing at me, I push the equally annoying bimbo back into her limo and get behind the wheel.

Chapter Two

Circa 11:00 PM

A long, stressful day is over, and I'm in Mira-Me's hotel suite watching a rugby game on a living room couch while she sips a third *margarita* and scrolls through her notifications in a connecting bedroom. Although she didn't make a personal performance today since it was more of a have-you-seen-me gathering of celebrities before the film première, she got her fill of camera flattery and, I quote, "super cool" response from fellow artists before she ended the evening celebrations by herself here at the hotel. By herself but not alone, as she keeps her zillion-something Instagram followers updated about important details such as dresses, hairstyles, shoes, purses, earrings, handsome young men, and the scandals everyone's going to talk about in the next few days.

She's in her happy place now, but she's not happy with me. After the annoying situation on the street earlier, she has seized every chance to criticize my "bullyish behavior" and call me "the worst person ever." She literally regrets employing me. I've got to hand it to her, for someone so fake and self-centered, she can offer great empathy and compassion to a stranger when she wants. Why? Because the clown charmed the crowd, because she thought he was funny? I have no idea. Young people nowadays only do or say certain things if they see a profit.

Her constant criticism bothers me. One, because she's been nagging me like an old hooker and I've had enough harassment for a day, and two, because deep inside I know she's right. She argues that the clown was only doing his job and it's not his fault we were late for the première or happened to be in the line of cars passing through that street. It's true. It wasn't anybody's fault and yet the situation happened. Do I regret it? Kind of. I don't like to think of myself as a bully. I don't want to be that man. Maybe I should take an anger management course. Or stop drinking.

Yeah, but first, the bad memories need to fade.

Every evening, a fierce and merciless thirst for alcohol takes place in my gut and won't let go unless I feed it. I don't even need to think about the stuff that happened in the past for the thirst to show its ugly face. It's an automatic urge, and tonight is no exception. I've already emptied the selection of Spanish beers in the minibar and I'm debating whether to go for a scotch or a gin next. Mira-Me doesn't mind me drinking as long as she's got what she needs and I can interfere if her own consumption gets out of hand. I'm never so drunk I can't take care of her. She's my boss *and* protégée.

Okay, tonight is an exception. I'm restless and uptight and I'm downing more liquor than usual. It's the damn clown, he continues to irritate me even after so many hours. I can't get him off my mind. On one hand, I want to apologize, don't want to be seen as an asshole who can't admit his faults and weaknesses. We live in the unforgiving age of the soft man, and if you can't talk about feelings with the opposite sex, you're in deep shit.

On the other hand, he intrigues me. Just the touch of his strong muscles beneath his clothes has me wondering who the hell he is and what he does when he's not being the clown. And the way he rubbed his ass against my crotch! Oh, man, that was hot. Way hot. You'd think he knew I was gay (well, bi to be precise) and took advantage of it … but of course, there's no way he could know.

During a pause in the game, I grab my phone and

lazily thumb through my Facebook feed. I'm far from being as social media savvy as my young boss and have no intention to be "connected" at all hours of the day, but I do have an account to keep somewhat in touch with family and friends back in the US.

A symbol announces I have a new message. From a certain Joe Keane. I don't recognize him from my friends list. What's odd is sometimes I get new friendship requests from people I know remotely, but this guy sent me a message without requesting to be friends. Hmm. The name rings a bell, but my brain is mushy and I can't locate him in time or place. An ex-colleague? Someone I went to school with? A distant cousin?

I thumb the message open. It starts with, **Hi, Zane, how are you?**

Mira-Me squeals from the other room, interrupting my read. The cry is more a sound of joy than fear, but it still causes a shiver to creep up my spine.

I put my phone on the coffee table, get up trying to ignore my tired body's complaints, and go stand in her doorframe. She's in bed propped up against a mass of pillows wearing pink and yellow PJs, likely inspired by the latest *Barbie* movie, and donning the happiest girlie smile.

Across her room hangs a vanity mirror on the wall, and it reflects the image of my torso. It's not a pretty sight. Ruffled blond hair, baggy eyes of undefinable color, and deep lines traced into my skin revealing my years. Not exactly going to make me feel better. The only thing I'm pleased about is my strong build. I run and work out every day to stay fit for the job. Cut out cigarettes years ago, too. The booze, on the other hand…

Something moves in my side vision. "I know who he is," she says.

I focus on the girl in the bed. "Who?"

Blue gaze sparkling, she waves her phone at me. "Robin the clown. He's not a clown, by the way, he's a harlequin. A *street art harlequin*, according to the description on his website."

"I can't believe you Googled him." The fact she thought about him at the same time as me and actually did something about it is baffling, but I conceal my excitement behind a yawn. "It's getting late, *chica.* We have a long day tomorrow. Do you even know the difference between a clown and a harlequin?"

Of course, she doesn't. Today's youth are illiterate and don't care for a minimum of general cultural knowledge. Ignorance and superficiality are the new norm.

To my surprise, she taps something on her phone and reads, squinting, "A clown is a mischievous buffoon that performs comedy, usually at a circus, and typically wears flamboyant clothes and exaggerated makeup with a big, red nose."

I conceal a smile. I'm not sure she knows the words "buffoon" or "flamboyant," but I'm impressed she bothered to look this subject up—and even spelled the words right.

"A harlequin," she continues reading, "is a more sophisticated and romantic pantomime that wears checkered clothes." She looks up. "What's 'checkered'?"

A small grin escapes me. For someone so invested in the fashion industry, her question comes across as odd. "You ever seen a chess game?"

"Maybe?"

"Imagine a diamond-shaped pattern of black and white."

"Oooh!" Her face lights up like she just discovered a new, cool gadget on her phone. "But that's what the clothes he wore looked like. Black-and-white diamonds."

"Duh," I say with a small laugh, mocking her generation's favorite word.

"Duh." She sticks her tongue out at me. "I'm not stupid, you know."

"No, just ignorant. I've never seen you open a book. What are you going to do when you're in your thirties and start putting on weight and your influencer career is over?"

A bag of *jalapeño*-flavored potato crisps sits by her side looking very alone. I lean down and snatch it before she can protest. It's funny—and nice—how she and I have managed to develop a sort of father-daughter dynamic during our year-long professional relationship, despite our age and cultural differences. Sometimes we can't stand each other and stick strictly to the job (her being bossy like a Nazi officer), and other times we silently agree to play the roles of close family members bantering and sharing everyday-life issues and pleasures.

"Huh, ignorant," she huffs. "Even you called him a clown."

I heave a shoulder. At the peak of my irritation earlier, I honestly didn't care what the heck he was, I just wanted the obstruction out of my way. A potato chip finds its way into my mouth, then another. Once I get started, there's no stopping me. My teeth crush the chips to mush, a fatty but delicious *jalapeño*-flavored juice spreading over my tongue.

She looks down again and uses her finger to scroll. "Gawd, he's hot!" she exclaims. "There's a pic of him without the makeup."

"Oh? Sh—" I was about to say, "Show me," but that would reveal a certain interest, and I can't let her know I have any thoughts whatsoever about this guy.

Instead, I say, "Shut up, you're too young for that stuff."

"Hey, you're not my father. Besides, I can have any guy I want." She purses her lips and reads on. "I think I can find out where he is, there's a phone number for his management."

I blink. She's pushing this too far. "Why on earth would you want to find out where he is?"

She rolls her eyes. "It would be your chance to apologize! Duh."

A chill traverses me. That girl is capable of doing the craziest things when she sets her mind to it, and she'll drag me through the most troublesome situations. Unfortunately, I signed a contract clause stating I can't refuse a direct order.

She jumps out of bed faster than I can blink again. Not the least shy, she turns to the wall and strips out of her pajamas.

I look away, set the bag of crisps on the bed—suddenly lost my appetite—and cross my arms. "Would you care to explain what the hell you're doing? At this hour?"

The sound of ruffling clothes behind me tells me the damn girl is getting dressed to go out, I'm sure of it, and I'm not liking it. She's set to doing something I don't want to be part of, cruising through town at night and looking for someone I don't want to meet.

Although Robin the harlequin—I'll call him that from now on—did intrigue me on some level, and if she does manage to find him, it might give me the chance to redeem myself. I'd hate to look back on this day for the rest of my life reminding me I'm an asshole.

Then again, I'm not sure I'm up to it. Nope, I'm exhausted and would rather have a good night's sleep between now and the moment I face that guy again to offer my apologies. It would suck if I showed up feeling and looking like a cadaver.

Quick as a whirlwind, she passes me by with a whiff of watermelon-bubblegum scent and heads to the main door. She's put white jeans and a Tina Turner-tribute tee on and styles them with a turquoise Aimee Song purse. "There's a program on his website, says he's doing an indoor show with another harlequin this evening. Let's go."

Fuck. I hold out an arm. "You're forgetting something, *Boss*."

"What?" She swivels and stands in my face with a raised eyebrow.

Up close, her eyes are a startling blue, and they stand out in the dark tan of her skin like two shiny opals. You'd think she was wearing lenses, but she's not. Her eyes are the only parts of her body that are real yet look fake, sadly. They remind me of the harlequin's green-colored eyes and how they stood out in his white facial paint, full of humor and mischief.

Ugh, why does he keep coming to my mind? I am *so* not ready to see him again. "I can't drive," I explain, glad to have an excuse. "I've had a couple beers."

Her inquisitive gaze wanders over my shoulder, at the couch behind me. "More, it seems."

I take a deep, calming breath. "And in Spain, you can't drink and dr—"

She waves a hand. "Oh, that's not a problem. The venue is a few blocks down the road."

"You mean you want to walk? You, who had to be driven in a limo earlier? Which is the reason why I got into all that trouble in the first place?"

She gives me a shrug that says, "*Whatever*."

I shake my head. "Seriously, I'd rather go tomorrow. I'm *super* tired." I stress that adverb in the hopes she'll hear the misery in my voice and relent.

A frown. "No, tomorrow they're going to another town. They're on tour."

Chapter Three

"What do you want from him?" A woman wearing the same costume as Robin the harlequin stands in the hotel reception with her arms crossed and glares at me. Her English is good but with a heavy Spanish accent.

After looking for Robin at his show and finding him gone, Mira-Me asked personnel at the venue for help. They directed us to a hotel not far from ours, but the receptionist refused to give us a room number. We thought we were lucky when a female version of him appeared in the reception to buy a soda from a vending machine, but she doesn't seem very friendly. Or rather, she seems to know exactly who I am and downright resents me.

She must be good at reading thoughts, too. "You're all over YouTube," she spits, her yellow-brown tiger eyes sending me darts of contempt. "You should read what people say in the comment sections. The hate level is through the roof."

I can feel defeatism sneaking into me. What the hell am I doing here? It's creepy enough standing in an obscure hotel late at night, all dark, ancient wood and cracked stone floor from another century, with the acrid smell of old lacquer making my nose twitch ... but to be the recipient of another person's hostility when I'm tipsy and overtired is a different story.

I turn to Mira-Me with a deep sigh, ready to give up and bolt.

She proves to be a smooth talker. She pulls a hundred-euro bill out of her purse and waves it in front of the female harlequin's face. "He's here to apologize. As for me, you saw me inviting Robin into the limo, right? And taking pics with him? It was so much fun." She flashes a white-toothed smile.

After a short stare down, the woman snatches the bill. "It's this way."

She leads us out of the reception and up three spiraling, creaking flights of stairs so narrow you have to climb one at a time. The third landing is a balcony, its wood floor squeaking and dancing under our feet as though suspended from the high, tower-shaped ceiling of monochromatic sheet glass above our heads. As depressed and suicidal as I can be sometimes, I hope this isn't the last day of my life.

At the end of the balcony, the female harlequin knocks on a thick, wooden door. The space is unlit, so when the door opens, a sudden flood of light blinds me. Mira-Me pushes me inside a cramped interior reeking of musty, old carpet and dust. I blink to adjust my vision.

A human figure disappears behind another door. "I was about to have a shower. Just got back from the show." An American accent! Our harlequin is even more intriguing. A quick pulse beats in my neck. Who is this guy? And what is a fellow American doing here in the Spanish *pampa*?

The woman and Mira-Me push me further in so they can fit inside and close the door behind them. The tiny room has just enough space for a small-sized double bed and a chestnut side table with a vintage lamp on top. But not an additional three people. Mira-Me and I stand awkwardly at the foot of the bed making ourselves small while the woman raps on the bathroom door. "They're here to apologize!"

A muffled, "What?" comes through the wood pane before it opens again. There's Robin the street harlequin in full circus galore, makeup and costume and all, but looking very human with thin eyes indicating tiredness and sweat beads down his temples leaving traces in the white paint. "Sorry, what did you say?"

"He—" The woman turns to point at me. "That guy over there, he wants to apologize for his rude behavior."

Oh, yeah, I'm the center of attention. Three pairs of eyes fix on me, waiting. I wish I hadn't had those beers earlier, so my head was clearer now that the moment has arrived for me to man up and apologize. I take a deep breath and splay my fingers. "Well, I'm sorry I bullied you. I went over the line."

Robin nods, but the two women stare at me as though my apology is too short or something.

I tell them with a frown, "I didn't mean to be a brute, okay? I was stressed, but it's not a reason to—"

Robin raises a hand and smiles. "It's all right. No harm done. Thanks for coming." He indicates the bed. "Why don't you make yourselves comfortable?"

You don't need to ask Mira-Me twice. She lies on the mattress like it's her own, leans against the bedstand, and pulls out her phone. "This is so cool. I gotta post it to my story."

Robin tilts his head. "As long as you don't take pictures of me."

"Or me." The female harlequin plops down beside her with a yawn, using the remaining bed space to spread her long limbs. "I'm *beat*. The last show was a killer."

Her facial makeup makes it impossible to guess her age, but judging from her flat boobs, slim waist, and hips that can't possibly have carried a child, she must be in her late twenties, early thirties. Oh, and judging from her behavior, so at ease on Robin's bed, she must be his girlfriend. The smallest hint of jealousy teases me, but I ignore it like most times that I see a hot guy and know he's taken.

Well, this leaves me to stand a bit alone in the tiny

hallway. I lean cross-armed against the wall and watch Robin as he turns back inside the bathroom with the door left open.

He takes off his pointy clown hat, revealing dark, sweaty curls plastered to his head. He sets the hat on the toilet seat and proceeds to remove the makeup. The mirror reflects the image of him using cotton pads to slowly uncover his real face, the person behind the mask. But just one side—before suddenly looking at me in the mirror and giving me a broad smile.

Okay, caught me staring. But it doesn't bother me. I'm amused. Even now when he is tired, he plays the clown and I find it charming. Half his face is tanned skin covering high cheekbones, with a Roman nose over full lips and a glowing emerald for an eye. A feline eye but void of danger. His gaze exudes warmth. And humor. And depth of soul. Mesmerizing.

He says to me in the mirror, "You didn't answer my message."

"Where?" I blink. It takes me a second to process the memory. "On Facebook? That was you?"

A nod. "You read it but didn't reply."

I slap my forehead. "I just saw the first words, then Mira-Me interrupted me." I nod my chin to the girl on the bed. She's still texting, but her eyes are heavy with sleep. "I'm sorry I didn't reply."

"It's okay. I thought you were angry with me and I wanted to apologize."

"You? Apologize?"

A smile. "Yeah, for pulling your leg. I went over the line, too. I should've stopped when I saw how upset you were becoming. I should've understood and let you go. But it was too tempting, with that fancy limo of yours and all."

I grimace. "It's hers. She's the boss." Kind of an

odd thing for a grown man to say about a young girl. If I wasn't so thick-skinned and careless about my life, our opposed roles could very well be an embarrassment.

"Figures, from how you two behaved." He picks up a cotton pad and removes the other side of his face paint, little by little uncovering handsome, manly features.

I can't say I'm not impressed. My heart thuds in my chest and I don't want to tear my eyes away from the mirror.

When he's done, he rubs his face in a towel and sends me a look. "Do you recognize me?"

I frown. There's something in the back of my mind saying I've seen him before, but it's the same as with his name—which I can't even remember now (you know me and my beer brain). I can't place him. I've seen a lot of people in my thirty-eight years, especially during the time I was a cop.

He gives a sad shake of his head. "You don't."

"Where from?"

Instead of replying, he pulls on his shirt and struggles as sweat glues the fabric to his torso. He stops pulling when half the shirt is over his head with his arms stuck. It's actually quite funny. He stumbles out of the bathroom unable to see anything and groans a curse. "You mind giving me a hand?"

This is out of my league. We're strangers. I send his girlfriend a questioning glance.

She pulls a face. "Um, no. That thing is drenched. *Eww.*"

"Come on," he insists, groaning. "I'm stuck."

Killing a smile, I step forward and pull at his wet shirt until he's able to peel it off over his head. When his arms finally slip out of the sleeves, he straightens and blows a puff of relief, displaying his naked chest. What a fit man, with neat muscles in all the right places and an amazing washboard for a stomach. He must be working out regularly, I refuse to believe otherwise, but he's not pumped up like weightlifters because his muscles look lean and natural. His tanned skin glows from sweat and fills the intimate space between us with wet heat and the ensnaring scent of musky maleness. Black hairs over the waistband of his stretch pants glue to his stomach.

To say he's sexy is an absolute understatement. I am hereby sexually assaulted, and my body reacts accordingly, my cock coming to life and my breath hitching. I hope he doesn't notice, but on some crazy level I don't really care—or maybe I even hope he *does* notice. Then what?

I send a new glance to the bed. Mira-Me has fallen asleep, head lolling to a side, mouth open. The female harlequin shows she has a good side, too, brushing hair away from Mira-Me's eyes with a motherly smile.

Thank fuck, having to take care of my protégée means I've got a reason to step away from Mr. Sex on Legs. Besides, I don't want to create a problem between him and his girlfriend. The last thing I need is for this couple to accuse me of harassment in addition to the previous bullying situation.

He follows my look and asks, "What are we going to do with her?"

"I'll wake her up and we'll go to our hotel. It's not far from here."

His girlfriend counters, "No, she's just a child. Leave her be. She can sleep in my bed."

Her bed? Do they have separate bedrooms?

Before I can think this through, she slips her hands underneath Mira-Me and lifts her into the air like she weighs nothing. She passes me with the girl in her arms, presses the door handle, and goes out onto the dark landing.

"Need any help?" Robin calls.

"Nope. Don't do anything I wouldn't do, guys," she throws over her shoulder with a wink and leaves.

I'm majorly impressed by what that slim, young woman just did. When the door closes, I burst out, "She's incredibly strong!"

Robin nods. "We exercise every day. She can carry my weight."

I widen my eyes. "She what?"

"We do acrobatics. Come to our show and you'll see. She lifts me and I lift her."

"That's insane."

He gives a loud sigh. "Well, I really need a shower." He returns to the bathroom, sits on the toilet seat, and proceeds to peel off his stretch pants, which stick to his skin. Looks like he uses all his strength, arm muscles bulging, to pull the pants down his thighs—and these thighs are equally muscular. Long and firm, not too hairy.

That's it, I've seen enough. The man's extreme sexiness confuses the hell out of me.

I retreat and have a breather on a miniature balcony. The roofs of the block buildings are connected to each other, forming a square, inner court, with moss covering the ancient, seamless terracotta tiles. It's dark, the city lights creating ghostly shadows. Sleeping pigeons aligned on a rooftop are silhouetted against a tableau of a thousand blinking stars in the night. A chilly, humid draught creeps up from below. The balcony's cast-iron fence looks solid enough, but I dare not lean over it to look down to the ground.

Now would be a good time to have a cig, but I've quit and need to keep my promise. The booze, however

… just from thinking about it, the thirst invades me, and I know my efforts to ignore it will be fruitless.

Every hotel has a minibar, no? The fucking craving grows, unquenchable, bad, and ugly like a beast. I hurry back inside. Through the now-closed bathroom door drifts the sound of running water splashing on tiles. I don't know if it's my cop nose or what, but I instantly locate a small door in the closet section that indeed holds a fridge with a nice selection of mini-bottles. I pick a gin, down it, and wait for the effect to hit me. It always takes some time, so the clue is to wait patiently.

Eh, but that's another thing about me, I have no patience. I uncork a mini-whiskey and swallow it in one go. Still no effect. The producers ought to work on that problem, increase the alcohol percentage or something.

"You should wait a bit," Robin's voice says from behind me.

Startled, I swivel on my feet. Was so busy drowning my thirst, I didn't hear him open the door.

He stands in the doorframe, his body the stunning beauty of a Greek god, with only a towel tied around his waist. "I know," he says with a sad voice. "I've been there."

Chapter Four

The effect of the alcohol hits me seconds later, dulling my senses and slowing my movements. I close the minibar and sit against the closet door, sucking in a deep breath and savoring the delicious heat that rushes through me. It's as smooth and soft as the carpet under my ass.

Robin kneels by the bed and opens a suitcase of clothes. Problem is, he's pointing his very sexy butt in the air, albeit covered by a towel, and I can't help getting hard from the enticing sight. I'd give a lot to slide my hard cock into his firm, puckered hole and do him until...

Okay, enough. I extend my legs to ease the growing pressure in my groin and slur, "You really need to do something about that shexiness."

"I *what*?" He turns to me with laughter on his face.

"Never mind. It's the booze speaking." I point a thumb backward, to the minibar. "Don't tell your girlfriend."

He has a moment of hesitation, before shaking his head. "Oh, you mean Lola? She's not my girlfriend."

I blink. "No?"

"We're colleagues."

Oh, well, that changes everything. Maybe at some point I can make a move, then. It's been a long time since my last fuck. I fill with more heat, my brain swimming. Then again, nothing tells me he's gay. What if I make advances and he rejects me?

He gives me a long stare. "You sure you don't recognize me?"

"Well, to be honesht, there's something familiar about you, but I can't pinpoint what. Shorry." I pull my wallet out of my back pocket, pick a twenty-euro bill, and set it beside me on the carpet. "This is for the drinks."

His emerald gaze lowers to the money but his features show no reaction. He sits on the bedside, facing me. "Remember art school? We were eighteen."

Of course, I remember art school, but it happened in another life. I slap my forehead. "Eighteen! Dude, that was twenty years ago!"

"I took dancing classes, and you music. You were gonna be the next rock star."

"Yeah." I chortle. Becoming a rock star was one of the many dreams that never happened. But I knew a dancer at the time? At the same school? I squint and concentrate on digging in my long-buried school memories.

"We weren't hanging out much," he says, "so I'm not very surprised you don't remember. I probably didn't make a big impression. But I remember you well."

He lets that last line hang, and although curiosity nearly has me pull my hair out, I don't want to push him. Something tells me he'll explain in due time.

What I do remember from school is being so bewitched by my gorgeous girlfriend that nothing else mattered. The other pupils, the teachers, the classes, everything is a distant blur.

His stomach grumbles. He mock-punches it and exclaims with a sheepish clown expression, "Oops, even a harlequin needs to eat. Let's order something." He reaches for his phone on the side table and scrolls with a finger. "You like *tapas*?"

"Thanks, but I'm not hungry." A blatant lie. Alcohol always awakes an insatiable hunger for snacks, but I don't want to make him order anything for me. I honestly don't know what to think of us at this moment. I'm attracted to him like hell, but I'm also afraid of provoking a rejection that will be a hard lesson to pay and only cause me to drink more.

"Okay." He sighs and puts his phone down. "They should be here in fifteen minutes."

"Right."

An uncomfortable silence settles. Maybe I should be going. But Mira-Me is asleep in a room nearby, and I can't leave her like this. Should I wake her? What if she's too tired to walk, will I have to carry her all the way back to our hotel? I'm not sure I'm up to that.

Robin folds his hands in his lap and breaks the quiet between us. "So, I wanted to be a dancer, but a toe injury stopped me from pursuing that dream. I dropped out of school and wandered around without a goal or purpose. Lived on the street, traveled from town to town. That's when I was drinking." He pauses to send me a nod, referring to what he'd said earlier. "One day, I came across a circus and made friends with one of their clowns. He inspired me to learn juggling, balancing, and tightrope walking, and he taught me goofy clowning skits, which was a lot of fun. But instead of staying in the enclosed circus world, I wanted to go broader and do my tricks as a street performer. It allowed me to be more in touch with people, and I could use a lot more improvisation. Which is very liberating, but also a constant challenge. I love that duality. It keeps me sharp."

"But you're also doing acrobatics?"

"Yes, Lola and I are doing indoor shows. Usually booked by town officials or private promoters. Otherwise, we wouldn't be able to make a living."

"Impreshive. I didn't know this way of life still exishted." I stifle a yawn. The booze is making me sleepy. "Well, the musichian dropped out, too, went to polishe academy, was a cop for a few years until they kicked him for shubstance abuse, then converted to bar goon and bodyguard slash chauffeur. Long shtory short."

"What about women? Are you still with that Kathryn beauty you were dating?" He throws me a pillow. "Here, be a bit more comfortable."

"Thanks." I prop the pillow behind my head and shoulders. But shouldn't have done that. The heavenly comfort of the fluff makes me even sleepier, my eyes closing. "No, Kathryn no more. No more." And it doesn't even hurt to say her name.

****

I wake up from a warm hand on my arm.

"Zane, you're having a nightmare," Robin's voice says.

I blink, at a loss. "Where am I?"

"On my bed. You fell asleep and you had a bad dream."

"Damn." I am indeed on his bed. I sit up and gaze at him with what must be a wild look. "How... how did I get here? Did I walk in my sleep?"

He smiles and turns to the side table, on which is a plate of cheese cubes, *chorizo* slices, and olives. "No, dummy. I carried you. Are you hungry?"

"Oh, damn. You really are strong."

"Are you hungry?" he repeats, using a toothpick to pick up an olive.

"No, thanks."

"You don't remember anything?"

"From what? My dream, or our days in art school?" I've sobered up during my sleep, my thinking clear again.

He gives me a long look full of brotherly warmth.

I nod, images slowly coming back to me. "I dreamed about my kiddo. I saw him in the hospital, tied to machines with doxorubicin slowly dripping into his artery." I pause to explain. "It's called that because of its ruby-red color. It's extremely toxic, it can damage the heart." A new pause, as the images reappear before my eyes. "I dreamed that the machine started pumping faster and faster so my kid became all inflated and red-faced. I wondered when it would stop, whether he would burst like an overfilled water balloon or something. Then you woke me up."

Silence.

I check Robin's reaction. He's livid, his green gaze wide and blurry. "Oh my God. Are you saying your son is undergoing chemotherapy?"

"He was. He passed." I suck in a loud breath. Talking about him and reviving the trauma used to hurt like a mother, but the regular consumption of alcohol has helped to control my pain.

Correction. Sometimes, alcohol gives access to the pain, like an evil bastard sending a line down to the darkest enthralls of my soul to locate the most atrocious feelings for me there—raw despair, fear, anger, profound sadness—and then enhancing them to such an extent I scream and cry until I pass out from exhaustion. But most times, the numbing effect of the alcohol helps me stay afloat above the abyss. I know it's there, the pain lurking right under the surface, but I'm swimming around happily unconscious.

I guess I must have put on some kind of face, for Robin's eyes fill with tears. "My condolences," he croaks. "It must've been awful."

"It's okay. I'm all right. I've learned to live with it." I hate to have hurt him, I need to work on concealing my feelings better. One thing is how I am inside, another entirely is how it affects my surroundings.

A tear rolls down his cheek, tracing a lone wet

line on his skin. "Was he Kathryn's son?"

"Yep. That's when our relationship went downhill. She couldn't deal with it all. We ended up divorcing."

He wipes his cheek. "I'm sorry."

"Don't be. We're both in a better place now." Wishing to change the subject, I ask, "What about you, and your love life?"

"Oh. Well." He sniffs and studies his hands. "It's not much to brag about. There was a time when I had the hots for a guy in school, but he was—"

"A guy?" It takes me a second to process the information. Wow, to think he's into men is downright baffling. My curiosity is piqued to the highest possible level. Gone is the pain, the bad dream.

A nod. "Yeah, but he was busy being a popular rock dude playing the electric guitar and dating the most beautiful cheerleader, so my feelings toward him never led to anything. It was a difficult time for me."

"I'm sorry to hear that."

"I was envious of his girlfriend." He sends me a direct look and seems to wait for a reaction.

"I can understand that," I blurt out, at a loss for anything else to say.

"Her name was Kathryn."

"Kathryn?" I blink several times. "What the hell are you telling me?"

"Don't you get it?" He rolls his eyes, like he can't believe the level of my stupidity. "I had the hots for you, dummy."

"Well, I'll be damned." I'm so surprised, I'm tempted to bark a laugh. But he's serious, and I don't want him to think I'm making fun of him.

"Uh-huh," he says. "But you don't recognize me. You don't remember." His eyes shine like two pure jewels in the semidarkness of the room.

I let some time pass returning his intense look. I'm in a hotel room in the middle of the night with a hunk so hot I struggle to keep my lust at bay, and now he's telling me he crushed on me twenty years ago. Judging from his long silence, there's more, and it's difficult for him to talk about. I wait, having completely sobered up.

He speaks up after a moment of twining his fingers. "What if I say we went to a party once, at a friend's house. In April 2003 or something. His parents were out."

I rack my brain. A party? There were several at the time, but at a friend's house? "What was his name?"

"Alex, I think. We were all a bit wasted. At least, I was high enough to get up the courage to talk to you when I stood in line for the bathroom and suddenly you came along."

Alex, my garage band drummer... Images come back to me. Of beer, loud music—it must've been Pantera or System of a Down—everybody thrashing and head-banging and growling their hearts out. The place was a mess. I can't believe his parents dared to leave the house to a bunch of dickheads.

Speaking of which. Another memory hits me. "I was so pissed, I tried to drink from an uncorked bottle." I chuckle.

"So, you remember?"

"Yeah, sorta. But it was a rock metal party. Why would you be there if you were a nice boy attending dance class?"

He ignores the tease. "'Cause some pals wanted to go. And I knew you'd be there. So when you came to the bathroom and there was just you and me left in line, I asked you if you wanted to hang with me."

"Hang, like...?"

"Hang, like go out with me. Like, date."

I swallow. He'd asked me out. It must've taken a lot of courage. "And?"

"You really don't remember that part?"

"Dude, there were so many people, and I was drunk out of my wits. How could I—"

"You laughed and then you said..." He pinches his lips.

"What? What did I say?"

His hesitation tells me it had to be bad.

Aw, shit. Now I see it. Me laughing at the face of some guy in a hallway. Was it him? I'd thought he was a little weird. Effeminate. I'd needed to pee bad, and he'd stood before me in the line. I'd just wanted him out of my way—like today, when he stopped my car—so when he'd suggested something totally insane, I'd used scorn to get rid of him. I'd spat, *"I'm not a fucking fag,"* then shoved him out of my way snickering and gone to the bathroom. Never saw him again, and I know why now.

How could I forget about this incident? And Jesus, how could I bully him in such a nasty manner? Poor guy... An ache spreads in my chest. Of guilt, of remorse. My view troubles. I look down at my hands. Man, this breaks me. I never meant to hurt anyone.

The mattress moves. He sits beside me and puts light fingers on my arm. "You okay?"

"I remember," I grunt.

"Oh." Just that, no comment.

"But I don't understand how I was able to behave like that. It's not in my blood. I resent the notion of bullying."

"You were drunk, pal."

Don't make excuses for me.

I guess I was high on myself, maybe I wanted to be cool and impress my friends. But such despicable behavior is unforgivable nonetheless. I peek at him, eyes stinging. "I'm really, really sorry. I don't know what else to say to make it right."

He smiles. "It's okay."

"Yeah?"

A nod. "The heart forgives, you know."

Well... His grand gesture helps ease my guilt. And to think I'm the one who's attracted to him after all these years! I wasn't homosexual back then, but I'm definitely bisexual now.

Should I tell him? Can I let the cat out of the bag? I draw a deep breath. "Okay, I've got a small confession to make. I've changed since those days. I'm actually bi—"

A rap sounds on the door, eerily spooky and startling both of us.

He gets up and reaches for the handle.

The door opens with a plaintive creak, a platinum-colored head poking in. Mira-Me, with mascara leaks under her sleepy eyes. "Zane, we should be going. We got stuff to do tomorrow." Her gaze widens as it trails to Robin's broad, naked chest, then down to his stone-chiseled six-pack before ending at the towel around his waist, tied tightly enough to reveal the outline of his cock. The young girl's mouth forms a silent, *Whoa,* of admiration.

I grin. I was right about him. He's the hottest stuff to walk the surface of planet Earth, and I'm going to make him mine.

Chapter Five

After a short night, a lazy breakfast at nine, an influencer interview at ten, a live broadcasted earplug review at eleven, and a manicure session at noon followed by a boring fashion show, Mira-Me and I have decided to drive south to the historic city of Segovia and watch Robin perform—this time as an audience.

We seek shade from the baking sun at the foot of the two-thousand-year-old Roman aqueduct guarding the old town. There're people everywhere, tourists and locals alike elbowing for the best spot. Town officials have prepared for the popular harlequin's street performance, placing fences and policemen in yellow vests along the length of the Via Roma, an avenue sloping down from the aqueduct. You'd think Robin was a national pop star, or a football hero returning home with a trophy.

Mira-Me and I wear light summer clothes and sunglasses like everybody else. How will Robin recognize us? My heart beats out of tune, I'm so excited to see him again. And *noivous,* as Jack White sang. After we separated last night, I haven't been able to think of anything other than our next meet and how I'm going to tell him about my attraction. Then what? That's the big question. He thinks I'm hetero because I married a woman, he doesn't know I'm also into men. And who says he'll accept my advances even after I tell him? A teenage crush that ended in disappointment and sorrow doesn't survive twenty years.

We've waited for about an hour in the afternoon heat, with an endless line of cars, motorcycles, trucks, and buses passing us, when a taxi halts in the middle of the road, effectively blocking traffic. Out climbs Robin the harlequin! My excitement shoots to the roof. He waves to the crowd, people around me cheering loud and throwing hands in the air.

We're instantly carried away by his goofy antics. Using the same facial expressions and gestures as a circus clown, he stops cars, teases passengers, snatches smartphones to take selfies or exchange them with other people's phones, opens trunks to make fun of personal items, orders vehicles to drive with the severe waving and whistling of a policeman, or gets on all fours and starts yapping when he sees a dog.

My admiration for his talent grows by the second. Now that I'm not stressed nor the subject of his pranks, I find him very funny, a mischievous buffoon with an ingenious sense of improvisation as he observes situations and uses them to create new ones. He feeds on the audience's response and loves making them laugh, and they adore him for being hilarious and naughty. It's a marvelous dynamic between an artist and his fans. I understand why hc's doing this for a living.

Every time he passes our spot in the crowd, I try to make eye contact with him and Mira-Me shouts, "Robin!" to the top of her lungs. But there are so many people along the fence shouting his name and gesticulating, he doesn't notice us. Besides, he is continuously up and down the avenue, jumping into a minibus, climbing up on the roof of a van, throwing his handkerchief up on a car hood then running after it in panic because the car speeds away.

The next time he appears before us, Mira-Me's high-pitched shouting finally attracts his attention. Recognition lights up his face, and he hurries over to us with an exaggerated clownish smile. That's when he sees Mira-Me recording him with her phone and stops in his tracks to lower his pants a little, pointing his butt to her as if posing for a porn shoot. People scream of laughter.

He's such a goofy seducer, I can't help cracking up, too.

His focus moves to me, green gaze sparkling in the white face paint. He releases a flirtatious wolf whistle that says he likes what he sees and moves his hips in a slow, sensual dance. I bark a surprised laugh. To the crowd's delight, he then morphs to a timid clown, giving me a shy smile the way Charlie Chaplin would with his head tilted to the side, eyes twinkling, hands between his crossed thighs.

I laugh again, digging his antics and giving him a smile full of heat and desire. I don't care that the whole world can read the happiness on my face. I'm attracted to him on so many levels and I want him to know. Although it's sad I don't remember him from school, it doesn't matter anymore because we don't need a twenty-year-old crush to have a connection today. I can't wait for his show to be over so I can take him someplace for dinner and flirt unabashedly until we go to a room and…

Suddenly, he climbs up on the fence, leans over to me, grabs the sides of my face in his gloved hands, and kisses me. Ha, the devil must have read my mind. I'm stunned, paralyzed, but accept the intimacy of his black-painted lips on my mouth. The crowd breaks into a collective scream, making my ears ring. They probably expected me to be bothered by his kiss and squirm away, but my counterreaction is even cooler and drives them ecstatic. Mira-Me is going wild at my side, screaming in my ears, and jumping up and down. And *he* knows I've got the hots for him. He knows.

Someone pulls at him from behind. He turns away from me with a grimace of fear and climbs down the fence. It's Lola, the female harlequin. Wearing the same black-and-white checkered clothes but playing a silent pantomime, she pretends to be his wife, mock-slapping him with an angry expression and rebuking him for being "infidel." More laughs arise.

Several motorcycles appear in a long line. Robin whistles sharply and pulls out his handkerchief. He uses it as a race car flag to indicate where the bikes must stop at an invisible line and be ready to compete down the avenue. Ever the goof, he sits behind one of them. Lola does the same thing, arms flailing in the air to show she's terrified. The crowd cheers in anticipation.

Robin waves the flag up and down and whistles, "*Uno, dos, tres!*" The bikes growl and jump forward at the same time, quickly picking up speed. He puts his hands in front of his driver's eyes as a prank, but only for a couple seconds. No worries.

Lola mimics him, except her driver must not be used to being distracted, for he hits the brakes and his bike skids to a side with a strange roar. He's going to lose his balance! The driver jumps off in time, but not Lola. The bike tips over and slides for a few meters, crushing her underneath.

Oh, no! Pulse drumming, I jump over the fence, run to her, and with the help of other men lift the bike off her. She lies on the asphalt in a contorted position, eyes closed. No blood. I put a finger to her throat and find a beat. My cop training says she shouldn't be moved in case of back injuries, but I can't leave her like this. With the traffic congestion, it's going to take an ambulance a small eternity to get here.

I lift the unconscious woman in my arms and ask the shocked faces around me, "Where's the nearest hospital?" I don't even know how to say this in Spanish. Never bothered to learn basic phrases.

A policeman points to the aqueduct. "*Te mostraré el camino!*"

I don't know what the fuck that means. I repeat, "Hospital!"

"*Sí, sí, el centro médico!*" He waves for me to follow him.

I throw a look over my shoulder. Where's Robin? Fuck, still on the backseat of a motorcycle down the avenue. Guess he hasn't heard anything because of the motor noise. I can't wait. Mira-Me will have to tell him.

The policeman frays a passage in the dense crowd and leads me through one of the aqueduct arches then onto a shopping street. The wounded woman is heavy, but I carry her as fast as I can, aware that her very life is literally in my hands.

After a few more hundred meters, I start heaving for air. Pathetic. I should have better health if I want to save someone's life. Better fucking endurance, better fucking strength. It's the alcohol's fault I feel so miserable, so out of breath. I swear this is it, I'll cut out the booze entirely or there's no point in playing the hero. Might as well let someone else take care of her. Like her harlequin colleague—at least, he stopped the drinking and pulled his act together. What am I? A clown in the metaphoric sense. A joke.

The policeman points to a modern brick building. "*El centro médico.*"

"*Gracias,*" I utter, huffing like a seal on land, sweat coating my clothes and running down my temples.

He ushers me through sliding doors into a chilly reception and calls out in Spanish. Several people in white hurry toward us and take my precious human package away. He shakes my hand and leaves me standing in the empty room in a sweat, out of breath, very lonely and helpless in a foreign world.

After a short moment, the doors slide open again and Robin stumbles into the reception, shocked out of his mind. "Where is she?"

I reach out for him, my heart hurting because he is

hurting. "Doctors are looking at her now."

"Oh God, it's insane." Breaking into tears, he throws his hat to the floor, pulls at his hair, and rubs his face, smearing the makeup all over. "It's not fucking worth it."

"Stop." I put an arm around his shoulders and bring him to a restroom. After closing the door, I wet paper towels and clean his face with a little soap.

Sobbing, he checks his haggard reflection in the mirror over the sink. "I can't believe I let this happen. We gotta stop doing this street thing, it's too dangerous."

"You didn't *let* it happen."

"Pfft. I almost fell off the roof of a truck 'cause it accelerated too fast. And a bus nearly ran me over 'cause he was pissed that I stopped the traffic. Every day, our lives are on the line."

I put a hand on his arm. "Dude, accidents happen all the time, and it's not our fault. Even my kid dying from cancer wasn't anybody's fault. It happened, and we had to accept that it did. Or else it wasn't possible to continue living."

"You think she's going to be okay?" He turns to me and stares into my eyes as if pleading me to tell the truth, but of course he knows I don't know. Voice gruff, he adds, "She's like a sister to me."

I give his shoulders a gentle shake. "She's strong. You need to have faith."

Tears flood his deep-green eyes again, and he wipes them with a hand.

It's moving to see someone caring so much for another person. At the same time, his despair breaks a barrier inside me, one that has held me back from making advances. I lean forward, circle my arms around him, and peck his lips. Maybe I can provide some comfort, or a distraction from his pain.

He has a slight moment of hesitation before kissing me back, slowly opening his mouth to me. I let my tongue enter him like a dagger, searching, roaming, licking every hot, wet part of him.

Changing roles, he takes command and pushes me backward, and for the first time I can really feel his full strength as he plasters me against the wall with the length of his body and grinds his hardness—chest muscles and washboard stomach and cock and all—against me. It's incredibly sexy, an all-consuming feeling, and I let him invade me, take over. I swim in the pleasure of sexual excitement and wish for only one thing: to be swept away by this insane arousal and fly high until I reach a level so intense, I have to ejaculate everything I've got stocked up in my balls.

A hard knock on the door freezes us. We gasp, eyes wide, releasing each other and creating distance between our heated bodies as though caught in the act ... but of course, no one could see anything from outside.

A new knock. "Hello?" a man calls through the door in a heavily accented English. "Are you the one who brought in the woman-clown?"

I stutter, "Y-yeah, give me a sec."

"I don't have time to wait," he says. "I have fifteen other patients to..."

"Okay, okay, I'm coming." I throw a glance to the mirror, flatten my tousled hair, and wipe the sweat off my flushed face before opening the door wide enough to slip out, all the while keeping Robin hidden behind it.

A bearded man in a white uniform stands in the hall with a folder in hand. He gives me a glacial stare.

Uh-oh, I hope he doesn't mean bad news. I suck in a breath to calm my nerves. "Doctor, how is she?"

He takes a moment to regard me from the length of his nose before replying, voice icy, "She's awake.

She's lucky, there're no broken bones, no concussion. She can thank her excellent physical fitness for that. She'll only feel a little bruised."

The door behind me opens. Out comes Robin, face livid. "Will she ever be able to—"

"What?" the doctor barks. He glowers from him to me a couple times, telling us he knows what went on behind that door.

Voice sheepish, Robin explains, "She's an acrobat and a contortionist."

"Well, she needs rest for at least a full forty-eight hours. And you can pay at the counter in the reception." With that, he spins on his heels and leaves, white uniform flapping.

Chapter Six

The next happened as I had hoped. Once Lola had been released from the medical center, a bit shaken but in good health, we all went out for dinner in the Old Town of Segovia. In truth, I had hoped for Robin and me to be alone at a romantic table, but we couldn't exactly exclude our two women friends from the party.

It's evening, the setting sun filling the narrow streets with languorous heat. This is tourist season, and all the restaurant tables are taken. Luckily, Mira-Me made a call to a manager earlier, offering top promotion on her Insta and Snap profiles and thus obtaining a nice table for four on a terrace overlooking the majestic Gothic cathedral. I've got to hand it to her, the girl has proven to be useful more than once.

My decision to stay off the booze meets some serious challenge when Robin, who sits across the table from me, orders a bottle of *rosé*. "We're going to celebrate that Lola is fine," he states, looking appeased and confident. It took him a while to get back to his normal self after the accident. "You have no idea how relieved I am."

A waiter brings a pink bottle and fills our glasses. I put a hand over mine. "Um, thanks, but I'm not having any."

"Why not?" my friends ask in unison, brows raised.

"I've decided to do something about my drinking problem." There, it's out, and those who didn't know I had a problem now know.

Mira-Me doesn't care. She stares openly at the waiter, a Spaniard with the looks and charisma of a young Antonio Banderas. I can understand her attraction, but I already have one right ahead of me, and it takes all my strength not to lean over the table, grab his shirt collar, and kiss him the way we kissed in the restroom. That steaming hot scene will stay very live in my mind and keep me lusting for a long time. Unless we do something even crazier.

The object of my desire studies me, hands folded on the table, his emeralds holding a strange radiance. "You know, it's possible to 'quit drinking' and still enjoy a glass once in a while."

I shrug. "I don't know. I'm afraid I can't stop at one."

"Why would you want to stop at one?" Mira-Me asks at my side, adding a small laugh.

"Because it has become a problem. I'm in such bad shape, I had trouble carrying Lola earlier. I wasn't *breathing*, I was making sounds you'd only hear in your worst nightmares." I grin to show I'm half-joking. "It's pathetic, and it's due to my daily alcohol consumption."

Lola, who without the facial paint reveals Latin features of great beauty, sends me a warm smile. "Don't underestimate yourself. You saved my life."

"Nope. Your extreme physical fitness is what saved you. You're all muscles, lady."

"Whatevs." She waves a dismissive hand. "You're my hero. You beat all of them trapezists and tightrope walkers and musclemen breaking chains etcetera at the circus. You even beat Robin, who's *almost* as strong as me." She elbows him in the ribs.

He chuckles, enjoying the gentle banter. It's nice to see them behave like loving siblings—I recall what he said at the medical center, how she's a sister to him.

A hollow settles in my stomach. I'm an only child and don't know what it's like to have a sibling. I don't even know what it's like to have parents anymore. Mine are cold and distant, back-talking me and fretting over petty issues.

Robin slides his wineglass across the table and sets it in front of me. "Have some and tell yourself that's all for now. Take control of your urge. I know, I've been through this."

"You have?" Mira-Me asks, voice high-pitched and gaze big as her loop earrings.

I nod my head to her and tell him, "Careful what you say, this bimbo will broadcast anything that can increase her numbers of *likes* and *comments*."

He laughs again and winks at her. "Oh, but she knows I have enough followers to crush her numbers."

"That's actually true," I agree, teasing her. "If you add up your followers on YouTube, Facebook, Instagram, Vimeo, your blog, and—"

She sticks her tongue out at both of us, then finishes her glass and raises it to the waiter, who serves other guests nearby. "*Uno más, por favor.*" One more, please.

He replies with a charming wink. "*Sí, un momento.*" Yes, just a moment.

Lola leans over the table and pushes Robin's wineglass closer to me. "Come on, have a taste. For me. And for you, because you were there for me." She sits back in her chair with fingers crossed over her stomach and her yellow-brown gaze full of humor and expectation. "Cheers, buddy."

That draws a smile from me. I appreciate her friendship. Yesterday, she practically jumped on me with her claws out because I'd been rude to her friend-brother.

The waiter returns with the bottle of *rosé*. All smiles, Mira-Me lifts her glass for him.

He thins his gorgeous black eyes and asks her, "Have I seen you somewhere?"

The girl beams as if the sun itself has taken residence in her. "Of course you have, Sweetheart. I'm an *influencer*." She puts emphasis on the last word, giving it more importance. "I'm all over the world."

He refills her glass with a mysterious smile.

"*Gracias*," she coos, fluttering her eyelashes. Thank you.

When he's gone, she gapes her mouth wide-open, staring at us around the table. "Oh my Gawd," she exclaims, ecstatic. "Did you see how hot he is?"

Lola laughs.

"He's even hotter than Robin," Mira-Me continues. "And *he* is hot."

Robin shakes his head, as if to say she's being silly.

"Right, Zane?" she asks, turning to me and flashing her teeth.

"With those mimics," Robin throws at her, "you could pass for a clown."

"Seriously, Zane is single. In case you're wondering."

"Oh, shut up," I groan and rub my face.

"Hey, everyone saw what was going on over the fence earlier."

"It was just a prank." I'm not ready to talk about the kiss with such a superficial person.

"Right," she scoffs. "Cheers, Zane."

"Cheers." I consider the glass of *rosé* in front of me. It's tempting. Light from the setting sun traverses it, giving the wine a rich, red-pink glow. The scent of sweet grapes and the woodsy sting of alcohol sneak into my nostrils, and my body knows a few swallows of this beverage can make me feel more joyous. Can I have this one glass and stop at that? Do I absolutely *need* more, or has the drinking just become an annoying habit I can control if I set my mind to it?

I started drinking because seeing my kid endure cancer treatment and all its ugly facets tore at my heartstrings worse than anything I'd experienced before. The pain of witnessing his hurts and fears, and the inability to help him—save him—destroyed me bit by bit, day after day. Long after his death, I continued escaping the horrors. Downing liquor until I was senseless wasn't an addiction but a means of survival. I was a broken soul who had been too close to Hell's furnace too long, and the edges of my wings had begun to burn.

I take a deep breath. I can't tell any of this to my friends, because it would chill their good mood and I don't want to ruin the evening.

Something strokes my leg underneath the table. I freeze but refrain from looking down. Was it a cat? Robin's voice brings me back to him. Warm and soothing. "We've got you, partner. It will only be this one glass."

"Yeah," Mira-Me quips, "and if you don't want it, I'll have it. Ha-ha. *No problemo.*"

I guess I can do it. I can decide not to give in to the thirst. It's like saying no to cigarettes, it's a matter of controlling the brain. Then with time, the body will adjust and accept, too. The urges will become a distant memory.

But do I want to say no? Or am I afraid of losing the assurance of knowing I can always seek refuge in a bottle, should my blues get too bad?

A new stroke of my leg, gentle but lasting longer, has me think it's not a cat but Robin, because over the table he is eyeing me with an inscrutable look telling me something intense. What? It's not only about the drink, is it? I need to ask him—my heart is screaming for understanding—but not here in the company of the two women.

"Okay, I trust you guys." I clear my throat, grab the glass of *rosé,* and raise it in a toast. "To Lola, and to us. May this day be a new beginning in our lives." And I don't only mean the control of my addiction.

"Cheers," the two women say, toasting.

I put my lips to the glass and taste the *rosé* on my tongue. It's sweet, it tastes fruity, and the sharp fumes tease my nose, mouth, everything that is used to consuming without restraint. I'm walking danger, I can drink anything so long as it contains a certain percentage of alcohol and a promise of carefree bliss.

Oh, but I'm not doing this to get high tonight, I want to enjoy a nice evening out with my friends. I taste some more rosy wine in my mouth before returning the glass to its owner. "Thanks, it's delicious, but I'm good."

Robin gives me an approving smile, but Mira-Me gets up with a huff, her chair screeching on the floor. "Oh, you party pooper. I'm gonna go see if that waiter is as fun as he looks." With that, she leaves, long platinum hair waving behind her.

Lola yawns and stretches her arms. "You know what, guys? I'm gonna call it a day, too. It was nice to go out and all, but I'm beat, *literally.* And the wine makes my head spin."

Robin's brows furrow. "You didn't eat."

"I'm not hungry. I'm feeling a bit nauseous after what happened earlier. But I'll be better tomorrow." She gets up, leans down to peck him on the cheek, and waves a few fingers at me across the table with a smile. "Good night."

"Good night, hope you sleep well."

"You, too." She slips away between the tables, leaving Robin and me alone. This time, she didn't add, *"Don't do anything I wouldn't do…"*

We sit in odd silence for long minutes, looking

around at anything and anyone but each other. Latino music fills the quiet between us. Laughter arises from a neighboring table. The dark of night settles in the narrow streets, along with a creeping chill.

I don't know how to make the first move. I don't even know what I want—a lover? How is that going to work if I'm employed by a rabid influencer bent on conquering the world of social media, while the man who now owns my heart is touring city after city doing street performances for a living? I grind my teeth, this situation is so difficult. What are the options? Not to engage in a relationship with him? Ugh, that would undermine my resolution to stay off the booze, I know it. To resume my life with a self-absorbed Mira-Me and not have anyone else to keep me up, will send me down the drain. I shoot him a tortured glance.

He meets my look and reaches across the table. "We're going to be okay." His dark-green gaze shines in the low light of the terrace.

I accept his warm hands and twine my fingers with his. "I'd like to believe it, but how?" My voice sounds plaintive, and I hate it.

"How long are you going to stay in Spain?"

"I don't know. For now, I have a one-year contract with Miss Celebrity, which ends in a month or so."

"Are you going back to the US after?"

I shrug. "Don't think so. Got nothing there holding me back."

"No family?"

"I have no siblings and pretty much no relationship with my parents."

"Why?"

"Oh, it's complicated." I let out a deep sigh. "We were an ordinary family until I went out with Kathryn, and my parents didn't like her for some reason. Maybe 'cause she was outgoing and liked to have fun, while they'd hoped for a more serious daughter-in-law. I had to protect my marriage, so our relationship with them turned sour. My kiddo practically didn't know them."

Robin frowns. "That's sad."

"Then when he got sick, suddenly my mother sorta woke up and became my liaison to the rest of the world 'cause I was too exhausted to do it myself. Except she spammed me with texts every day, pushing for information about his scan results and such when my angst level was already sky-high, so I ended up telling her to give me space. Which of course she didn't like, so she started back-talking me and my wife. Then when the kid died, she stopped talking to me altogether. It's like there was nothing left between us."

"I'm so sorry." Gaze blurry, he rises from his chair, leans over the table, and pecks my lips.

I close my eyes and savor the intimate gesture. He knows exactly what to do when I need it most. I return the sweet kiss and ask him, "What about you?"

He sits back on his chair and runs a hand over his face. "Me? I was adopted at birth. Went in and out of institutions 'cause I was a 'difficult child'. Was saved by the circus people, who became the family I'd never had. There's the story of my life in three sentences." He pauses, drawing a deep breath. "But my brothers and sisters are spread across the world now, so to answer your question, I have no one. Except Lola, who lives here, and I don't see myself leaving her anytime soon."

"You two have a strong bond."

"We're 'twinsies,' like Mira-Me would say. But we're not lovers."

At that, we hold each other's looks. We are two orphaned, grown men who know what we have in our lives, what we risk losing, and how much we can gain from taking a chance.

His face breaks into a goofy clown smile. "C'mon, let's do something about it."

Chapter Seven

The Spanish like their *fiesta* and they know how to party. Pulsating music and cheerful laughs accompany us as we wander hand-in-hand through the dark streets of the Old Town. The scents of food, beer, and cigarette smoke permeate the air.

It's such a good feeling, to be with someone. I've had a few fleeting relationships after my divorce, but nothing involving romance. Loneliness is a treacherous friend, and in my case, it conspires with my nemesis the liquor. Not tonight, though. Tonight, my soul is singing.

We walk by stone buildings from medieval times, ghostly shadows in the night, their arches and spires silhouetting against a star-sprinkled canvas of blackness and eternity. I could feel at home here and anywhere in the world so long as I'm with someone able to make my pulse beat a wild cadence in my veins.

I'm acutely aware of Robin's presence by my side, my body sizzling and on edge. I don't know what the rest of the night has in store for us, but from his lighthearted enthusiasm and easy gait, he's not about to abandon me anytime soon.

"I'll show you where we were supposed to perform this evening," he says, as if reading my mind. "It's an old theater. About this way, I think." He tugs on my hand and leads me through a narrow, unlit alley. Our footfalls echo between walls. At the bottom, a dome appears before us, wide as a circus tent and a bit alone in the dark. The moon rises over the city, slowly casting white light into the maze of streets and revealing the theater entrance: a double door framed by two Greek pillars underneath a banner. "Shall we have a look?"

I ask, "It must be closed, no?"

"I've still got the keys to a side door." He turns to me with a grin, the moonlight complimenting his handsome features. His angular chin, strong nose and cheekbones, generous lips, and in place of eyes, deep-green glass marbles mirroring his soul.

My heart skips a beat. He's so special, how can I possibly deserve him? And what if his interest in me fades after he learns to know the new me, the burnt me, a different person from the young rock star wannabe he crushed on twenty years ago?

"Don't worry so much," he whispers, reaching up to caress my cheek. "We're going to be all right. Take a day at a time."

"Yeah." I let out a nervous chuckle.

He leans forward and kisses me, lips soft and oh-so-gentle. His fragrance of musk and cologne fills my space. Before I can respond to the kiss, a *ding* from my phone says I've received a text. I want to ignore the interruption, but Robin says, "It's okay, answer it."

"Pfft. It can only be Mira-Me." I pull the phone out of my pocket and thumb it open. Sure enough, she's sent me a selfie of her cheek-to-cheek with the charming Antonio Banderas lookalike and the words, **Don't wait for me.** I show it to Robin with a laugh.

"He-he, I guess this means we have the night to ourselves. But first, can I show you something?" He gestures for me to hand him the phone, taps the YouTube app open, and types "Robin and Lola" in the search section.

A long list of videos appears on the screen. He picks one where the two harlequins are bathed in purple light against a black backdrop. It must be filmed during one of their acrobatic shows, where they do a great number of acts you'd never imagine were humanly possible, he lying on his back and she using his extended arms and legs in the air for support to do extreme contortionist splits and dances. "What we do there is called an adagio."

"Wow." I gape. I am baffled by the way their movements are clocked and synchronized to perfection like machinery, having probably been rehearsed a thousand times, and how the duo relies on each other's physical abilities and balance. The video continues, now Lola lifting Robin the same way he did, and he standing upside down using solely her up-reached hands for support. I blink, this is so crazy. "That girl's strength is insane!"

"I told you she could carry my weight."

"And your balance is just..." I can't find the right word to express my admiration.

He laughs and returns the phone. "Now, let me show you where we had planned to do this."

He goes to the side of the theater, unlocks a steel door, and slips inside. I follow him into what looks like a small hall, the door clicking shut behind me. He fumbles in the dark before finding a switch. Light floods our constricted space, blinding us. "This way." The hall ends with a heavy red curtain. He pushes it aside. "Ta-daa!"

His voice echoes in a vast, round room towered by a domed ceiling. The lights are off, but moonlight pierces through a window revealing row after row of red-cushioned seats, balconies, and in front, a wooden stage. I recognize the smell from our hotel in Aranda de Duero—century-old lacquer and musty carpets, and maybe also a hint of candlelight. There is an oppressive quiet in here, as if ghosts from the past are watching us from the shadows.

Before I can say anything, Robin takes his shirt off, folds it over a seat, and removes his shoes—then hops up on the stage. What is he up to?

Eyes closed, he lifts a leg and spins around on the tip of his toe. Once, twice, in a slow then quickened rhythm as if following the leads of some classical music in his head. The low light filtering from the ceiling puts on display every single muscle of his torso and floating arms as he dances across the stage, swirling, jumping, gliding with utter grace.

"What are you doing?" I whisper, in awe. "A show? For me?"

I lean against a low, wooden fence separating the stage from the audience seats and hold my breath, his dance is so beautiful. I understand, now, that performance is his world, his life. The wooden stage floor creaks under his weight, but he seems so at home in this magical universe of the theater, like a crucial keystone the old building needs to feel alive, too. Where will I fit in?

Slowly, he melts down to the floor and lies there for a moment, arms spread, chest heaving for air and pelvis lifting in tune with a melody only he can hear. In profile, his body is a masterpiece of sculpted forms and proportions. Whoever created man must have had sex on his mind, for this man's gorgeousness sends me spiraling into a haze of lust and need. My body tenses, straining against my clothes as if they've become too small.

Seems as though Robin is feeling the same thing, for he arches his back like a bow, unbuttons his pants, pushes them down his legs, and kicks them off one foot after the other, giving me ample time to view the outline of his cock in his briefs. He must be aroused, how else can it be so long and thick? Surely, the low light isn't playing tricks on me. As if he's heard my thoughts, he turns to me with a dazzling grin and runs a hand over his erection.

Fuck, he's bad. Fierce arousal slams into me, my cock growing rock hard and tenting my jeans. I return the grin and tell him with my eyes, *Go on!*

He nods a silent, *Okay*, and gets up with the fluency and ease of an acrobat. Then goes to the side of the stage, grabs a rope hanging from the ceiling, and pulls it toward the center. The rope must be about twenty-five feet high, but he crosses his legs around it and climbs fast as an ape before stopping mid-height and suddenly spreading his arms, letting himself fall backward.

No! I gasp and plunge forward to catch him, colliding with the raised platform of the stage. But he's okay, his legs are locked around the rope, and he swirls round and round, head upside down, looking like an angel whose wings have given up a flight.

My heart hammers in my chest as I lean against the stage and suck in a deep breath. And calm enough to reckon he's got the most impressive human body I've seen, natural muscles bulging and not an ounce of fat. In addition to an innate sense of coordination, weight, space, and balance. Stupendous. Oh, yeah, and that hard rod in his briefs is still very visible, its veined profile enhanced by the moonlight, a supplement of maleness that has me salivate and lick my lips.

As quickly as I jumped to his rescue, I'm back into sex mode. My stiff cock presses against the wooden platform, the pulse in its veins pounding. I squeeze it to ease the pressure then rearrange it in my pants.

He straightens, glides down the rope, and at the bottom forms a limbless human ball rolling on the floor a couple times until he reaches the edge of the stage. Stopping inches from me, he spreads his long limbs again in a seductive position, dark gaze fixed on me, muscles trembling, his broad chest going up and down with each breath. Heat oozes from him. A thin coat of sweat covers his skin, which glows a dark bronze in the low light. Irresistible.

My turn to play. The show's over, and the performer must be thanked accordingly.

I grab his chin and pull him to me a little rough-handedly before covering his mouth with mine in a hard kiss then diving in, roaming, exploring. His gasps for air only urge me on. I curl my tongue around his in a teasing dance and lick the wet inside of his mouth, his tongue again, his teeth. Everything is mine. He breathes heavily through his nose, moaning in my mouth.

I release his swollen lips to give him some air. "Don't let anyone else kiss you like that," I warn, my voice hoarse and deep in my throat.

Cheeks flushed, he pants as he lifts his pelvis and reaches for the waistband of his tented briefs.

I put a hand over his and order, "Let me."

His eyes shine with such intensity, my breath hitches. They tell me he wants to come hard, he wants to shout out, but he also wants to be loved and not be let down. Like me, he's a lost soul struggling to stay afloat, a spirit broken again and again and now silently looking for a meaning to simply exist.

My heart bleeds for this man, but it's also full of a love I have not known in a long time. Love I can share if he's the right one.

Wanting to show him my attraction is not all about sex, I move my hand to his taut pectorals, stroking them with a finger following the deep lines between them. Fuck, he's such perfection, I need to have a taste. I lean down and tease a nipple with the tip of my tongue, then the other, gently nibbling the erect bud and sucking it in. His skin tastes salty, the ensnaring scent of male filling my nostrils.

He shudders, ragged puffs of air escaping his parted lips.

I run my hand down to the tight, warm muscles of

his glistening stomach and draw the contour of each washboard ridge. Then hook a finger into the waistband of his briefs and pull them down over his hips, uncovering a furious boner. Thick, firm, and so needy it's jerking. My fucking God, what a sight.

I press my raging hard-on against the stage in an attempt to soothe the pain. Then lean down to place a gentle kiss on the mushroom-shaped head of his cock before going in for an assault—not in a mean way, but a little rough, because I want him to be swept over the top like a roller-coaster wagon shooting into the air.

I close one hand around the base of his hard rod and grab his sac with the other. I stroke the full length of the firm, velvety shaft up to its bulbous head and down, milking and pulling his foreskin back and forth, all the while massaging his balls. The sounds of pleasure erupting from his throat encourage me to bend down again and let my tongue glide back and forth along the veined underside. I lick up to the tip and swirl it around in small circles like a slow dance, each stroke leaving a wet trace on his stretched skin. I tease and toy with the tip, curling my tongue around and dipping into its wet slit. Salivating for more, I take him into my mouth and suck him in and out, then form a tight ring with my closed lips before letting it glide out again. I pump up and down the shaft before taking the tip into my mouth again and swallow as far as my throat can take, adjusting the angle of my neck so I can take him in deeper. The thick cockhead bumps the back of my throat.

To increase his pleasure, I move a finger to the small, puckered hole in the slit of his ass, circle the hole and apply light pressure. When I think he's gotten used to the intrusion, I dip my knuckle past his ring muscle into his tight, hot depth. He tenses against my finger, but I work the ring with slow moves until he's relaxed enough for me to push deeper, curling my finger upward and stroking the flesh inside.

There! He bucks and groans, his pelvis lifting in the air. His pulsating cock fills my mouth with warm, creamy semen.

I swallow mouthful after mouthful, his cum thick and salty on my tongue. So fucking erotic. His orgasm has heat rushing through my hard dick and warm pre-cum leaking into my briefs. Fuck, too soon. My balls are so full I'm about to burst, but I want to wait. I hold my breath and savor the amazing feeling, though, leaking more. Heart pounding a wild beat, I let his cock slip out of my mouth and straighten.

Sweat rolls down my body. My shirt sticks to my clammy skin, so I lift my arms to take it off, damp heat drifting from my armpits.

"Fuck, that was hot," he groans, panting. Sweat pebbling on his face, his gaze roams over my naked torso, followed by a wicked grin that says he likes my looks. Guess I don't need to be beefy as hell to please him. I work out just enough to look natural.

"Are you ready for the main course?" I unbuckle my belt, unzip my jeans, and show him my cock in my fist, twitching with excitement. Drops of pre-cum drip from the tip. "I'll let you have the honors." I find a rubber pack in a pocket and hand it to him, before letting my jeans and boxers drop to my feet.

"You're amazing. So, so hot." Voice husky, he laughs and licks his lips with a glowing stare. That's all I want, for him to feel great. Better than great, I'm going to devote the rest of my life to make him a happy man.

Dick still hard, he scoots over to the edge of the platform, jumps down, and kisses me. Our lips melt together, his tongue meeting mine and curling around it.

With a happy chuckle, he rolls the condom on his

cock, gathers drops of cum from mine, and smears it on the rubber before pushing me to lean against the stage. Jesus, this is unreal. Just at the thought of his cock penetrating me, my ring muscle contracts.

Trembling with need, I stretch one arm ahead of me on the stage floor and wrap the other around my burning length.

The firm tip of his cock pokes at my hole. I brace for the invasion, but he eases into me inch by inch, stretching me with care. When the hard head passes my ring, my nerve endings come alive, a sting of pain shooting outward. He waits for me to relax before he lets his slick shaft glide further in. Halfway in, he grabs my hips and shoves deeper, burying his cock completely.

I let out a gasp, my inner muscles clamping around his shaft, enhancing our friction, and heightening my arousal. Feels so good with my ass stretched. He fills me so nicely, giving me an incredible sensation. I'm tense and full at the same time, can't believe how well we fit. My core tingles with need. To come even harder, I rub my cock base-to-tip with long, urgent strokes in the same rhythm, on and on.

He rides me with such ease, pulling in and out with slow, calculated moves and almost slipping out before thrusting in again. He groans and pushes deeper, faster, and I relish the feel of his thick cock gliding in and out of me at a quick, rhythmic pace, pumping me over and over. Sweat slicks our linked bodies, each rough movement making his balls slap my butt cheeks and slamming me against the stage. It doesn't stop me from giving myself a major jack-off. That, combined with the friction against my ring muscle and the gliding sensation of fullness in my ass, is going to make me come so hard. I'm going to be blown away like crazy.

His rapid breaths fill my ears. He's chasing a new

orgasm. I couldn't be happier for him, I want him to experience this again and again.

My body trembles. My balls ache. The more he increases the speed and friction inside my ass, the harder I'm going to explode. I gulp air, bracing. Then climb higher and higher until I have to spray all of that burning cum out of my cock.

Oh, it's happening! Heat shoots through me, and I blow up with a cry. Arching my back, squeezing him with my ass, I release all the searing hotness from inside my balls and shoot long spurts onto the stage wall.

He convulses at the same time, growling to the fucking silence around us.

It takes me a long moment to come to. And when I do, I laugh, leaning back against my lover's large, heaving chest and looking up to the domed ceiling of the theater where he was supposed to perform for an ecstatic audience tonight.

The cheeky harlequin did perform all right—he seduced *me* to the moon and back with his act—but the truth is, he is now mine, all mine.

The End

REDEEM MY HEART

Megan Slayer

Copyright © 2024

Chapter One

"You want me to do what?" Will stared at the paper proposal. He hadn't seen a proposal for art done on paper in forever. Everything seemed to come through email or mass shared files. The paper version was so … archaic.

He scanned through the information and his brain damn near misfired. Carsten Gold. He hadn't heard that name in a long time. A shiver ran the length of his spine. Back in the day, Carsten had been mighty handsome. Unlike Will, he hadn't had a gangly teen phase. Nope. Carsten always looked hot. Now that he had ten years on his frame, he looked even better.

But Carsten Gold wasn't all that shimmered. Not in the least. Carsten had been the bane of Will's existence. He'd done everything possible to make Will feel like an outcast.

Not that Marissa needed to know his life history.

He turned his attention to his fellow professor. "First, I thought we only did digital props. Second, when did we start catering to celebrities? Third, no. I'm not doing this." He refused to take part.

"I'm sorry?" Marissa Kline shook her head. "You're the best with graphic design and the artist demanded you."

Sure he did. Probably to demean him again. Or to give him ten tons of shit. No, thank you. He set his jaw. "Artist?" He was an artist. Carsten was a creator. "He's a musician. That's not art." It was, but now that he'd lost his temper, little coming out of his mouth would make sense.

"Why are you so bitter about this?"

If she only knew. "No reason. I'm just not feeling the spark for this project. Not being inspired."

Marissa sighed. "Not feeling it? You're kidding me. It's a simple poster. The management is trying to rehab his image after coming out, so he's doing campus shows. It's not that complicated. He wants a basic poster and in your style. How hard is that?"

She was right. The concept wasn't hard. The execution wasn't either. Dealing with Carsten ... now that was the hard part. If she knew how Carsten had treated him, she might not be so welcoming. But she had no idea and he wasn't going to disclose.

She might not be cool with the job if she found out he was collaborating with his former bully. Then again, she might push him harder to do it.

He scrubbed one hand across his forehead. "Fine. I'll do it." To be honest, he couldn't look away from the image of Carsten. The man had only grown hotter with time. The same chiseled features, same mischievous grin on his face, and those biceps … but Carsten peddled in handsome. He had to in order to sell tickets. His music was good, but he had to have the I to go with it.

If only his attitude matched his overall look.

"So you'll do it?" Marissa asked.

"Yes." She'd push until he agreed and part of him did want to work on the project.

"Great." She grinned. Her green eyes sparkled and the spring returned to her step. "I'll get the rest of the files over to you today. Some of it is in digital form, but the initial proposal was print." She shrugged.

"Sure." His stomach churned. He wasn't thrilled. Hadn't been since he'd seen Carsten's face smiling back at him. Why did he have to come back into his life? Why now?

He'd thought he'd moved on. Thought he wasn't ever going to revisit his past. Then Carsten happened.

He could still hear Carsten's taunts. *"You're so gay. You're so boring. You think everyone loves you."* Carsten hadn't been right, but that hadn't stopped him. Then there was the time he'd pantsed Will in front of the football team. Real nice. Carsten had hit him, too. *"I'll knock you right into next week just for existing."* What a gem.

"You know he's cute." Deanna sat beside him. "And single."

"And gay?" He'd heard this song and dance one thousand times before. A cute, single gay man must be his next conquest. Except his shyness tended to win out and he wasn't interested. "I'll pass."

"What?" Deanna squeaked. "You can't."

She was a sweet girl and the best grad assistant he could ask for, but he wasn't about to turn to her for dating suggestions. "Not my type." It was a lousy answer, but it'd do for now.

"No one is."

He pulled a folder onto the photo of Carsten, blocking the view. "What's that supposed to mean?"

Deanna folded her arms and leaned against his desk. "You really want to know?"

He didn't, but he couldn't help himself. "Yes."

"You've been single for a year. Stan isn't single. He also wasn't any good for you. He never deserved you and you deserved better. It's time you stopped being cranky and hiding away. It's time you put yourself out there. Why not give this guy a chance?" She tapped the folder with her manicured nail. "He's passing through and might be a good way to get back on the horse, so to speak."

"You're assuming a lot." Too much, really.

"You don't know that."

"What if he's not interested? He might not be. What if he's not single? He could've found a boyfriend in the last few months. To be honest, he might not even look my way." Knowing Carsten, he'd take one look at Will and laugh, then run. Or he'd take up where he'd left off ten years ago. "He's just passing through, but he might not want the complication of a relationship, even for a night."

She narrowed her eyes and sighed, but didn't speak right away. Instead, she simply stared at him. The longer she stayed quiet, the more he wanted to run away. Shit. He didn't need her thinking too hard on this.

"Just because he's passing through doesn't mean he won't be interested. He could be," she said. "If he's got any brains, he'll see you and want to snap you up."

Oh, God. "What makes you think he's even looking?" He hadn't kept up on Carsten, but he doubted Carsten would be single for long.

He glanced down at the file and a few ideas ran

through his mind. He sort of knew how he wanted to tackle the concept art and should start pulling the ideas together to create a mock-up.

"Well…" She shrugged and crinkled her nose. "It's possible."

"You haven't answered my question." He opened his laptop. "What gives you the idea he would even want me? What if he doesn't want a one-nighter? What if he's not even looking?"

She rounded his desk. "You've got an idea, don't you?"

"I have a few I'd like to work up for this." He opened the graphics file and the layout he wanted to try first.

"Then okay. I think he'd be interested because I read an interview he did last week about being lonely. He said he wanted a boyfriend—someone quirky, sweet, and unique. Someone not like the rest. He said he'd keep looking until he found that person, too. That could be you."

Could be a hundred other people, too. "You're pushing too hard. Last week you tried to hook me up with that theology professor who said I had cute shoes. He wasn't even gay and he meant your shoes." She had to stop.

"I thought he was talking to you and I'm sorry." She snorted. "Look, I'm tired of seeing you mopey. You're miserable."

"Maybe I like being that way." Not really, but there wasn't much point in the argument. She wasn't listening to him.

"You do not."

"You're right. I don't."

"Then why be that way? You're not happy. You're lonely, too. Wouldn't it be so cool to have two lonely souls come together? It'd be like a movie." Her eyes twinkled. "I'd love a romance like that."

"I'm sure you would." But it was completely impossible. "That's not how this stuff works, though. Love isn't that possible."

"But what if it could be? What if you could have it?"

"Deanna." She needed to let this go.

"You don't understand."

"No, I don't." He pushed away from his desk. He'd never get any work done until she gave him space.

"I just mean you have a chance at forever."

"You think I do," he corrected. "Carsten Gold never said he wanted to date Will Rohr. He said he's tired of being lonely. You don't know that he's coming here for me. For all you know, he's coming to town just to play a show and move on. He wants to play and get paid."

She winced. "True."

"What happens if you get all invested in this relationship you want me to have, into me being with him, but you find out he's not interested? What if he doesn't want to see me? What if there's no connection?" He'd never survive it.

"Okay." She groaned. "You take the fun and romance out of everything."

"I have to because it's my job. I'm not here to fall in love," he said. "I'm here to create art and teach students to do that, too."

"I know."

"So why should I get hooked up with someone? I'm busy and happy." He was busy, but the happy--not so much. Didn't matter. He needed to focus on his work.

She stared at him and he knew she didn't buy his line of bullshit.

"What?"

"You're a terrible liar."

"So?" He had to keep this in check. She might be his grad assistant, but she wasn't his social coordinator.

"You need to get over Stan and move forward. I have a feeling about this one." She grinned. "And I might have talked to him. Bye." She ran out of the room before he could argue.

"Wait." She'd talked to him? Why? How? Jesus. Will could only imagine what she'd told him.

Or what Carsten had said in return.

His stomach lurched again. His past tended to come back to bite him in the ass. Now that Carsten was in his orbit, he'd be in big trouble. He'd fall for Carsten's blue eyes and crooked smile. He'd want to fall into his arms, too.

A piece of his heart belonged to Carsten. Back in the day, despite the harsh treatment, he'd been a sucker for Carsten. Was he still infatuated with him? He'd never know until he saw him, but he had the feeling he was in trouble. He'd fall and have his heart broken, then torn apart. All because he liked Carsten Gold.

Did he really want to get burned again?

Why did love have to be so difficult?

****

Carsten sat on his tour bus and swiped through his messages. He hated the nitty-gritty of running his social media now that he'd fallen out of favor with his management's social media team. The people he'd worked with before didn't want to associate with a gay man. He'd surrounded himself with shitty people and they'd shown their true colors. They wanted money and fame by association. None of them had taken the time to know the real man.

Unfortunately, the real man was more

dimensional than they'd given him credit for being.

He read the rest of the messages and switched to his social media streams. Most of the feedback was now positive, but when he'd come out, it'd been bad. Really bad. No one wanted to associate with him. Some even told him he wasn't a real man. The announcement damn near ruined his career. Being himself would be his downfall.

He turned his attention to his personal email. Ashley was supposed to be managing them, but with over five hundred unanswered messages, he guessed she hadn't gotten around to it. He scrolled through the mail, but swiped most to delete it.

His phone pinged with a personal notification. He'd almost forgotten about his other phone. He dropped the tablet in favor of the smaller device.

Jesus Fuck. He should be making music, not doing this kind of housekeeping. He should be practicing his scales and keeping his fingers limber. Should be composing. No, he had to oversee correspondence.

He read the first two emails on his phone. One email concerned the contract for his show at Northern College. Good. He'd been waiting for that one to be completed. The second email involved the layout for the arena at the school and how his stage would be set.

Everything was so standard—the stage, his setup and the building, a basketball arena at the college. Fine.

He looked at the third email, but before he could really read it, his thoughts turned to his time in school, particularly high school. To Will.

His heart squeezed.

Will had been his problem in so many ways. Will was everything he wanted to be and had been such an easy target. Will was different. Will wore bright colors and had pink hair for a while. He created art and sang so well. He also had no problem being out. He'd taken the abuse for admitting he was gay, but never lost his cool. He'd never lost that smile.

God. Carsten closed his eyes. He'd been so jealous of Will. The guy seemed to have everything going his way.

A burst of pain washed over him. He'd hated Will for having everything in place—the grades, the look, the circle of friends and supportive family. Will had everything he wished he could have.

But that was life. Sometimes it wasn't fair.

He could still hear the things he'd said to Will. *"I hope you die."* Who said things like that? *"You dress like a girl."* Jesus. *"You do realize no one's wearing those shoes now?"* He remembered the time he'd tripped Will at graduation practice. Everyone saw and most everyone laughed. At the time he'd thought he'd done it to be funny, but he'd been cruel and oddly thought Will falling at his feet would make Will fall for him. Hardly.

He'd wanted to make Will pay for being gay and being out. Carsten couldn't forget the way his parents looked at him when he came out. When Carsten had tried to come out, his own father beat the fuck out of him. He could still feel the tender spots from the bruises, even if they were long gone and only phantom pain. For six months straight, his father managed to beat him in one way or another, inflicting pain in what he called an attempt to make Carsten not gay. When that hadn't worked, they'd kicked him out of the house and only asked him back when he made it big. They didn't want it to look like they didn't support their son. They hadn't encouraged his music career and only wanted in on the fame he'd earned.

He hadn't had the greatest circle of friends, either. None of them encouraged him until he made it big. Then they all wanted to be around him. They wanted to hang out with him when he'd played football because he'd been a star receiver and the center of attention. He liked the adulation on stage, but not his personal life. The women he'd dated hadn't made his heart race.

Hadn't made him want to settle down.

The music made him want more.

The music made him better.

So did Will.

Goddamn Will. Why did Will have to have such a hold on his heart? It wasn't fair.

Will had to hate him as well. He'd done everything in his power to insult and belittle Will. God, he'd been so immature. He regretted what he'd done because he'd been cruel. Not that he could take any of it back. He couldn't.

How could he explain to Will that he'd been hurting so bad and wanted someone else to hurt, too? It would've been easier to just let Will in on the pain, but also the attraction. He might have had an ally. Might not have been so alone.

He might not have written such deep love songs, either. His career could've been terrible or nonexistent. Did that mean he owed Will a debt of gratitude for his career and songs? Maybe. Maybe not. He could've had his heart broken by someone else and had the same trajectory in his life. Didn't matter, though. He'd have to apologize to Will when he saw him in public. By God, he'd see Will. He hadn't chosen to play Northern College for the fun of it. He'd done it to see Will. He missed Will.

The whole situation was odd, since he hadn't actually been with Will. Could he now? Would Will even give him the time of day? He'd only find out if he took a chance.

He scrolled on his phone and looked up Will's page on the college's website. Will had aged well—at least he had in the photo. He still had his hair. He now wore dark-rimmed glasses, which accentuated his dark eyes. He'd aged a bit, but he still had the same overall look of youth and carefree attitude. He wondered if Will was single. He couldn't be. He was too cute to be alone.

A call interrupted his scrolling and walk down memory lane. Marissa Kline.

He hesitated. He'd connected with her and Will's grad assistant concerning the art for his show. Truth be told, he'd done it to get intel on Will, but he hadn't gathered much information. He swiped to answer. If he left her waiting, she'd either call back or quit on him. Everyone else seemed to have given up on him already.

"Hello," he said. "How can I help you?"

"Mr. Gold, hello. How are you?" she asked. "I wasn't sure I'd be able to reach you."

"I'll always make time for you." It was a fib. He didn't know her well, but he'd learned to foster a polite and accommodating attitude with people in charge of his art and venues. The attitude got things done. He'd learned the hard way to conduct himself with a cordial spirit.

"We have some movement on your poster art," Marissa said. "The artist has some ideas mocked up and I need you to approve of the art before we can move forward. We'd like to start promoting the show as soon as we can."

"Sure, right." He nodded. "You can email it to me."

"Perfect. I've got the file heading to you now so you can look it over. There are two mocks and you're free to make suggestions. Mr. Rohr is working hard to create the art as you've requested."

"I can't wait to see them." Mr. Rohr. That sounded so official. "The professor?"

"Yes. I've known him for so long that he's still Mr. to me," she said. "I'm going to include his email so you can contact him directly if you want changes."

"Sounds great." He barely contained his excitement. He had an unavoidable reason to speak to Will. Good, good.

"The link should be in your inbox shortly. You can download the files from there. Thank you," Marissa said. "I hope it meets your expectations."

"I'm sure it will." He'd seen Will's art at the college and knew his work. The man was good with graphics and creating emotion in a poster. "Thank you and have a good day. I'll be in touch." He waited for her to hang up, then tossed his phone onto the seat.

He draped his arm across the back of the sofa and stared out at the landscape going by in a blur. Nothing else in his world seemed to matter but creating this moment with Will. He'd get to talk to him again and might even have a second chance to make a better impression.

Country love songs could be about the impossible being possible. His dream of redemption just might be coming true.

Cheers to second chances.

Chapter Two

Will strode past the poster on the digital board outside of the art building and cringed. He prided himself in the work he'd done for the art. The poster was eye-catching and accentuated Carsten's stage presence. If he had to admit it, he'd say it was one of his best works. As much as he liked the poster, he wished he never had to see Carsten's face again. Every time he looked at Carsten, his heart ached. He'd been treated so poorly by this man and now he was creating art for him to help his career.

He shook his head and made his way into the art building. He had meetings with students today for their mid-semester grades. The meetings never bothered him, but the inevitable crying and complaining always got on his nerves. Some students completely focused on their work. They did as asked and had no issues. Others thought they should fly through the courses without having to pay attention to deadlines or restrictions. Some simply had too much on their schedule to keep up. He hated having to give them the tough talk, but someone had to do it.

He hustled up the steps to his office and checked his bag to ensure he had his tablet with him.

"If it isn't Will Rohr in the flesh." Carsten leaned against the doorframe to Will's office. "It's been ages, hasn't it?"

He bristled and stopped in the middle of the corridor. He had to be dreaming. Or was it a nightmare? Carsten was in his life and standing before him.

"Don't you talk? You've always been so loud and funny." Carsten remained against the doorway. "Cat got your tongue?"

227

"No," he managed. He summoned his courage and stiffened his spine. "You're here."

"I am."

He strode up to his office door and unlocked it with his key card. "How can I help you?"

"I hear you're the artist behind my poster for the concert here on campus." Carsten followed him into the office. "It's sold out."

"I know." He hadn't tried to get tickets, but he'd been encouraged to do so. Why see someone he detested?

"Are you coming to the concert?" Carsten closed the door behind him. "Do you get special tickets because you did the art?"

"I'm not going." He positioned himself behind his desk. "I'm not into country music." Never had been. Maybe because Carsten was a star in the genre...

"I'm sorry to hear that." Carsten frowned and the crinkles around his eyes added to his attractiveness.

Shame, really. Carsten was even better looking in person than he was in his photos. Will understood why the fans rushed to him and why he was so popular. His music wasn't half bad, either. His attitude destroyed the illusion, though.

"I came by to congratulate you on the art. It's better than I thought it might be," Carsten said. "I worried it wasn't going to turn out well."

"Because I hate you?" He might as well be blunt. "Because you treated me like shit and I never forgot?"

Carsten's eyes widened, but he regained his composure within seconds. "You haven't forgotten that, have you?"

He had to be kidding? "Forgotten it? You made my life hell in high school."

"I was hard on you, yes."

"Hard?" he blurted. The gall of this man. "You

told me I was slime and needed to die."

"I…" Carsten shut his mouth.

"Yeah. Forgot that, didn't you? Or how you told everyone I was fucking half the football players because we lost that playoff game. I had nothing to do with the football team and only paid attention to them because I was in the marching band. You pantsed me and punched me." He'd kept this venom under control for so many years, but seeing Carsten made the hurt rush right now. "You made my life miserable."

"It's always about you." Carsten shook his head. "You think you were so poorly treated. You brought it on yourself."

"What?" He needed Carsten to leave right now. He rounded his desk and stepped into Carsten's personal space. "Get. Out."

"Why?"

"This is my office and I have appointments this afternoon." He regained his composure. If he let Carsten bother him again, he'd never forgive himself. He was a professional. "Excuse me. I have work to do."

"You do." Carsten didn't back away. He met Will's gaze. "You're supposed to be meeting with me."

"Pardon?" He knew his schedule and Carsten wasn't on it.

"You're to be meeting with me until one." Carsten hooked his fingers in his front pockets. "To discuss the art and see an old friend."

"Old friend?" Jesus. "You've got the wrong person. I did the art for you because it was a job. I have no desire to be friends with you."

"I really hurt you that badly?"

He had no clue. "It was hard enough to be gay in a small town where being gay was frowned upon. I did my best to do my thing and not bother anyone, but you went out of your way to make fun of me. You insulted me, you tried to throw me into a locker, and turned people against me. Was it you that drew devil horns on my photo in the hallway when I did the musical? Was it you that booed me when I sang my big solo? Or were you directing people to do that for you? Couldn't dirty your hands that way?"

Carsten held up his hands, then slid them down Will's shoulders. "There's so much you don't understand."

"I have my doubts." He didn't want Carsten to touch him, but he couldn't seem to pull away. God Almighty, why did he have to be attracted to him? Even after all this time, the attraction was still there.

"Do you know where I was living during my senior year of high school?" Carsten asked.

"Wasn't my business." Even if he'd have asked, he'd have been assaulted so he didn't bother.

"I lived with Nick Clain's family because mine threw me out."

Nick Clain? He remembered the guy. A soccer player with a nice ass and sweet smile. Nick wasn't gay, either. But if Will remembered correctly, Nick and Carsten had been friends for years. "Why did they throw you out?" The last he knew, Carsten had everything going for him. He was the picture of what any Brookville kid should be—handsome, well-adjusted, and straight.

Except he wasn't straight.

"They threw me out because I admitted I was gay back then." Carsten kept his hands on Will's shoulders. "That's why I treated you so shitty. I hated that you were so able to be out and no one hated you for it. I hated that you had parents that fucking loved you. Everything went your way. I said I'd punch you into next week because that was something my father always said to me. Sick, isn't it?"

He had to be talking about someone else. Things hadn't gone his way in school. He'd had to learn to handle the backlash for his sexuality and how to be his own man. Yes, his parents had backed him all the way, but he'd never questioned that. They were his parents and had always been his biggest supporters.

"I hated that you were even on the prom court because I wanted to be the king," Carsten said. "You were good at music and art."

"But you're good at football and must be good enough at music or you wouldn't be on tour." He didn't understand what was going on or why he couldn't seem to pull away from Carsten.

"You don't get it." Carsten shook his head. "It's so plain, but even I didn't get it back then."

"Get what?" He hated when people spoke in riddles. "You were beaten, weren't you?"

"My parents didn't want a gay kid. They wanted a successful one. My father beat the ever-loving fuck out of me for being gay. You never saw the bruises because I tried so hard to hide them. When I took the time to learn my guitar and practice writing music, then got some actual success, they began to like me," Carsten said. "I'm not anything to them if I can't give them money."

"That's sick." Truly.

"They hated that I was gay. My father left me bruised and battered."

"That's sicker." And a piece of his heart broke for Carsten. He didn't know what it was like to have parents who didn't support him and couldn't imagine being in Carsten's place.

"It is and I hated myself, which made me hate you. I was so hurt and I wanted you to hurt, too. You were everything I wanted to be," Carsten said.

"Everything I wanted. So confident in your own skin. I had to hide mine."

He paused. He had to have heard Carsten wrong. Everything he wanted? That made no sense. "What did you want?"

Carsten remained close to him and caressed Will's shoulders. "You."

Now he knew he'd been dreaming. Carsten hadn't wanted him. He'd treated him like shit. "Huh?"

"And I wanted to do this." Carsten didn't give him time to think. Instead, he bridged the gap between them and pressed a kiss to Will's lips.

This was really happening. Will didn't bother to close his eyes. He barely moved. The shock of being kissed was too much to process, but the kiss was too good to stop. God, he was so fucked.

He almost liked Carsten. Almost understood him. Almost.

****

Carsten had waited so long for this moment. He'd dreamed about kissing Will back in school. Treating Will like shit to get him to like him was fucked up, though. In hindsight, he wished he'd been clearheaded about the attraction and his motivations.

Will was the one he'd never forgotten. Now he had his work cut out for him. If he was going to convince Will to give him a chance, he had to redeem himself. He slipped his arms around Will, loving the way he felt in his embrace.

Why had he waited so long to make this kiss happen?

Fear.

He swore he'd be rejected. Hell, he still could be. Will hadn't pushed him away and hadn't screamed, but he could.

He memorized the softness of Will's lips, the silkiness of his hair, and the way he whimpered when he was kissed. He wanted to run his hands over the planes of Will's chest, but he couldn't mistake the bulge in Will's jeans. Was he turned on, too?

Will broke the kiss. Wildness shimmered in his eyes. Pink infused his cheeks and he averted his gaze.

"You hated that." Carsten should've guessed. He'd been told by men and women he wasn't good at kissing. He pushed too hard and wanted too much.

"I didn't say I did." Will put space between them and sat on the edge of his desk. "I wasn't expecting you to kiss me."

"No?" What had he expected?

"I thought you might punch me." Will folded his arms and crossed his ankles. "You hated me so much."

"I did." He hadn't missed the way Will canceled himself out and put up barriers. He wished he hadn't been so terrible to Will.

"What time is your concert?" Will cleared his throat. "You don't want to be late."

"Not until nine." He had plenty of time until he had to be at the venue. "I looked at the hall this morning. It's a good but standard space. Decent acoustics and plenty of room for fans. I have no idea if I've sold out, but I doubt it. I haven't sold out in ages."

"Why not?" Will relaxed just a bit.

"No one wants to listen to a country musician who's gay and lied to them for ages about his sexuality. They want the stereotype." He shrugged. He'd gotten used to the hate mail. The fans didn't rush to his concerts like before. They wanted something else from him—to see him as the sexy attainable man. Being gay meant he might not be as attainable.

"That's ridiculous." Will didn't shift positions,

but he loosened his stance just a bit. "The music doesn't change because you did."

"You tell the fans that." Was Will softening to him? Sure felt like it. Even if only a tiny shred.

"I've heard the music. I'm more of a rock man myself, but I've heard your albums and they're not bad." Will narrowed his eyes. His blush evaporated and he sighed. "They're good love songs. It's not perfect, but I've heard them and I can see the appeal. I've also seen your stage show."

"You have?" No way. "Have you come to my concerts?" He hoped so.

"YouTube."

"Oh." Just as well.

"You're good. I can see what drew the fans in and why you've got gold records." Will unfolded his arms and rested his hands on the edge of his desk. "What exactly did you want by coming here? I did the art for you. What more do you want?"

"Redemption."

"Ain't happening."

"Why not?" He hadn't thought this through very well. He'd simply assumed he'd hit it off with Will and things would be fine.

"You treated me like shit. No kiss is enough to erase that." Will cocked his head. "I still don't understand why you did it."

He had to be honest, even if it killed him. "You were more popular than me."

"You're kidding?" Will rolled his eyes. "It was because I was nice to everyone. Do you know how many people knew my name but didn't know me? They thought they were my friends because I was nice and said hi, but none of them got to know the real person. It was enough to be friends on a superficial level."

"But you were popular. The only reason I got elected to prom king was because Lucy had the vote fixed." It wasn't his best moment.

"You're fucking kidding me." Will rolled his eyes again. "That's sick."

"It is, but Lucy offered and I wanted to be on top. That's the only way I thought I could be."

"Didn't want to be second to a gay man." Will shook his head, then stood. "You're ridiculous."

"I am. I was and I am." He wasn't going to deny it. "I've told you I hated you. I did because you had everything I wanted—parents who supported you for real, friends who seemed more authentic than anyone I hung out with, you were musical from the start and could be yourself. You weren't stuck in a box the way I was."

The muscle in Will's jaw twitched, but he said nothing.

"I said it before and I'll say it again. I wanted you to hurt like I did." His voice clogged in his throat. Damn, being honest wasn't any fun. But it'd make for a good song. He'd channel his pain and frustration into a tune tonight.

"What were you going to accomplish by hurting me? You made me look like a fool. I used to want to hide and I found ways to avoid you," Will said. "You treated me like dirt."

"I wanted you to confront me and ask why I was so mean. I thought you'd ask and I'd be strong enough to tell you. When I told you, you'd feel sorry for me? A kinship? You'd see it wasn't so much that I hated you, but that I wanted to be with you?"

"Why would I see those things?"

"Because they were the truth." They are the truth.

"What?" Will shook his head again. "I didn't get the feeling you liked me at all. Quite the opposite."

"I was wrong."

"No shit."

He deserved that. He hooked his fingers in his front pockets again. "I was a mixed-up kid. I was led to believe if I treated you like crap, you'd see it as interest and you'd talk to me. If you talked to me, then we might be friends. We might have things in common. But I was wrong. It was the wrong tactic and it failed me. Then I hid who I was because it was easier to hide than to be honest. No one wanted the real me—not even my parents."

"That's not fair." Will's shoulders sagged and the anger seemed to evaporate within him. "I'm sorry it happened."

"Would you have given me the time of day? If I'd have been honest?" Carsten asked.

"No."

He should've known.

"Not because I wasn't interested, but because you'd treated me so poorly up to that point," Will said. "That wasn't the dance I wanted to do with you. If you'd have treated me like a person and confided in me, we could've been friends. I'm sorry your family was trash to you and if I'd have known, I'd have tried to help."

The words made him pause. Would've helped? "Were you attracted to me?"

"Depends on how you define *attracted.*" Will ducked behind his desk, putting space between him and Carsten. "Did I think you had a great body? I did. Would I have loved to have a guy like you interested in me? I would've liked to have explored the possibilities."

"But?" There had to be a but.

"Your attitude put me off."

"It should've. I was a dick."

"You were."

"Does it help to know I'm sorry? I regret everything I said and did?" he asked. "It's the truth. I wasted a lot of time and I hated that I did it because I was miserable and I see just how miserable I made you. You're right. It wasn't fair."

"No." Will rested his knuckles on his desk. "If you're looking for forgiveness, then you've got it. We all make mistakes and you've seen the error of yours. I commend you for being so honest with yourself and now me."

"Thanks." He didn't want simple forgiveness.

"You're free." Will settled on his chair. "Go out there and do the best concert you can because your heart is free."

"It's not." Far from it. He rounded Will's desk. "I want something more from you."

"Are you going to hurt me?" Will winced. "I don't fight."

"Who said I wanted to fight?" He turned Will in his chair to face him and grasped the armrests.

"What do you want, then?" Will's eyes widened.

Up close, Carsten noticed the flecks in Will's eyes, amber among the dark brown. Noticed the thickness of his lashes and the dusting of freckles on the apex of his cheeks. He even saw the slight growth of whiskers on the hollow of his cheeks. "I want one night to prove to you that the attraction between us is real and you know it. One night to show you we could have one hell of a time. One night to prove we should've gotten together back in the day because we're better as a twosome."

"You've got to be kidding me. We're in totally different worlds. You're famous and I'm a professor."

So he was considering it? Carsten could work with that. "So?"

"It won't work."

He knew better. "What if I told you it could? Would you give me a chance? One night?"

Will stared at him but said nothing. His mouth opened and closed, despite his lack of sound.

"Because that's what I want. One night to redeem myself and prove you and I should've been together all this time. We're meant to be."

Will sagged in his seat, but continued to stare at Carsten. "Fuck me."

Chapter Three

Will swore his heart dropped to his toes. He hadn't meant to say "fuck me." Hell, he hadn't planned on agreeing to Carsten's suggestion they get together. Carsten hated him, had treated him like shit for years. Now he wanted to have a relationship? Even if only for one night? It had to be a trick. Had to.

Men like Carsten weren't attracted to men like him. It wasn't done. That happy ending didn't come true.

"You have a concert tonight. You can't let those fans down," Will said. There. He'd given Carsten a reason why the one-night thing wouldn't work. It had to be enough.

"Except there's plenty of evening after the concert. What do you think I do when I leave the stage? Stay there all night?" Carsten continued to stand over him. "I don't have a guy in every town, if that's what you're implying."

"I wasn't at all." He hadn't even considered it.

"I didn't plan this concert just to play at this college. I did it to see you." Carsten leaned into him again and pressed another kiss to Will's lips. "I knew you'd be the one doing the art. I requested you personally. Marissa begged me to pick someone else because she said you weren't thrilled about my request, but I insisted. I can be very persuasive."

"So can she." To the point of driving him to the brink. "She's protective, too. She doesn't like to see me upset. She saw what happened when Stan and I split and I'm guessing she doesn't want to see it again, so she's extra protective."

"I know, but her persistence didn't pay off. Mine did because I'm here with you." Carsten bobbed his eyebrows, then his smile fell. "Stan?"

He didn't want to hash this out right now, but he doubted Carsten would let the topic drop. "Stan was my boyfriend. We lived together for a while and he decided he wanted more from life than I could give him. He moved out about a year ago."

"What more could he want?" Carsten stood, then grabbed the chair in front of Will's desk. "You're a catch. A professor, you've got your own place, your own car … what's there not to like?"

"I have a cat, for one. He hated cats. Monet is a sweet cat and gets along with everyone."

"Except Stan."

"Yeah."

Carsten nodded. "The cat has a sixth sense about people."

"I guess so." He relaxed a bit. "Stan kept trying to convince me to rehome Monet. I refused and that led to us splitting."

"Had to be more than that." Carsten reclined a bit in the chair and propped his left ankle on his right knee. He folded his hands on his flat stomach. If Will didn't know better, Carsten looked right at home—like he'd been in the office a thousand times.

"I got promoted to the chair of the graphic arts department, but he thought I should be the dean. I don't want to be the dean. I want to work with students." Will raked his fingers through his hair. "There's something to be said about collaborating with other artists. I like that so much more than being behind a desk."

"Makes sense," Carsten said. "I looked up your one man show, too. You're good. Your graphic works are fantastic. That's what made me want to work with you."

He had to believe Carsten, even if the whole situation seemed far-fetched. "Why didn't you just tell me you were hurting back in school? Why treat me like shit?"

Carsten sighed and re-laced his fingers together. "I was ashamed and I just wanted you to notice me."

"How could I not?" Will hated the way he felt. The more Carsten talked, the more he softened toward him. It wasn't fair. Part of him even considered taking Carsten up on his proposal. It might be fun to be with someone for the night. Might be hot.

"You were the most colorful," Carsten said. "I was jealous of you."

"You were?" It wasn't possible.

"I was. Once I came to terms with who I am, with what I did, and decided to make amends, I knew there was one person I had to see first. You. I've apologized to everyone else and done my damndest to fix things. You're the one I can't forget and the one I owe the most to."

"And you're convinced one night will do the fixing?" A big naive on Carsten's part, if he did say so.

"No, but it would prove to both of us that we should've given each other a chance back in the day. I believe it could work now, too." Carsten sat up and lowered his foot, but kept his hand folded. "If that kiss was any indication, you feel it, too."

"What if I do?" He'd almost said he did. God, he had to get a hold of himself. "You'll leave tomorrow. That's not the way I operate. I'm not a one-night-stand kind of guy."

"That's another reason Stan left, isn't it?"

"What's that supposed to mean?" Carsten had cut too close to the bone for Will's comfort.

"I've known a few men like Stan and I've never actually met him. They want what they want for now, demand they get it, then when you can't deliver because it's either impossible or decidedly unfair, they jump ship. They want what they want and no one can make them happy." Carsten shook his head once. "For me, it was Kip."

"I'm sorry. Truly." He didn't wish the hell Stan had put him through on anyone.

"Kip met me after a show. I hadn't come out yet, but everyone around me knew. They weren't happy, but as long as I kept it quiet, they dealt. Kip wanted to be with me, for what I *thought* was me. Turned out he played the long game and was only hanging on because he thought I'd get him a recording contract. Hang around the concerts, meet people, show up on a record or two, get some credibility and parlay it into something for himself. It almost worked."

The wistfulness in Carsten's voice stuck in Will's mind. So did the story. "What happened?" He hated to admit Carsten had him riveted.

"I overheard him giving the same speech he'd given me the night we'd met."

"Who was he talking to?" He rested his chin on his hand. The last time he'd been able to simply talk to someone like this and forge a ... was this a friendship? It sure felt like the start of friendship.

"Howland Moore, the guy currently at the top of the country music charts."

He'd heard of him. He wasn't familiar with the artist's music, but he'd heard the name. "Okay?"

"He couldn't get me to do what he wanted, so he got Howland to do it for him. Howland doesn't seem to care that he's being used. He'll probably toss Kip aside in a month. That's how he works. Not me."

"No?" Will wished he could take the blurted question back as soon as he asked it.

"I have that coming. I've been a dick in the past

and I'll work for the rest of my life to make up for it," Carsten said. "He wanted to use me and when I didn't let him, he moved on. I'm glad he's out of my life, but I'm not glad I got my heart broken. I actually liked him."

"I'm sorry."

"So am I." Carsten stared at him. "But the situation taught me to be more observant. I realized just how much of a dick I'd been and it was a turning point. I didn't want to be the man I'd been for the last almost thirty years. I wanted to be better. Someone people could look up to. Someone a man wanted to love. Someone I could respect."

"You are." He was as a musician and a man.

"I'm trying." Carsten didn't speak, but instead seemed to appraise him. His eyes shimmered and a slight smile pulled at his lips.

Something had changed between him and Carsten. He wasn't sure what, but things were different.

"What do you say? Are you interested in giving me a chance?" Carsten asked. "At least for one night? You're convinced I'm the same dick I was before and I would love the chance to welcome you into my world, to show you I've changed and to give that spark I know is burning between us a chance to blossom."

He hesitated. He wanted to believe Carsten would respect him, but he'd been burned. Did Carsten deserve the chance to prove himself?

Didn't everyone?

"Well?" Carsten asked. "What do you say?"

He had to answer. Had to make up his mind. Go with his gut and push Carsten away, or give in to the simmering passion and give him a chance? It was time to do something for himself. "Yes."

Carsten snorted. Will would have to make him

wait. Nothing would be easy with him. But that was okay because he'd wait for someone that special. He'd waited this long. A few more minutes hadn't killed him. Now he had the chance to have a night with Will.

He'd dreamed of this moment for so long. Dreamed of the chance to touch him, to caress him and find out if the passion was something that could last.

He pulled the backstage pass from his pocket and offered the card to Will. "Put this on and wear it wherever you want around the arena. If anyone questions you, show the pass and they'll let you through. Promise. If anyone has a problem with it, then ask for Leroy and he'll fix it."

"I don't need a fixer," Will said. "I don't have to have special access."

"I would like you to join me during the warm-ups and after the show. The only way you'll get back, other than the ridiculous stickers the radio stations pass out, is to have the pass." Being a semi-public figure was a pain in the ass sometimes.

"Oh." Will accepted the plastic card on the lanyard. "You're really famous, aren't you?"

"I had four number one songs and a number one record." He hadn't believed he was famous. Just a guy who got lucky and could make music for a living. "I would love it if you'd come to the concert and see what I do. You've made me look damn good in that poster. Now give me the chance to show you I'm not the confused young man you remember."

Will exhaled. "I have appointments with students today, but I'll keep it in mind." He toyed with the pass. "Thanks."

"You're welcome, but I should be thanking you. If I had my way, I'd have you do all my promotional art. You're fantastic."

"You don't have to butter me up." A smile flashed across Will's face. "You've got sound checks, don't you?"

"You know the lingo?" And his schedule? Interesting.

"I've gone to some of the concerts and a few of the professors here in the art department have a band, so I know they have to do sound checks. On a much smaller scale, I'm sure." Will finally smiled. "And I might have looked at your schedule in the information Marissa gave me so I knew when and where to avoid you."

"Do you still want to avoid me?" Based on that kiss, he'd bet not.

"No," Will said. "I'm still wary, but not totally willing to avoid."

"I'll take it." He'd been given an inch—more than he deserved. "I'll see you later?"

"I'll think about it."

"I'd like it if you did." He winked, then forced himself from Will's office. The place had more of Will's personality than he'd expected. The splashes of color, the eccentric lamp with the multicolored glass shade, the thick rug and books all over the place. He knew Will loved to read, but the things he hadn't expected in the small office were the three laptops and the drawing board with the male nude displayed on it. Sexy man, no less, but it made conversation hard. Thinking about Will made him hard, too. He wanted to run his hands over Will's thin body and learn the planes and nuances of him.

He'd been a fool to treat Will so poorly in the past. Will would've been an asset. Hell, they might even have gotten together and could even still be a couple all these years later. Damn. Realizing that made him want Will even more. Made him want to forge the relationship even more, too. He'd get his chance. He just knew it.

Carsten tugged his hat down and ducked as he left the art building. He doubted anyone would really recognize him on campus. According to the schedule plastered on the fan pages, he should be chilling out in his bus right now, not roaming free. He'd planted the news to allow him time to seek out Will. Sometimes, he appreciated his savvy with social media.

"You're him." A young woman rushed up to him. "I know you are. You're here early."

He stopped short. "Hi."

She fumbled in her backpack, then retrieved a pen and piece of paper. "I'd ask for a selfie with you, but you don't do them." She thrust the implements at him. "For Stephy."

"Sure." He scribbled his name onto the paper, then added the words *To Steph.* "Spell it."

"Oh." She shrugged. "S-T-E-P-H-Y."

"Thanks." He added the Y, then *with love*. "There you go." He offered the pen and paper to her. "Will you be at the concert tonight?"

"Wouldn't miss it." She stuffed the items into her bag. "I love the comedy show."

"Comedy?" He liked to joke with the band, but it wasn't a comedy show.

"Oh, yeah. The trainwreck that's your career. You tanked it when you came out." She shrugged again. "You know no one's coming to hear the music. They're coming to see what you'll do."

"Play music." He nodded to her and winked. "I'm glad you'll be there. See you at the concert." He walked off at a brisk pace. He wasn't in the mood to deal with another fan tonight.

Once he reached the venue, he ducked in one of the back doors, then made his way to the stage. The band was already there and setting up. Dorian, the soundman, rapped his knuckles on the stage.

"Are we about ready? I know you just got here, but we have everything set up for you." Dorian flattened his hand. "Should be plug and play, but we need to do the checks."

"You bet." He picked up his favorite guitar and ran through his finger exercises. He loved playing and hadn't done the exercises in so long. Stretching his abilities this way pleased him. He'd rather have Will there watching, but he couldn't be sure Will would show up.

"Great." Dorian hurried back to the soundboard.

Within half an hour, Carsten had limbered up and Dorian had his levels. Carsten jammed with the band for another few minutes, running through some of the songs on the playlist. It'd been so long since he'd played simply for fun, not to pay the bills. He loved the thrill of making music. Songs filled his head and some weren't even from the playlist. A new tune added to the mix. He hadn't heard this one before. He'd have to write it down when he got the chance.

He finished the jam session, then left his guitar on the stand. "Nathan?"

His slide guitar player glanced over his shoulder. "What's happening?"

"Someone knew we were here." He sank onto the stool next to Nathan. "She said she was coming to watch the comedy act."

"Goddamn." Nathan folded his arms. "That's harsh."

"Is she right?" He didn't want to think so.

"She's not, but she was trying to get a response out of you. The papers want dirt on you. The word got out that you're looking for the guy you went to school with and you're expecting to meet him here. They want to see you get a happy ending. She probably wanted to tip them off."

"You could be right." He hadn't thought of that.

"It might have gotten out that you treated that guy like shit in the past and you're trying to make amends, too." Nathan moved the guitar aside. "Are you really tying to make up for what you did?"

"I am." He might as well be honest. If the word was out, then it was. "I used to tease him pretty good when we were teenagers. I thought it would make him like me if I made fun of him. It was stupid and stereotypical and I wish I hadn't done it. I was miserable back then. My parents hated me for being gay, I didn't like my life and I wanted someone to hurt, too."

"That's deep and rough." Nathan stood. He covered the guitar with a sheet, preparing for the show. "Is he even open to the idea of forgiving you?"

"Kind of?" He wasn't sure if Will had forgiven him. "We're talking at least."

"That's something." Nathan narrowed his eyes. "Did you invite him to the concert?"

"I did."

"That's romantic." Nathan grinned, then laughed and the sound echoed through the room. "I knew you could be. After Amber and that farce of an engagement you tried to have, I knew you could really be romantic and it sure looks like he means a lot to you. I hope he understands that and is open to giving you a chance."

"It would be nice, but I'm not banking on it." He knew better than to bet on something that wasn't guaranteed.

"If he shows up, I want you to point him out to me. I bet he's handsome," Nathan said. "He must be something special."

"He is." He considered his friend a moment.

"You're not upset that I'm gay? The rest of the original band hated it."

"They wanted to get paid and they thought you'd tank." Nathan stuffed his hands into his pockets. "I never cared either way because I know you're damn good on the mic and on the guitar. You hold your own and that's what matters. You're captivating on stage and your sexuality shouldn't make a difference. As long as you can entertain and bring in the crowds—which you can because tonight is sold out—then that's what matters. I want to play with someone who wants to play. You."

"Thanks, Nate." He appreciated his bandmate's honesty. "I wish I'd have known the truth."

"That's why we had to find the new band members. Your reputation wasn't as trashed as you think and the gang wanted to play on this tour."

"But that's why no one was honest with me, isn't it?" Carsten asked. "I thought they jumped ship because my sales were tanking and my reputation was in the toilet."

"Sadly, it's true for those guys, but not these. Look, I knew you were gay all along, Car. You've got to be true to yourself. The band is behind you and I'm on your side. We've got this." Nathan clapped him on the shoulder. "And if this guy is any kind of gentleman and he sees you for who you are now, then he's a fool if he doesn't snap you up."

He laughed and the tension left his body. "He is, and thank you."

"Let's get dressed for the show and grab something to eat. Before we know it, it'll be showtime." Nathan walked with him from the stage. "You've got to shine like a fucking diamond tonight."

"Damn right." He wanted to knock Will's socks off, pour his heart out with every song, and show his former rival that they were meant to be together all along. Not impossible, but quite the long shot.

Good thing he liked his odds.

Chapter Four

Will stood outside of the convention center and debated his next move. He could go inside and give his heart a chance to be happy. A piece of him craved Carsten. The man was everything, physically, he wanted. Tall, blond, handsome, and those eyes... He'd longed to investigate them back in high school and feel Carsten's arms around him. If he had known Carsten needed him, he would've given him a shoulder to cry on. He'd always been a sucker for Carsten and big goofy guys with sad eyes.

But part of him wanted to turn and walk away. Good God. Carsten had treated him so terribly. Like shit, really. He'd made fun of him in front of everyone, tried to push him into a locker or two, tripped him, and called him names. He'd been cruel.

Had he really changed?

Will shook his head. Why was he thinking so hard about this?

Because he couldn't forget that kiss. His skin tingled as he remembered the way Carsten took control, kissed him senseless, and made him feel safe. Made him feel treasured. He hadn't felt that way in so long.

"Are you going in or are you standing outside?" Stan opened the door leading from the overhead walkway into the foyer of the convention center. "I didn't think you liked country music."

He stared at his former lover. "What are you doing here?" The last time he'd spoken to Stan, his ex-boyfriend told him to get fucked and die.

"I like this guy. He's hot and out and on the market." Stan stepped into the foyer. "I thought I'd try to catch his eye."

"He'd be interested in you?" His hands shook. It was so like Stan to try to step in, even if he had no idea Will was interested in Carsten.

Holy shit. He was interested in Carsten.

Him being here wasn't a fluke. He wanted this one-nighter with Carsten. Even if it was only to get him out of his system. He wanted him.

"How could he turn me down?" Stan swept his hands over his body. "I'm in perfect shape, I'm available, and we'd be hot together."

"Right." He snorted. "Everyone is so attracted to you because you're hot. You think everyone wants you. Have you ever considered attraction has more to do with emotions and appearance, not just how you look? Have you considered anyone else's feelings but your own?"

"Why?" Stan rolled his eyes. "One look at me and he'll beg me to come backstage. I'm the arm candy he needs."

"Please." He didn't know Carsten well, but he knew Carsten wasn't going to fall for Stan.

"Are you jealous? You did have a hard time when we split," Stan said. "You do realize I needed to move on. I wanted someone who could stand up to me and wasn't going to bend over all the time. Someone with some confidence."

"You're an asshole." He'd been pushed around for long enough and wasn't about to lose this chance with Carsten—not even for Stan. "I had plenty of confidence until you showed up in my life. You tore me down and ripped out my heart, then thought I should let you back in. I'll never date you again. I know my worth and you're a fucking waste." He surged past Stan through the foyer to the security team scanning tickets. He pulled the pass from his pocket and offered over the code.

"You've got a backstage pass?" Stan rushed up to

him. "Take me with you."

"Sorry, sir. This pass is for one and exclusively states Mr. Rohr. This way, Professor." The guard ushered him through the door, closing it just as Stan tried to follow.

"You need to bring me along," Stan shouted.

Will wanted to look back but didn't. He refused to lower himself to Stan's level. Besides, he'd come to the realization he wanted to spend at least one night with Carsten. For all he knew, nothing would happen, but if the kiss was any indication of the attraction, then he was in for something fantastic.

"Where do I go?" Will asked the guard. "I've never had such a pass and attended the basketball games as a spectator."

"This way. I'll show you." The guard led him through the building to the main floor and up to the stage. "Let the guys see your pass and you'll get the rest of the way to your seat."

"Thank you." He hesitated. "You were in my digital design class, weren't you?"

"I was." The guard grinned. "I had to quit college to raise my daughter, but I loved that class. I use what I learned to create graphics for the school security team."

"Good. I'm glad you're able to use it. Thanks for helping me." He swore the guard's name was Tate, but didn't want to call him that if it wasn't.

"Enjoy the concert." The guard walked away, leaving him at the velvet rope leading to the gated area.

"You must be the boy toy." Another guard, this one in all black, unclipped the rope. "There's only one of those passes and I haven't seen Car give it out lately. You must be special. This way, Mr...?"

"Rohr." He followed the second guard through the area to a space cordoned off with black curtains. "You're permitted to be in here."

"I am?" This was so complicated. He ducked into the secluded space. No one else was in the area. This had to be wrong.

"The woman and her friend who won the radio contest will be joining you, as well as the dean and her wife. I believe another couple have a special pass, too." The guard dipped his head, then left Will alone.

Will rubbed his hands on his pant legs. This was wrong. He didn't belong in such a special area. He wasn't special.

"Will." Carsten gestured to him from the other side of the curtained-off space. "Come here. I didn't think you'd show up."

"I wasn't going to, but something drew me here." He crossed the expanse to Carsten. "Shouldn't you be warming up?"

"I will in a minute." Carsten tugged him through the curtains to the other side. People milled around and guards waited while Carsten kept walking. He didn't let go of Will's hand. "You're supposed to be backstage with me."

"I am?" He kept asking that, but the whole situation was surreal. "Carsten."

"I know. It's too much, right?"

"Yes." He stopped short. "We just started talking and I'm still scarred about the way you treated me. Who says I wanted to be backstage? I just wanted to listen a while." God, he was lying, but he wasn't ready to let Carsten off the hook so easily.

"I..." Carsten paled, then sighed. "Tell me that attraction isn't palpable."

He folded his arms. "What if it's not?" He couldn't help but lie because he wasn't ready to give in yet.

"That kiss meant nothing?" Carsten's eyes flashed.

He winced. Shit. He'd pushed too far and would feel the sting of Carsten's rotten nature again.

"Will?" Carsten curled his fingers under Will's chin. "Wait. I thought there was a spark. Thought you'd give me a chance. I blew it, didn't I?"

He measured his words carefully. "You've blown it for a long time."

Carsten nodded, then hooked his fingers into Will's front pocket. He said nothing and tugged Will into a dressing room.

"Where is everyone else?" Will tensed as the silence enveloped him. "Carsten?"

"I have a lifetime to make up for the shit I've done and I want to do it right now." He dropped to his knees before Will. "Let me prove I'm not the same man."

"Carsten?" He swore the world spun as he gazed down at Carsten. This man, the one who'd bullied him so many times in school, was on his knees before him.

Carsten fumbled with the buckle on Will's belt, then popped the button on his jeans. He fixed his gaze on Will's as he tugged the zipper. When he licked his lips, Will groaned.

"Gonna make you fly." Carsten pushed the front of Will's boxers down, exposing his cock and balls. "My God. The quiet ones are always packing."

His cheeks flamed and he moaned. "Carsten." This wasn't happening, yet he didn't want to miss a moment. He threaded his fingers into Carsten's hair. "If you're going to do this, kiss me first." He needed to feel that kiss again.

Carsten managed to stand and slipped his arms around Will. "My pleasure." He snagged Will's mouth in a kiss and stole his breath at the same time.

Will wanted to fight this. Wanted to fight and not melt into him, but damn. This kiss was everything he'd ever dreamed a kiss could be—sexy, hot, craving, and full of passion. He sucked on Carsten's tongue, learning his taste and the scent of him. He opened his eyes to memorize every detail of the moment.

Carsten whimpered and shoved his hands under the hem of Will's shirt. With one hand he caressed Will's back and with the other he toyed with Will's nipple.

Christ in Heaven. Will wouldn't be able to handle this. No way. He'd combust first. He couldn't wrap his head around the fact that this person had teased him and been terrible toward him, but now teased him in a great way, making him want more.

He wrenched his mouth away and panted. "Carsten." He couldn't think straight.

"Like that?" Carsten tweaked Will's nipple. "I crave you."

He nodded, unable to form a coherent sentence.

"I need more of you." Carsten sank to his knees again, then cupped Will's balls in one hand. He wrapped his free hand around Will's shaft before smearing the pre-cum on the blunt head of Will's erection on his mouth.

Seeing Carsten on his knees with his lips shiny from pre-cum was just about the sexiest thing Will had ever seen. Will embraced the power in his veins, knowing he was making Carsten happy, and threaded his fingers into Carsten's hair again. He groaned as he rocked his hips.

"Yes." Carsten sucked him into his mouth and met Will's gaze. Pink infused his cheeks and fire lit in his eyes. He bobbed his head with abandon, taking him deep before nearly withdrawing. Within minutes, he worked into a steady rhythm and the passion in his eyes increased.

Will kept his fingers in Carsten's hair, allowing Carsten to set the pace, but also fully joining in on the fun. He panted and widened his stance a bit. The sensations running through his body were more than he could handle. Blood coursed through his veins and the tingles settled in his dick. He wanted to strip naked and allow Carsten to have his way with him.

A ragged cry stuck in his throat. He couldn't breathe.

Carsten increased the ferocity of his bobbing, then raked his teeth along Will's shaft. He buried his nose in Will's short curls before pulling back and withdrawing long enough to suck on Will's balls.

"Jesus." Will bit back a moan. He'd never last. Not like this. He tugged lightly on Carsten's hair. "More."

Without a word, Carsten resumed sucking on Will's shaft. This time, he moved with more gusto and hummed.

The sound, compared with the heat in his veins and the desire coursing through his body, overwhelmed him. Will cried out. "Fuck, Carsten." He bowed his head and closed his eyes. He needed the second to think and keep himself in check.

Why the fuck was he trying to hold back the orgasm?

He wanted the moment to last. Why? He might not get another.

Carsten pulled back again. "Let go for me, Will. Come apart."

He hadn't needed much encouragement, but Carsten's words sent him right to the edge. Holding back wasn't going to happen. He cried out again and rammed his dick into Carsten's mouth. The way Carsten curled his tongue around his shaft pushed Will the last bit over the edge. Will trembled as he embraced the orgasm and came down Carsten's throat.

The world seemed to move around him, but his little corner went at a snail's pace. His head swam as he opened his eyes. He gazed down at Carsten. If anyone would've told him his life would change this much and he'd reconnect in a good way with Carsten, he'd have laughed. He wobbled as Carsten licked him clean. Carsten withdrew again, but this time he helped Will to one of the overstuffed chairs.

Will sank into the plush material and stared at Carsten. "Wow."

"Yeah?" Carsten winked. "That's only the beginning."

Holy shit. If that was the beginning, then he'd never survive the middle and end.

Who needed survival anyway?

****

Carsten stayed between Will's knees with him as he came down from the orgasmic high. He loved that he was able to give Will this pleasure. It wasn't nearly enough to make up for the years of torment he'd given Will, but he'd gladly work to balance things out. Hell, he might even work for the rest of his life on it—if Will would let him.

"Carsten." Will scrubbed the back of his hand across his mouth. "You're due on stage soon."

"I've got another fifteen minutes." Carsten sat back on his heels. "The opening act is warming up the crowd."

"Oh." Will nodded and his lips remained parted a bit.

"I never thought you'd show up. I had hope, but I didn't believe you'd come through because I didn't think I deserved it." Carsten massaged Will's thighs. "I'm glad you're here."

"Uh-huh." Will sighed and blinked a few times. "I need to put my dick back before someone comes in here and catches us."

"They won't." If they did, he'd fire them. Carsten licked his lips. He loved the lingering taste of Will with him. "This is my time to center before the concert. Everyone leaves me alone."

"Oh." Will managed to tuck his cock behind his underwear and zip his jeans. "Good to know."

"It is." He stared at Will. "You're not used to doing things like that—being blown backstage at a concert."

"No." Will sat up a bit straighter and righted his shirt. "I'm not the kind of guy who has one-night stands, either."

"There's nothing wrong with that." He rather liked knowing Will was a relationship kind of guy. He could use the stability in his life.

"Are you a relationship guy?" Will asked. "We've gone a million miles an hour and haven't had a chance to really talk."

"No, I guess we haven't." He sat back on the floor and crossed his legs. "What do you want to know?"

Will toyed with the thick silver bracelet around his wrist. "What's your favorite color, favorite song ... do you have other dreams than music? Do you want to fall in love? Do you regret what happened? I don't know."

"You do." He let the questions wash over him a moment. "My favorite color is black because it goes with everything and I have yet to see a man who doesn't look good in black. My favorite song is 'Rhapsody in Blue.' I know, it's nothing like what I'd normally listen to or play, but it's a beautiful song and I love the way it swells and ebbs. Brings a tear to my eye. I bet you wouldn't have expected that."

A wistful look filled Will's eyes. A half-smile curled at the corner of his mouth. "No, I didn't. You're much more than I ever thought you'd be."

"So are you," Carsten said. "To answer the rest of your questions, I do regret what I did and how I conducted myself. I wish I'd have come out earlier and been true to myself. I also wish I'd have told you I liked you, rather than treating you like shit. As for falling in love, I have but he had no idea. I never had the guts to tell him."

"That's sad, but sweet. I bet if he knew, he'd be honored."

"Because of my position?"

"Because you're more than you give yourself credit for and it has nothing to do with your celebrity." Will scooted forward in the chair and offered his hand. "Who is he? We should get you connected with him."

"You'd never believe me if I told you." His heart hammered. Will wanted him to be honest. Doing so would be the biggest gamble of his life. He'd fallen in love with Will back in school and never forgot the attraction. Seeing him now proved those feelings hadn't died. They'd grown stronger with time.

"I bet I can guess. Someone from your previous band?"

"You knew I had a new band?"

"I might have done some research on you when I was working on the poster art." Will half-shrugged. "So, someone from your band? Nelson?"

"No." He hadn't been attracted to his drummer. "I don't mind tattoos, but I don't want to kiss a smoker."

"Oh." Will nodded slightly. "Klay?"

He shook his head. "He's married and has three

kids. He's devoted to his wife and I believe they're trying for a fourth kid." Besides, he wasn't interested in a fiddler.

"Huh." Will sank back in his seat and frowned. "Someone from school? Or someone you dated while you were in the closet?"

"Both." He didn't want to make Will guess for much longer, but Will seemed to be having so much fun.

Will narrowed his eyes and crinkled the corner of his mouth. "Whoever he is, then, he's a lucky man."

"Why do you say that?" He wanted full honesty again. He'd already made up his mind, but he still wanted to hear the words.

"Even after a few hours, I can tell you've changed. You know what you did in the past wasn't the best and you're trying to make up for it. That's huge. It's also huge because you're wearing your heart on your sleeve. I admire that," Will said. "That's why whoever is with you and whoever is the object of your affection is lucky."

"You're observant." But he'd always known that about Will. Will might have acted the part of the social butterfly, but he had a keen sense of observation and a tender heart.

"I call them how I see them." Will leaned forward again. "You've made strides since we were in school— expected, since that's ten years ago."

"Over."

"Over," Will repeated. He grinned. "Who is it? Who is this lucky man? I want to know who to avoid."

"Why?" He didn't want to put any more space between him and Will.

"You just gave me head. Once this guy finds out you're interested, he's not going to want to share you with anyone and I don't want him to get the wrong idea.

You're not in love with me. He's the one you want. I'm just a hot time backstage."

"You're never just anything," Carsten said. "Not when you're the one I fell in love with. Yeah, you." Let him chew on that.

Chapter Five

Will stared at Carsten. Carsten was in love with him? He had to be hearing him wrong. Had to. Carsten wasn't in love with him. It was a joke. A farce. A lie to get him to sleep with him tonight.

"When I was eighteen, I wasn't smart enough to know I'd done something wrong. I wasn't savvy enough to admit my truth. I'm not that kid. I didn't come here to Northern to play just because I had to rehab my image. This is the last stop on the tour for a month and I chose this college because I wanted to see you. I wanted the chance to pour out my heart and soul in person and on stage. I didn't ask you to give me tonight just because I wanted to fuck. I did it because I wanted the chance to be with you."

Will reeled. He had to be hearing this wrong. Carsten ... nothing made sense, yet it felt so right.

A knock on the door split the silence in the room. "Car? It's nearly time to go on. The band is playing the last song and our guys are getting ready in the wings."

"Who is that?" Will whispered.

"Frank, my stage manager." Carsten stood. He offered his hand to Will. "I'd love it if you'd watch me play. I saw all your productions and concerts. You might have thought I hated you, but I didn't. I was transfixed."

Will allowed Carsten to tug him to his feet. "Every one of them?"

"Uh-huh. You were fantastic as Tommy in *Brigadoon* and the sexiest Scarecrow in *The Wizard of Oz*." Carsten winked. "I need to head out. Frank will show you to your seat. I promise it'll be a great show."

"I had no doubts." He reached for Carsten's hand, moving on instinct. When he grasped Carsten's fingers, electricity shot through his body again. For a second, he was transported back to high school, but not the one they'd attended. A better version. The version where he and Carsten were together. Where they were a team and could face anything. A place where he and Carsten were a couple, just as they should've been all along. "I can't wait."

Carsten beamed. "Neither can I." He kissed Will, lingering a moment before stepping back. A warmth filled his eyes and a blush spread across his cheeks.

"Have a great show." Will didn't want to release his grasp on Carsten's fingers, but he had to let him leave. The crowd didn't want to see him show up late. Will stayed back, giving Carsten time to take the stage.

Frank stood in the doorway after Carsten left and grinned. "So you're the infamous Will."

"Should I be afraid that you know my name?" Or that he was infamous? "I created the art for the show."

"The posters, I know." Frank's grin widened. "You've also been the inspiration for at least a third of his musical catalog. He's been inspired by you for so long."

"You're joshing me." He shrugged. He wanted to say something snappy, but the words didn't come. "He's not that taken with me."

"He is. When you listen to him tonight, think about who he's singing for. It's not the woman in his life. Not his latest boyfriend. It's deep, longing love … it's for you." Frank waved his hand. "This way. You've got a performer to inspire."

"I guess I do." He followed Frank back to the curtained-off area where two velvet-covered seats waited. "Am I sitting with anyone else?"

"Nope. This is all for you. He wanted to be sure you'd be comfortable. I guess he thought you'd have someone with you. Good thing you don't." Frank lingered another moment. "Do you want a drink or anything? Snacks?"

"A beer?" He hadn't known he could get anything. "How much?" He withdrew his wallet.

"You should know better than that. Whatever you want is on the house." Frank left, then returned a moment later with a bottle of beer. "Just don't throw it at him."

"No." Why would he do that? He wasn't without manners. Jesus. "Thank you." He debated sitting or standing. The chairs sure looked comfy, but wasn't it concert etiquette to stand? This wasn't an instrumental concert. He could stand, dance, and cheer if he so desired.

The second the curtain rose, the spotlight shone on the lead guitarist as the music swelled. Will's excitement increased. He'd never been to a concert like this. The electricity was palpable. The guitarist played, then nodded over his shoulder. The larger set of curtains parted and the spotlight converged right on Carsten. Seeing him on stage stole Will's breath.

No wonder Carsten was a star. He oozed power and charisma. The more he listened to Carsten sing, the more he fell under his captivating spell. He swayed to the music and drank in the atmosphere. Carsten knew how to work the crowd, singing to the attendees not only in the first row, but throughout the arena.

Will sank onto the chair and embraced the sexual magnetism coming from Carsten. He'd thought he was immune to Carsten's charms, but he hadn't been. No blowjob could cement his feelings this way. He hadn't been with Carsten as a simple tryst. Something deeper had happened. Was he in love? Hardly. But he'd known this man for a long time and saw the changes within him. Carsten wasn't that kid from school. He might be cutthroat in the music business—Will wasn't sure—he hadn't been around him during business meetings. But his heart was different. He knew his shortcomings and had tried to make up for them.

Before he knew it, the concert ended and Carsten ducked backstage as the lights dimmed. The crowd didn't leave. Instead, they chanted his name. Will glanced around, expecting either the crowd to jump the stage or for Carsten to return.

The lights came up slowly, but Carsten wasn't on stage. His slide guitarist and the drummer sat on stools. The drummer played a small set of bongos while the guitarist strummed a regular guitar. Will didn't know most of Carsten's music, but this song sounded different.

The crowd cheered more and the lights dowsed again. When the spotlight came up, it focused right on Carsten.

"I wrote this song a few weeks ago and we've been tweaking it ever since. The guys don't know who it's for, but I do. We're still working on it and it's a little rough, but bear with us." Carsten sat on the stool between them. "This is called 'Redeem My Heart'." He broke into the first verse of the song.

Will paused. A new song for someone … the second he heard the title, he knew. Carsten met his gaze and winked. Carsten sang:

"I came, I saw, I messed things all to hell.

I let my pride rule my life, despite knowing all too well.

You showed me how to be a man. How to love who I am.

My heart is in your hands.

I can't change how things have been but if you're ready, I need you.

Redeem my heart, I know you can. Redeem my

heart and be my man."

How could he resist? Will rose to his feet and moved to the leading edge of the curtained-off space. He held onto the railing. He was falling in love. He'd need lots of time and they'd have to sort out how this romance would happen, but he'd fallen.

Will remained at the railing for the rest of the concert and swayed with the songs. When the lights went out the last time, then came up to full brightness, he sighed. What an experience. He'd never be the same. Everything that had happened—the song, the blowjob, the revelations from Carsten—had changed him. He wanted to redeem Carsten's heart and keep it in his hands. Did he deserve it? No, but he didn't care. He liked that Carsten had chosen him.

Frank gestured to him. "I was supposed to come get you before the contest winners got to see him, but they were better organized this time." He shrugged. "He's dying to see you."

"After that song and declaration, I'd assume so." Will followed him, moving the curtain aside.

"How come he gets to go there?" a woman shouted. "We should get to see Carsten, too."

Will didn't look back, but tensed. He should've expected Carsten would get come-ons like this.

"Ignore them. There are all sorts of people trying to get backstage. They think if they shout and demand, someone will give in." Frank tugged the curtain into place. "The guys are on the other side of the velvet ropes surrounding the curtains. No one will get through."

"I wasn't worried they would." He continued to follow Frank. "They think they should have access?"

"Some want to declare their love for him, some want him to declare he loves them, and others just want to touch him or steal things." Frank knocked on the door.

When no one answered, he nodded once, then opened the door. "He's in the next room and will be over in a moment."

"Sure." He wasn't sure what to do with himself. Sit? Stand? Wander? He rubbed his hands on his pant legs and excitement thundered through his veins. His nerves frayed. He'd never been this on the edge before when he wasn't having sex. He didn't want to screw this up.

A moment later, the door opened. He whirled around to see Carsten. Sweat slicked his forehead and a blush infused his cheeks. His eyes widened and his lips parted. "Hi." Carsten sank onto the closet chair. "Good show?"

"The best." He marveled at Carsten. He'd never seen anyone sexier in his life. For all he knew, this would be his one night with Carsten, but he had the feeling it was only the beginning.

****

Carsten needed a few more minutes to catch his breath. He'd put his entire heart and soul into the show. "The fans demand a lot of attention. I must've signed a hundred autographs and posed for four dozen photos."

"I'm surprised it wasn't more pictures." Will dragged the wooden chair over and sat across from Carsten. "You were electric."

"You're biased." He brushed his knee against Will's and the thrill of touching him shot through him again. Singing about his feelings hadn't dulled them. Far from it. Singing about his attraction to Will only made it stronger.

"A bit."

He liked hearing that. "So you liked it?"

"You commanded the stage and were hard to look away from. You held my full attention." Will slid one of

Carsten's hands into his. "I felt the longing, the desire, and every other emotion when you sang."

"Then I did my job." Carsten patted his thigh. "I don't have the right to demand you come here, but I'd love it if you did."

"You have all sorts of rights." Will perched on Carsten's lap. "What don't you think you can do?"

"Kiss you." Carsten slid his fingers around the back of Will's neck and tugged him closer. "I want you." He'd been bold in his song, but speaking his mind felt right. Holding Will felt even better. He caressed Will, shoving his hand under Will's shirt. The second he touched Will's chest, his own heart raced. The scent of Will intoxicated him. He longed to taste him all over. The more he looked into Will's eyes, the more he fell for him. Sure, things happened for a reason, but he never should've taken so long to get with Will.

"Who says you can't have me?" Will asked. "I never said you couldn't."

"You did." But arguing with him wasn't going to get them anywhere.

"I did, but I've changed my mind. I heard every word you sang to me and I want to see where this goes."

He had to be dreaming, but he didn't care. He needed this chance with Will. "Then come to my hotel room tonight."

"Not the bus?" Will's eyes flashed. "Don't you do that sort of thing on the bus?"

"Not with half of the band right there." He squeezed Will's ass. "I like my privacy when I'm with the hottest guy I've ever known."

Will blushed. "I'm not the hottest."

"Want to bet?"

Will's blush increased. "I don't believe you, but I like the flattery."

"You deserve it." He patted Will's ass again. "Up. I want to take you to my place."

"Temporary." Will stood, then grasped Carsten's hands. "I want to take you to mine. If you're going to do this, then let's do this right. No hotels."

He liked the way Will thought. Plus, he wanted the chance to enter Will's inner sanctum. "Lead the way."

"Don't we need an escort?" Will asked. "I didn't bring my car. I'm still parked in the staff lot behind the art building."

"We can walk." Carsten let go of Will's hands, then tugged his sweaty concert shirt off. He grabbed another shirt from his bag, then donned a long-sleeved one over top of his undershirt. He picked up the rest of his clothes and jammed them into the bag.

"Do you need to clean up?" Will asked. "Let me help you."

"Stop." He'd done this a hundred times and wasn't about to let Will clean up after him. He checked the dressing table, then shoved the rest of his belongings into the bag. "I have to do this after every concert."

"I bet you used to have someone who did it." Will folded his arms. "Cleaned up after everything you did."

"You're correct. When I took a step back and looked at my life, I realized I could do my own dirty work. I didn't need so many assistants because I could handle my own shit."

"And it got too expensive when that shit hit the fan?" Will asked. He crooked his brow.

"You're too smart for me." He zipped the bag shut. "I have it coming. After the way I behaved, you shouldn't talk to me."

"Then I'd be alone and bored." Will shrugged. "You're more fun."

"I hope so." He ensured he had his phone and

wallet. "I'm ready."

"For?"

"Whatever you've got in store for me." He slid his arm around Will. "Now take me home and use me however you want."

"Don't say what you don't mean." Will led the way as they left the dressing room. "Where do we go? I don't know the bowels of this building."

"This way." He'd paid attention and memorized the directions when he'd paced the room preparing for the concert. He grasped Will's hand and tugged him through the labyrinth behind the stage to the rear door. The lights glittered and the trees lining the walkway threw shadows across their path.

Will tucked against him and fell into step with Carsten. "We're both so broken."

"We are." He caressed Will's shoulder. "Your ex was foolish for leaving you, but it's my good fortune. If I'd have been with you all this time, I'd have treated you better."

"You had to go through this journey to learn what you really want. I know I did." Will directed him across campus to the art building and the small lot behind the structure. "Here's my car."

He wasn't sure what he'd expected, but not the sports car. "This is yours?"

"I'm not allowed to have a fancy vehicle?"

"Not one so vintage or sporty." He waited as Will opened the passenger door of the black Jaguar, then Carsten placed his bag on the floor. He settled on the seat. "How do you keep it in such great shape?"

"A garage, and I can see the car from my office." Will closed the door, then rounded the hood. He sank onto the driver's seat. "That, and I've got one hell of a security system in it. If anyone touches it who isn't supposed to, the shrieking sound will split eardrums."

"Nice." He liked that Will took no prisoners with his car. He wanted to hold Will's hand, but saw that Will had to shift the car as he drove. "How far are you from campus?"

"Not far. Sometimes I ride my bike instead." Will drove out of the lot then wound along the streets of the college. Within a few minutes, he left campus and made his way down a tree-lined street to a simple Cape Cod home with an attached garage. "This is mine."

The house suited Will. Simple, but utilitarian and current.

Will pulled into the garage. "It's not fancy, but it's home." He parked, then shut the garage door. "Come inside?"

"You bet your ass I will." He hadn't even told his people he'd left the venue. He loved that he'd gone this far out on a limb with Will. The fear and excitement washed through him. For the first time in a long while— without music involved—he was having the best time. He chased Will into the house and stopped short in the kitchen. He swore he'd stepped right into the sixties. "What shade of blue are those cabinets?"

"Robin's-egg blue and white countertops. I know it's garish, but this was exactly the style in the house when I bought it and I can't bring myself to change it. I kind of like the funkiness." Will tossed his wallet, keys, and phone onto the counter. "At least I got rid of the carpeting."

"Good thing you did." He abandoned his wallet and phone with Will's then snagged Will in his arms. He pinned Will between his body and the counter. The second he had Will pressed against his body, he had to kiss him. Nothing else mattered.

Will eased his arms around Carsten and slid his

hands into Carsten's back pockets.

Carsten groaned. He grinded his hips against the growing bulge in Will's jeans. The scent of Will curled around him and the sounds of their combined groans filled the air. He couldn't breathe or think straight. All he wanted to do was make love to Will. He hefted Will onto the counter, then worked the buttons on Will's shirt.

There was so much he wanted to do and not enough time to make up for his mistakes. At least he had tonight.

Chapter Six

Will kissed Carsten, not wanting to miss a second. His balls were heavy and he needed release. When he nibbled on Carsten's bottom lip, desire filled his being. He pushed Carsten's shirt up, but Carsten stilled his hands.

"Want to see you." Carsten fumbled with the buttons on Will's shirt and caressed Will's chest. Within seconds, he helped Will out of the garment. "You're beautiful." He kissed along the planes of Will's chest and collarbone.

Will groaned. He'd never expected to hear such words from Carsten or to be in this moment, but he wouldn't trade it for anything. The second Carsten licked his nipple, his senses turned inside out.

Carsten tugged the button on Will's jeans. "Need to see you naked."

He wasn't about to argue with him. He propped himself on his hands and lifted himself up enough for Carsten to help him out of his jeans and underwear. Once he settled back on the counter, naked, Will shoved Carsten's overshirt off his shoulders.

He loved being naked for Carsten. A shiver ran along his spine. Being this way freed him.

"You have a tattoo?" Carsten grinned. "Since when?"

"Ten years ago." He'd forgotten all about the ink. "I wanted to look tough, but it doesn't look all that menacing." He tamped down his embarrassment. At the time, he thought the heart with numbers looked dangerous. Not so much now.

"Whoever said it wasn't tough is a dick. It's perfect." Carsten trailed his fingers over the ink high on

Will's thigh. "What do the numbers mean?"

"The date I came out." It was personal and close to his heart because he'd been true to himself.

"Beautiful."

"Carsten?" He hadn't expected to hear such things from him. Things were happening almost too perfectly. "I want to taste you."

"Later." Carsten resumed licking a path of fire along Will's chest. He gave special attention to Will's nipples, then down to his navel. At the same time, he stroked Will's shaft.

A strangled cry vibrated in his throat. "Feels so good."

"It'll get even better." Carsten shoved his pants to his ankles. He managed to kick out of his boots and wadded-up clothing to stand in his full naked glory before Will.

Will propped himself on his elbows and drank in the view before him. He loved Carsten's hard body, lean but muscled. God, he was strong. Carsten's upper arms were decorated in a collection of tattoos and had a sunburst tattooed around his navel. He had little body hair, but was fully erect.

Will's mouth watered. Carsten had girth and length … and if he knew how to use it, even better. "I need your cock."

"You can have it—after we find supplies."

Safety first, sure. He had to think straight. "In my bedroom." He wasn't like some men who had condoms and lube secreted all over his house. Hell, he hoped he still had supplies and hadn't run out being that he hadn't needed them in a while.

Carsten helped him off the counter, then chased him to the bedroom. When Will collided with the bed, Carsten collapsed on top of him. Will liked having the weight of Carsten on him.

"Where?" Carsten asked.

No finesse. Just desire. "Drawer." He tried to point in the right direction.

Carsten left him alone long enough to retrieve a condom and lube. When Carsten returned to the bed, Will rolled onto his back.

"Going to fuck me?" Will asked. He drew his knees to his chest in a silent invitation. "Please?"

"If I knew we'd get together and have so much fun, I'd have lost my fears back when we were in school." Carsten squirted lube onto his fingers and caressed Will's hole. He toyed and teased him, running the tip of his finger over the puckered skin. "I lost my nerve so many times, but I wanted to tell you all along that I craved you. Wanted to feel your hot body beneath mine, you riding me. I wanted to look into your eyes and feel like I'd come home."

Carsten's words struck a chord within him. They'd be his undoing. He relaxed as Carsten breached him.

"So tight." Carsten moaned. "I love it." He pumped his finger, pushing in and pulling out most of the way to prep Will.

So did he. Will rocked his hips, pulling more of Carsten into him. Being so vulnerable and having his mind so wide open pleased him. It was freedom, really. He could have everything he ever wanted.

What did he want?

Sex.

Not with anyone.

With Carsten.

Words filled his mind. Memories of the concert and the song Carsten sang played on a loop. The ice around his heart melted. He'd never really fallen out of love with Carsten, but this wasn't surface love. This wasn't teenage fantasy love, either. This was stronger. He'd need time to fully foment the love, but the start was there.

"Practically keeping me inside." Carsten kissed Will's right shin. "So fucking good. Better than I imagined."

"We haven't fucked yet." He knew damn well this could get so much better. He needed it.

"I know," Carsten said, his voice husky. "We will."

Will shivered and groaned. Goddamn. He couldn't wait for everything Carsten had to give.

He was ready.

****

Carsten panted. He loved the enthusiasm in Will's voice and also loved the way Will felt. Nothing was truly perfect—there were rough edges and scars on everyone—but he'd found someone who could accept him, imperfections and all. Will was that man.

Carsten withdrew his fingers and tore open the condom wrapper with his teeth.

"You'll kill your teeth that way." Will's eyes glittered.

"I know." He couldn't wait to be inside Will. He sheathed himself in seconds, then added more lube. "Ready?" he asked as he stroked himself.

"Born ready." Will exhaled and met Carsten's gaze. Light and hunger filled his eyes. He parted his lips.

"Good." He pressed the head of his dick against Will's hole. Excitement thundered through his veins. Desire overwhelmed him. The sizzle between him and Will was undeniable. He pushed slowly into Will. He'd dreamed of this moment for years. Unlike his dreams, reality was better than his imagination. He wasn't thrilled he'd waited for so long because he could've been loving Will all this time and had him in his life, but at least he'd finally made a move.

This was happening.

Will tensed as Carsten completely filled him. He shivered. "Oh, God."

"Yes?" Carsten began to thrust.

"Yes." Another groan vibrated in Will.

"Fuck." Carsten moved his hips, shoving to the hilt before pulling nearly all the way out. He built a steady rhythm. He leaned over Will and pressed his face to Will's neck, breathing him in. The healing in the act of making love filled his mind. His heart was stronger and his soul renewed.

All because of Will.

Within seconds, Carsten lost himself in the cadence of fucking Will. The man was still tight. Still delicious. When he looked into Will's eyes, he saw forever. He also heard the song he'd sang to Will tonight playing in his mind. Will did own his heart. He and Will had a long journey ahead, but he couldn't imagine having anyone else beside him for the ride. He pumped his hips, fucking Will with abandon.

"Oh, God. Love it." Will arched his back a bit and met him thrust for thrust. His cock bobbed between his legs.

"Stroke yourself for me. Get off with me." He continued to piston into Will. He held onto his lover's leg as Will curled his fingers around his own dick.

Will shivered again. He watched Carsten from under heavy-lidded eyes and stroked faster. He whimpered and the sound pleased Carsten.

Watching Will and knowing this had changed between them for the better, sent Carsten right to the edge. His thoughts centered around Will. He was at home and at peace with him. His mind at ease. Everything finally felt right.

"Fuck." Will dug his nails into his leg and tensed. "I need to come."

He continued to piston into Will. "Come with me." He didn't need much encouragement to climax. He was damn ready. "Do it."

Will said nothing. Instead, he cried out and yanked on his shaft. Cum spurted onto Carsten's chest in a hot streak.

Seeing and feeling Will come sent Carsten the last bit over the edge into oblivion. He surged into Will and remained there. This was where he wanted to be. He let go of Will's leg and sagged into him, smearing cum between them. He kissed Will, needing the extra closeness.

His soul was renewed and his past mattered, but it didn't define him.

He feathered kisses all over Will's face, making him chuckle.

Will threaded his arms around him. "You make this fun."

"What? Sex?"

"Second chances," Will replied.

Carsten let the words roll over him. That's exactly what he wanted. What he needed. The bully now ceased to exist. He'd been permitted to start over. "You redeemed my heart."

"For real?"

"For very real." He met Will's gaze. "Very."

A sad smile curled on Will's lips. "Good."

Not good. He wasn't done with Will at all. He pulled out and rolled onto the bed. Once he removed the condom and tossed the used rubber into the wastebasket, he turned over to face Will. "Why do you look so sad, handsome?"

"It's all over." Will's smile faded. "It is."

"What?"

"This. Us," Will said, choking out the words.

"No." Not a chance. He tucked Will to his chest. "Why would we be done?"

"Because you're a star and I'm a professor. I'm not leaving the college. I can't. It's the middle of the semester and you're in the midst of the tour. This is our one night and it's careening toward the end." Will blinked back tears. "When we were in school, I wanted two things—for you to leave me the hell alone so I could live my life, but also for you to see how much I secretly liked you. I wanted you to tell me you liked me as well. Now I know you did and I'll have to live with you leaving."

He laced his fingers with Will's and kissed his knuckles. "Slow down."

Will whimpered but didn't pull away.

"I wouldn't expect you to dump your life here at Northern. It's important and you're good at what you do. I admire your work and art. I also like you very much. I fell in love with you years ago and being with you tonight solidified those feelings. I want to make you proud."

"You do?"

"I do," he said. "I have to confess, though, that the tour is on a temporary hiatus."

"Why?"

"It was already planned, but I need a rest. I've been on tour for three years straight and it's time I took a break for some *me* time. Plus, I have a reason to rest. I want to see where this can go—you and me."

"You're serious?" Will asked. He propped himself up on his elbow and spread his free hand across Carsten's chest. "Car?"

"I am." He'd never been more serious in his life. "I've been a dick to you for too long and now that I've had a taste of you, I'm hooked. I need more. If it takes the rest of my life to prove my heart is yours, then I'll do it."

"I know you will," Will said. "I doubted you back then, but not any longer."

"You're willing to give us a chance?" Hope blossomed in his heart. "Will?"

"I am. It's crazy and this is happening quickly. I shouldn't trust or give you this chance, because you've hurt me in the past, but I know you're not the same guy you were before. You're not a bad guy."

"Not with you." He'd be a bulldog for Will, though.

"You were hurt so much when you were younger and I can't even begin to understand how you felt. I hate what you did to me, but you're a product of your raising. Now you're in control of yourself."

"I am." He found strength in Will because he was a good balance for him. An inspiration. "I'll need a place to stay. Might be nice to be close to campus, too. I'd like to take a class or audit them or whatever it's called." He'd never gone to college and wanted the chance to try it.

"Oh? You'd audit a class?"

"I would," he said. "And be close."

"To what?"

"You."

Will beamed. "You could probably teach some music classes."

He'd never considered that, but it sounded like a great idea. Teaching songwriting would be a good stretch for him. "I'd love that, but I need a suggestion as to where to live. I've called the bus my home for the last three years."

"I have a guest room," Will replied. "It's a start."

"Sure is." Close to Will, too. He wanted to move in right now.

"If you're planning on sticking around, you should get comfortable and sleep. I'm not going anywhere and you might want to get a feel for the area," Will said. He settled next to Carsten. "Life is funny, isn't it?"

"It is." Carsten snuggled up to him. He'd work out the living arrangement details later, but he had a direction and a plan for his future. He had a chance because he'd been redeemed.

Now he could move forward.

****

One Year Later

Carsten closed the notebook as the literature class concluded. He'd been at Northern University for two semesters and loved every second. He'd never thought he had what it took to be a teacher, but when he worked with the students in the music department in the songwriting classes, he found a purpose. He loved working with the students to hone their craft.

He even liked the classes on writing he'd audited because he'd learned so much.

The press hadn't hounded him and the students rarely did either. He could be himself and stretch. Hell, he couldn't imagine a better life.

He pushed the notebook into his satchel and allowed the day's discussion to percolate in his mind. He truly grasped why he'd been such a jerk in the past and why he needed to make up for it. Reading the stories of pain and redemption helped him, too.

"Are you going to sit there until the janitor sweeps you up?" Will asked. He sat beside Carsten. "I hear you're doing well in this class."

"I am." He draped the strap of the bag across his body. "What're you doing here?" He'd expected to see him at home for dinner.

He'd spent the last year getting to know Will all over again and falling deeper in love with him. He'd moved into the guest room, but quickly moved over to Will's bedroom. They'd created a homey life together. It was more than he could've believed he'd have.

Tonight, he needed to bare his soul to Will. It was time.

"I came here because you got a certified letter at the house." Will offered an envelope. "And the media is outside. They're trying to get in to see you."

"Why?" He hadn't done anything to warrant a certified letter. Hadn't been given a speeding ticket, caused trouble on or off campus or anything. He opened the letter and scanned the words. Shock ran through his system. "Well, shit. I've been nominated for a music award in the category of 'best song.' Seems my song, 'Redeem My Heart,' was used in a movie and gained the attention of the music business." He knew the song had been used, but he hadn't realized anyone had taken such notice of his ballad.

"Oh? That's the one you sang for me."

"I wrote it for you. The team recorded it the night I sang it to you and with their help, I put it out on an album. It was a single and did well, but I tried to play it cool with you because I worried the press would hound you." He'd followed every bit of the progress of the song after he'd released it and now after the movie version was used. The money had been nice, but he hadn't really wanted to share the song with anyone.

"Does your label expect you to tour with it now?" Will asked. "I won't hold you back. You should ride the wave."

"Will." He shifted in his seat to give Will his full attention. This was bigger than a song or an award.

"I won't hold you back."

He'd use that for a song, but not right now. "I know." He pushed his bag aside and held onto Will's hands. "I told you I toured for three years straight. Having this break is what I needed to reset my brain."

"But the song and your label…"

"Are my problems. The team recorded the song for me, but it's on my personal label. Why let a bunch of people have some control over my work when I could have most all of it and reap the biggest reward? I did the work and I'm benefitting."

"True." Will sagged in his seat. "I just thought you'd want to fly."

He'd have to use that line, too. "Before I found you, I might have taken off, but not now. If I decide to tour, it'll be our decision. We're a team." His heart thundered. He couldn't hold his secret in any longer. "Will?"

"Yeah?" Will tipped his head and said nothing else.

"I might be nominated for an award for our song and might get another bump in sales, which is all great, but it's not the thing I truly want."

"What do you truly want?" Will asked. He cleared his throat. "Tell me."

"You. Us. This life we've created. Will, I didn't come looking for you because I wanted to be cleansed. I did it because I wanted you. I'm still here because I want you. I like my life with you."

"But the fame…"

"I don't need it. I had the fame and it, along with my past, made me a monster. You make me better," Carsten said. "I love you."

Shit. He'd done it and said the words. No taking them back.

Will's eyes widened. "What?"

He and Will hadn't used those words—not since getting together. He hadn't wanted to rush this, but now was the right time. "I told you I fell for you back in school and this last year proved to me that the love has only grown stronger. I love you."

"I…" Will scrubbed the back of his hand across his mouth. He said nothing for a pregnant moment. Instead he opened and closed his mouth without sound.

"It'll take some getting used to, but it's the truth." Carsten leaned in and kissed him. "I'm the man I am because of you. Because of the changes I made to me. You're the reason—without you, the song wouldn't have happened." He loved Will big time.

"Carsten."

"It's okay. I didn't expect you to say it in return. It'll take time."

"No, Car. I love you, too. Always have." Will scooted closer to Carsten and threaded his arms around Carsten's shoulders. "I'm thrilled and stunned, but relieved. I'm whole with you, too."

"I bet you never thought you'd fall in love with your bully, did you?" Carsten asked. "Never imagined we'd be here."

"Honestly, I had a feeling we'd find our way to each other. Do or die kind of thing. We needed closure and to admit the truth and we did, because redemption goes both ways," Will said.

"It does." The man was so wise.

"I didn't know when or where, but I knew we'd see each other again. I knew I loved you, even if I hated you back then. Always will love you."

Those were the best words he'd ever heard. "So

we love each other and we live together. You inspire my music, too. Think you'll come with me to this award ceremony? I might not win, but I'd love to have some sexy arm candy with me." He wasn't sure he could go through with it alone. "I don't do insta-official, but I will if that's what you want."

"You don't have to do anything special for me," Will said. "I'll follow you anywhere, so yes."

Desire deeper than Carsten had never known filled his heart. He found his soul and his love in Will.

He found his redemption, and it was so sweet.

The End

EVERNIGHT PUBLISHING ®

www.evernightpublishing.com